THE SIXTH PRECEPT

DARK YORKSHIRE - BOOK 6

J M DALGLIESH

First published by Hamilton Press in 2019
This edition published 2020

ISBN (Trade paperback) 978-1-80080-432-6
ISBN (Large Print) 978-1-80080-726-6
ISBN (Hardback) 978-1-80080-560-6

EXCLUSIVE OFFER

THE SIXTH PRECEPT

"We are what we think. All that we are arises with our thoughts. With our thoughts, we make the world."

Gautama Buddha

CHAPTER ONE

THE CELLS on the spreadsheet merged as eye-strain overcame her. She pressed thumb and forefinger to the lids and gently squeezed them towards one another, meeting at the bridge of her nose. Blinking furiously, she waited until her eyes refocussed. Glancing at the mobile on her desk, she noted the missed call. The second of the evening. Checking the time, it was pushing eight o'clock.

She saved the document and resolved to pick up where she left off first thing in the morning. Closing down the applications, she switched off the monitor and detached the laptop from the hub, sliding it into her carry bag. Lastly, she turned off the desk lamp and got to her feet. Crossing the office and taking her coat from the stand, she put it on and slipped the straps of her bag over her shoulder and left, closing the door behind her.

The carpeted corridors were deserted and were now illuminated only by secondary lighting, in place to allow the contract cleaners to set about their routines. They paid her no attention as she reached the lift, accompanied by the grating sound of a vacuum cleaner. Summoning the lift to the fourth floor, she waited, checking her watch once more. Thomas would be annoyed. Another figure came into view, rounding the corner at the far end. Despite the lack of light, the sizeable frame gave away the identity of the night shift security guard. He smiled at her as he approached.

"Working late again, Miss Ryan?"

"Heading home now, Marcus."

"You work too hard."

"Isn't that the truth." A ping sounded and the doors parted before her. Entering the lift, she turned and pressed the button for the basement parking level. "Goodnight, Marcus."

"Goodnight, Miss Ryan."

The doors closed and the lift began the descent. Moments later, she stepped out into the underground basement. There were perhaps a dozen cars scattered around the parking level. Apparently, there were employees outdoing even her with their commitment to the cause. She moved to the left, her heels echoing through the parking level the only sounds that carried. Descending a ramp to the lower level, she set eyes on her BMW, parked in her designated space. Alongside was a transit van and she was irritated by the proximity of it to her own. To be fair, the spaces were narrow and not marked out with wider vehicles in mind but even so, she cursed the driver under her breath for being so thoughtless.

Approaching the car, the keyless entry system registered her presence and the car unlocked itself. Opening the boot, she placed the shoulder bag containing her laptop flat inside. Removing her coat, she lay that alongside it too. Shutting the tailgate, she was forced to turn sideways and slip down between the two vehicles. Whilst assessing how much of a gap would be needed to enable her to get into the driving seat, something in the corner of her eye caught her attention. Looking across the parking level, she tried to see what it was. For a moment she thought she'd heard something and seen a flicker of movement.

The level was well lit with only the huge concrete supporting pillars and the occasional parked car interrupting her line of sight for fifty yards in every direction. She waited, straining to see or hear what had alerted her – but nothing. Only the muted drumming from within the ventilation duct overhead could now be heard. Realising she was holding her breath, she dismissed her overactive imagination. The mobile phone in her pocket began to vibrate and she took it out. It was Thomas again. She directed the call to voicemail, putting the handset back in her pocket and grasped the door handle. The sliding door of the van opened and before she could react, something struck her in the back. Intense pain tore through her as her body went into spasm moments before her legs gave out and she collapsed, falling against the car on her way down. The fluorescent strip lights hanging from the roof appeared to swing from left to right as strong hands took a firm hold of her.

Then, there was only darkness.

SOMETHING WAS WRONG. Opening her eyes, her lids felt heavy. Gritty. The darkness of the night was all-encompassing. The smell of the outdoors; damp soil. Something was wrong... very wrong. Attempting to stand, she found herself held in place somehow, panic flared; she feared she'd been in an accident and was paralysed or worse still: dead. Her left ankle throbbed. Although unable to move her foot, any flexing of the muscles in her leg caused a sharp painful sensation. Relieved she could still feel all of her extremities, despite their apparent cold, she cast her mind back. Leaving the office, speaking to Marcus and arriving at her car... but then, nothing. Breathing was difficult. There was something restricting her mouth, taut and unforgiving. She couldn't move her lips. Trying to call out gave off a muffled sound, elevating to a scream. Only when trying to reach up with her hand to free her mouth did she realise that she couldn't move at all.

No amount of struggling or exertion, using all of the strength she could muster, could move her even the slightest. She cried out again, as loudly as she could, but her muffled screams passed into despairing tears as frustration turned to fear and then panic. A thud sounded nearby, not particularly loud but it drew her attention. Her eyes were slowly beginning to adjust to the darkness and she looked around but couldn't make out what had made the noise. Then there was another, only this time much closer. A third sounded behind her, a little way off. Then silence returned.

The wind whispered from nearby trees and then came the realisation. She was by woodland. The damp soil, the trees... the cold. Shadows moved. It was hard to judge but she thought it was a person, perhaps twenty feet away but she couldn't be sure. Craning her neck, she tried to make out any detail but moving caused her discomfort. All of a sudden, she was bathed in bright light. Screwing her eyes tightly shut, she screamed again. Slowly opening her eyes, she squinted against beams of car headlights. They illuminated everything around her.

Nearby, she saw a rock, perhaps the size of a closed fist. To the right was another. They looked somehow out of place, as if recently deposited. Another thud. Another rock, landing to the left of her head. She screamed. Something struck the top of her head sending a shooting pain across her skull. Her screaming ceased, replaced by confusion. Then another. This one struck her forehead before dropping to the ground in front of her. Liquid flowed across her eyebrow and trickled into her eye.

She was bleeding. Something else passed through her line of sight, striking her on the cheek. Horrified, she silently begged for help but none was forthcoming.

Another strike. Her vision swam... and the darkness returned.

CHAPTER TWO

Caslin followed the line of Garfield Terrace, picking his way along the narrow road. With cars parked on either side negotiating the small housing estate made up of Victorian semi-detached and terraced houses was not easy. Doing so on a Saturday morning, following a rather sociable Friday evening, made it even tougher. To the left was the railway yard, its lines feeding into both York Central train station and the National Railway Museum, whereas a short distance to his right they were further hemmed in by the river Ouse, winding its way through central York.

Reaching the turn at the end of the road, Caslin kept an eye out for Hunter. He had been making himself his second cup of coffee of the day when she had called. They were summoned to Stamford Street, a small cul-de-sac on the edge of the Holgate area of the city. The houses here were originally built for the railway workers but were now residential homes at the cheaper end of the scale. As cheap as houses ever got in York, anyway. A few of the buildings had been transformed into small businesses, Caslin spied a sandwich shop just behind him and he wondered whether it would be open on the weekend. The road angled to the right onto Garnett Terrace and immediately he spotted Hunter's vehicle parked half on the pavement, directly opposite the entrance to the street. As he approached, her driver's door opened and DS Sarah Hunter stepped out acknowledging him with a wave.

Pulling his car in behind hers, Caslin pulled on the handbrake and switched off the ignition. Getting out, he nodded towards her by way of greeting and he could see the effect of an early start written across her face as well. She reached back into the car and reappeared with a takeaway coffee, handing it towards him. Caslin took it gratefully.

"You took your time," Hunter said.

"I've barely been to sleep. So, what are we doing here?" Looking directly opposite into Stamford Street itself, uniform had already cordoned off the road with blue and white tape, signifying it was now a crime scene. Looking beyond the cordon, Caslin could see perhaps half a dozen houses. All were nondescript, of a uniform design and appeared largely functional in their aesthetics. Glancing at the neighbouring streets, the design was commonplace. None of the houses had driveways nor gardens to the front. Most of the houses still had their curtains drawn and of those that didn't, nets obscured the view of the interior. A handful of residents stood at the edge of the cordon speaking with the uniformed officers, present to maintain the integrity of the scene. Most likely, they were trying to find out what was going on.

"Your guess is as good as mine," Hunter said. "When ACC Broadfoot couldn't get a hold of you, he called me."

"Well, he can't have tried very hard."

"You didn't just ignore his call like normal then?"

Caslin laughed. "I'm not that bad. So, what did he say?"

"He gave me this address and said there was a situation developing here. One that might see a crossover."

"Crossover?"

"Yes. Seemingly an address that the drug squad has red flagged flashed up late last night, and the concern is that there may be greater ramifications as a result."

Caslin looked at her inquisitively. "And this concerns us how?"

Hunter shrugged. "You know as much as I do. Broadfoot told us to ask for DI Craig Templer. Do you know him?"

"No. Not someone I've ever come across. So, shall we go and see what's going on then?"

Caslin sipped his coffee as they crossed the street. The constable saw them approaching and, recognising them, lifted the tape. Both Caslin and Hunter ducked underneath and entered Stamford Street. Hunter glanced towards the constable who pointed in the direction of the crime scene. He needn't have bothered because the intensity of the police presence at the address made it quite clear where they had to go. There were three liveried police cars as well as a CSI van parked outside.

They were met at the front door by another uniformed officer. She stepped aside to give them entry. The hallway was narrow, allowing them only to pass through one at a time.

"We're looking for Templer?" Caslin asked.

"You'll find him in the living room."

"Thanks."

Reaching the door, set to the left of the hallway, they stopped and took in the scene before them. Two forensics officers dressed in their white coveralls were busy mapping the scene with a sketchpad. A third was taking photographs. To their right was another whom Caslin guessed was DI Templer. He looked too young to be a DI in Caslin's eyes. Mind you, as the years passed, he found himself saying that about his colleagues more often. Casting an eye around the room, Caslin could see what he assumed this house was; a drug den. Four people, three men and one woman were seated in the room. Two were on a sofa, one an armchair and the remaining body lay sprawled out face down upon the floor. All four were clearly dead.

Eyeing their arrival, Templer crossed the room and came to greet them. Removing his latex gloves, he extended a hand and Caslin shook it. The latter introduced himself and then DS

Hunter who Templer acknowledged with a brief nod in her direction.

"What do we have here?" Caslin asked.

"That's just what we are trying to figure out," Templer replied, gesturing for them to enter. Caslin stepped forward into the middle of the room and immediately paid closer attention to the nearest bodies, sitting on the sofa. One of the males and the only female present were alongside each other. The male had a thin leather belt tied around his left bicep that, although still in place, was no longer tight. The inside of his elbow was exposed and Caslin could easily tell that this man was a habitual drug user due to the number of scars, scabs and bruising in that area. Leaning over the pair he could see a syringe on the sofa between them. It was empty but the needle was still visible. Turning his attention to the woman, Caslin cast a glance over her uncovered arms and was not surprised to see similar markings on both.

Caslin looked to Hunter and indicated for her to check out the remaining deceased. She nodded whilst putting on her own forensics gloves to avoid contaminating the scene with her own fingerprints. Stepping past the photographer, she moved to investigate the body on the far side beneath the window overlooking the street. For his part, Caslin looked at the coffee table at the centre of the room. Visible for all to see was the paraphernalia that accompanied those with an extensive drug habit. On the table were syringes, spoons, with some kind of semi-translucent substance or residue left on them, and ruffled sheets of blackened aluminium foil. Dropping to his haunches, Caslin looked at the underside of the spoons and saw carbon residue on those as well. Most likely as a result from holding a naked flame beneath them. There were also a couple of packets of cigarettes, two lighters, a mobile phone and some empty wraps that Caslin knew from his experience would once have contained drugs. There were several small bags fashioned from clingfilm, rolled up and sealed at the top, and in them was a brown substance. Caslin glanced towards Templer.

"Heroin."

Templer nodded. "I would assume so. Plus, we found some crack cocaine along with mixed amphetamines and some synthetics. Probably spice but we'll have to wait for the lab tests to confirm that. But that's not all. Come with me." Templer beckoned Caslin to join him. He followed the young DI into the adjoining room. Caslin's eyes narrowed and he exhaled slowly as he entered. On the table were several foil-wrapped bricks. One of which was open and the contents appeared to be a block of processed heroin. Alongside these blocks were bundles of cash in used tens and twenties.

"This isn't your average crack house," Caslin said.

"No, it isn't," Templer confirmed.

"Hunter says you had this address flagged. Is that right?"

"Yeah. This is a known address for one of the key players in the North Yorkshire trade. We've been tracking his movements for months, watching him expand his operation in this direction."

"Expanding from where?"

"Eastwards, out of Leeds."

"This isn't the usual area for a place like this, is it?" Caslin asked, referring to the middle-class suburb they were in.

Templer shook his head. "No. The days of your average crack den being in a squat or some other semi-derelict location are long gone. For some reason they seem to draw less attention to themselves once they become established in suburbia. Most of the houses we find that have been converted to grow cannabis are usually rentals in the heart of affluent estates. It is amazing how they manage to go under the radar, but they do."

"Even so, this isn't normal."

"No, you're right. This is definitely not normal."

"Whose house is it? One of the victims?" Caslin asked, indicating back towards the living room with a flick of his head.

"No, I don't believe so. We can't say for sure who runs this particular part of the operation, as well as who owns it. Neither would be partaking of the refreshments, if you know what I mean? Not with this much gear," he added, indicating what was on the table in front of them.

"Good point." Caslin was in agreement. "Do you think they did a runner when that lot overdosed?"

"If they overdosed?" A voice said from behind them. Caslin turned to see Iain Robertson, the head of Fulford Road's crime scene investigation team.

"Iain," Caslin said. "I didn't realise you were here."

"Aye. That's because you don't recognise me with my clothes on," Robertson said with a grin.

"Forgive the assumption," Caslin said, "but I didn't see any wounds to indicate violence. Three of them appeared to die in the chairs."

"You're right there," Robertson agreed. "And the fourth managed to get up… just about."

"If not an overdose, then what are we looking at?" Templer asked. "A poisoned supply?"

"Unfortunately, you're both going to have to wait for that answer, but my guess would be a tainted supply. Now, whether that's intentional or accidental will be for you to decide."

"Instinctively?" Caslin asked.

Robertson sucked air through his teeth. "Well, judging by what all of them are missing, I would suggest the former rather than the latter."

"Missing?" Templer asked.

"I thought you two were supposed to be detectives? Go back and have a look at their right hands."

Both Caslin and Templer left the room and made their way back to where Hunter was examining the victims. She smiled as they approached. Obviously, she had overheard the exchange and found it amusing.

"Here," she said, indicating the man lying on the floor at her feet. Caslin bent over and immediately saw what he had initially missed. The index finger of the man's right hand was missing. There was a little bit of blood but not a great deal which indicated it had been removed post-mortem. Caslin glanced over towards the sofa where the man and woman were sitting. Templer met his eye and nodded in answer to the unasked question.

"They've both been cut off too," he said. "Looks like a clean cut."

"Surgical?" Caslin asked, as Robertson appeared at the threshold of the door.

"Possibly," he replied. "Could just as easily be achieved with a gardening tool."

"And the fourth?" Caslin asked Hunter, gesturing to the final victim with his eyes.

"Same."

"And have you seen this?" Robertson asked, pointing to the table. Caslin stood up and took two steps to come alongside him.

"What do you have?"

"The only thing of beauty in the house of the dead," Robertson stated flatly. With his pocket torch, he illuminated the centre of the table. In amongst the empty wraps, crack cocaine residue, razor blades and syringes, was the head of a flower. The centre was bright yellow and surrounded by layers of white petals that morphed into a hot pink at the points.

"What is it? Magnolia?" Caslin asked.

"Perhaps, not my speciality. Could be a waterlily of some type," Hunter suggested, going to stand alongside Caslin. "I agree with Iain. It seems a little out of place."

"You said they were moving into this area?" Caslin asked Templer.

"They are, yes."

"Any chance this is a result of the locals pushing back?"

"I would think that is pretty likely, yes," Templer said. "We've seen a number of places just like this being turned over in the last few months. There will always be some kind of response when these guys start crossing imaginary lines into the other's territories. That's to be expected."

"Anything quite like this happen recently?" Hunter asked.

Templer shook his head. "More commonly they trade blows at a lower level. Street dealers will get a kicking, perhaps the odd mule will be intercepted. This however, this is an approach I've not come across before. Poisoning someone's supply, getting into their supply chain before it reaches their network of dealers is a new one on me."

"Is that why we are here?"

"I don't need you to be here," Templer stated, rather dismissively in Caslin's eyes. "But someone upstairs thinks it might be bigger than just a turf war."

"You disagree?"

"Too early to say," Templer said. "I'm more than happy to run with it as a narcotics inquiry, all the same. Feel free to pass it back upstairs that you are not required, if you aren't interested."

"I didn't say I wasn't interested," Caslin replied with a smile. "Let's see where it takes us."

CHAPTER THREE

CASLIN STEPPED out of his office and drew Terry Holt's attention. The detective constable looked up from his laptop with an inquisitive raise of the eyebrows.

"What have you got from the scene?" Caslin asked.

"Robertson has sent over the detailed inventory."

"Anything interesting?"

"Obviously, we are still waiting on the pathology reports, but Dr Taylor has promised she will pass us the preliminary findings as soon as they're ready. Likewise, the chemical analysis of the drugs you found at the scene hasn't come in yet, but what I do have are the results for the mobile phones. I've already got the serial and telephone numbers over to the respective networks, along with a warrant and I'm expected to hear back from them very soon. Once I have that I'll start cross-referencing the call history logs, text and voice calls, and I'll start piecing these people's lives together."

"Good work," Caslin said, patting him on the shoulder. "Did Iain give you anything else?"

"Off the record, he was pretty certain their stash was interfered with."

"Yeah, doesn't take a genius to figure that one out."

The conversation was interrupted by Hunter walking into the room. "ACC Broadfoot wants to see you in his office."

"Now?"

"Now."

"Terry, can you bring Hunter up to speed and I'll be back as soon as I can," Caslin said as he left the room. Assistant Chief Constable Broadfoot's office was on the third floor but it was unusual for him to summon Caslin upstairs. Usually, he was left to his own devices and only checked in with the senior officer as and when he felt the need. Caslin's shoes squeaked on the polished stairs as he made his way up to the next floor, coming across DCI Matheson on the way.

"You've got visitors," she said in passing.

Caslin stopped. Turning to look at her he raised an eyebrow. "Anyone I know?"

"I don't," she said. "They look serious, mind you. Nice suits as well."

"They're certainly not from around here then. Thanks for the heads up."

"Any time," Matheson replied, resuming her course downstairs.

Caslin continued upward, leaving the stairwell at the next landing and entering the corridor housing the senior officers of Fulford Road. Upon reaching the office, Caslin sidled up to Broadfoot's PA, placing his hands gently on hers as she reached for the telephone receiver, presumably to announce his arrival.

"Who's in there?" he whispered.

"Nathaniel, you know better than to ask that," she said.

"Am I going to like them? You can tell me that."

Unfortunately, the question went unanswered as the door to Broadfoot's office opened and the man himself appeared.

"I thought I heard voices. Come on Nathaniel, we are waiting on you." Broadfoot glanced at his PA and without another word retreated into his office. Caslin followed, raising his eyebrows as high as he could, walking around the desk and towards the office.

Broadfoot's PA stifled a laugh and merely smiled as Caslin almost skipped past her. Entering the office, Caslin glanced around. Besides Broadfoot, there were three others present. He immediately recognised Templer but the other two were men unknown to him.

"DI Nathaniel Caslin, please meet DCI Sean Meadows and Detective Chief Superintendent Myles Henry. I believe you already know Craig Templer," Broadfoot said, indicating the youngest man in the room. Caslin nodded to the latter and then acknowledged the two senior officers. Eyeing the two men, Matheson had been right. Their suits were not off-the-peg. They were possibly not tailor made but at the very least, high quality. That set these men aside from the norm. If you had to guess, then he figured they were highly influential, possibly beyond their rank. Not least because Broadfoot appeared to behave differently towards them than any other senior officers Caslin could recall, not deferential, but respectful to a greater degree than usual.

"What can I do for you sir?"

"We were just discussing the narcotics investigation, Nathaniel," Broadfoot said.

"I'm glad you brought that up sir," Caslin said, before Broadfoot could continue. "I'm not convinced that this is a narcotics investigation."

That comment caused some consternation amongst the assembled people. "We brought you in," Meadows stated.

"Because you thought there might be a crossover between narcotics and major crimes," Caslin said. "Correct?"

"That's right, yes," Meadows confirmed. "Out of common courtesy if nothing else."

"But the early indication is the drug supplies have been tampered with."

"I haven't heard that," Templer said. "I'm the senior investigating officer until it's decided otherwise. Why wasn't I informed?"

Caslin shrugged. "I've only just been made aware myself. Perhaps you need to improve your communication channels."

"Gentlemen, please," Broadfoot interrupted the exchange. "What point are you trying to make Nathaniel?"

"Well, as DI Templer rightly pointed out yesterday, at the scene, rival dealers don't usually poison each other's supply chains in order to get the upper hand. Therefore, it follows that if the drugs have been tampered with in some way that led to four deaths, then we are looking at a multiple homicide. That's definitely major crimes and not narcotics."

"That's bull shit, Caslin," Templer stated, shaking his head with an irritated smile on his face.

"It's still major crimes," Caslin argued.

"And if the dealers are cutting their heroin with something else to increase a street value and that accidentally results in users dying, then it remains a narcotics investigation," Meadows stated, locking eyes with Caslin.

"And how many dealers do you know would flee the scene of an overdose, leaving their supply on the table, not to mention a shit load of cash?" Caslin said.

"It's not as simple as that, Inspector," DCS Henry said pointedly.

"Perhaps you could fill us in?" Caslin asked. The three officers from narcotics exchanged glances, something that wasn't missed by either Broadfoot or Caslin.

"Yes, perhaps you should fill us in?" Broadfoot said evenly.

Meadows and Henry exchanged something unsaid between them and the latter nodded. Meadows exhaled heavily. "The drug house in question is owned and run by Lawrence Metcalf. Metcalf is someone we've been tracking for a long time. His market share in West Yorkshire has been steadily growing over the last five years. He started out as a loyal lieutenant in another organisation until his own ambition got ahead of him and he branched out. Metcalf isn't your typical drug dealer. He's taken efficiency to a whole new level, reaching beyond the normal level of criminality to work in his business."

"How do you mean?" Caslin asked.

"He's not using your average thug for his muscle. He's recruiting ex-military, mercenary types and, in some cases, former police officers. He likes having the latter around because he feels it gives him credibility, window dressing to the public eye, and I dare say it's to stick one in the eye to people like us."

"Fair enough. He sounds like someone you'd like to take off the streets. If you know so much about him, why haven't you done so already?"

"Metcalf has moved ahead of his competition to such an extent that he is broadening his horizons, which brings him to York. We think he has ambitions to stretch his operation from the west coast of England to the east, hoovering up anything in between. Like I said, we've been watching him, building our case and when we're ready, we will take him down. But we don't just want Metcalf. We want his entire operation, from his dealer network right through to his supplier and all the links in between."

"Where do you think these four deaths in one of his drug houses come into it?" Caslin asked.

Myles Henry picked up the narrative. "The honest answer is we don't know, but what we do know is that we have an inside man and we believe he can help us."

"This inside man," Broadfoot began, "who is he and where does he fit into this?

"He's been working in Metcalf's organisation for the past eighteen months and he's been feeding us information. Quality intelligence since day one," Meadows said.

"This is an employee of Metcalf's?" Caslin asked. "An informant?"

"No, this is an undercover officer. We spent two years developing his back story and his experience, giving him a name that will allow him to freely enter Metcalf's organisation. He is both experienced and highly skilled."

"Have you been able to make contact with him?" Broadfoot asked.

Meadows shook his head. "He was supposed to check in with us last night. When he didn't, we followed protocol, which was to give him six hours, and if there was still no further contact, we were to follow up."

"And?"

"He didn't get in touch," Templer said quietly.

"Come on guys," Caslin said failing to mask his irritation. "You may as well give us the rest."

"Fowler was running Metcalf's drug house last night. As you know, he wasn't at the scene and we've been unable to make contact through the usual channels."

"Well, that certainly puts a different slant on things, doesn't it?" Broadfoot stated. "Information we probably should have been abreast of earlier." His tone was snippy.

"This doesn't change anything," Caslin said. "This is still a major crime's case."

"How the hell do you figure that out?" Templer argued.

"If you've got an undercover officer who was at this scene and has gone missing, then I would argue there is even more reason for narcotics to stay well away."

"And you can get to fuck!" Templer snapped, momentarily forgetting himself and then holding a hand up in apology towards the senior ranks.

"I think everybody can appreciate the sentiment that DI Templer is exhibiting, if perhaps a little overzealously," Henry stated. "Perhaps there is some accommodation that we can come to?" He looked to Broadfoot, seeking a compromise.

Broadfoot nodded. "I think major crimes should take the lead in this investigation, albeit with narcotics represented in the team." Caslin was about to interrupt and lodge an objection but one stern look from his superior nipped the protest in the bud. "Until such time as it becomes clear whose case this should be. As and when that is established, we can discuss it further. I suggest that Caslin here takes the lead and you assign a liaison to work alongside him, presumably DI Templer would suffice?"

Templer also looked ready to protest but any opportunity to voice his objection was immediately curtailed by Henry's agreement. "I think that is a workable solution, Kyle."

"That's settled then," Broadfoot said. "Perhaps, Nathaniel, you could take Templer aside and bring him up to speed with what you've already uncovered while we finish up here."

It was quite clear that the decision had been taken and the two junior officers were being politely pushed aside, whilst the high-level protocol was discussed between themselves. Caslin didn't mind. That was the element of his former position that he missed the least – the politics – and why he loved his new role so much. He said his goodbyes and went to the door, grasping the handle firmly. Opening it, he gestured for Templer to pass through before him. The younger man didn't seem as pleased to be leaving as Caslin did and it took another glance from his DCI before he reluctantly left the room. Caslin closed the door and smiled at Broadfoot's PA as they passed her desk.

"Thanks for that," Templer said.

"You're welcome." Caslin ignored the sarcasm.

"This was my case."

"It still is your case," Caslin countered. "At least, you're still on it, aren't you?"

"Anyone ever tell you you're an arsehole, Caslin?"

Caslin smiled. "Frequently."

Leading them downstairs and along the corridor, back to the ops room, the two men spoke little. If Hunter and Holt were surprised at Caslin reappearing with the detective inspector from the Drugs Squad, they hid it well. Hunter dealt with the introductions and Templer pulled up a chair, apparently burying his frustration at losing the lead role in the investigation.

"What can you tell us about your man on the inside? Has he ever done anything similar?" Hunter asked.

"You mean, like going off script?"

"Yes, exactly. Can you think of any reason why he would ditch protocol like this?"

Templer shook his head. "No, I've known him and worked alongside him for a long time, and I've been his handler since we brought him on board. He would have to have a very good reason to go to ground like this, and I'm at a loss to think what that would be."

"You said you don't think this will be a rival gang?" Caslin asked. "Not an act of retribution."

"That's right. I don't believe so."

"Is there a possibility he may have been abducted by a rival gang in order to make some kind of point?"

"The only friction we've seen between the groups has been at street level. You know, new dealers moving into areas, streets, that they haven't been in before but even that's been at a minimum."

"How so?" Caslin asked.

"Metcalf has been. He's been unsettling his rivals by disrupting their supply chains, which makes their street level dealer network more susceptible to switching. That way he isn't putting his guys up against theirs."

"He's just been recruiting their own dealers to sell his supply rather than that of his rivals," Holt clarified.

"Exactly. That way, his rivals are looking down the chain rather than up at him. So far, it's proved to be quite a successful strategy. Fowler has been in at the ground level since Metcalf has expanded eastwards. We've got names. We have places and we've been tracking his links back up through the distribution network to where his merchandise is entering the country. With some help from abroad, we are looking at bringing down his entire operation. We're so deep into his network that I'm very surprised at this turn of events. I mean, it's not the first time we've lost an asset."

"You had other people in his network?" Hunter asked. Templer nodded. His expression was grave. "And they've disappeared too?"

"Anyone that we managed to embed before has been uncovered in one way or another. Fowler was the first undercover officer we've successfully integrated. Previously, informants or employees we managed to flip have all been dealt with."

"When you say dealt with, you mean killed?" Caslin clarified.

"Some have disappeared, certainly. However, we've always had an inkling that something wasn't right and they've never caught us completely cold. They were managed gambles."

"With people's lives," Hunter said accusingly.

"Don't hate the player. It's the game."

"But this time it's different?" Caslin asked. The question broke Hunter's disgust at Templer's perceived intransigence.

"It would appear so."

"Did Fowler wear a wire?" Caslin asked.

Templar nodded. "Sometimes, but not always. Only when he figured he was safe to do so. Metcalf is no fool."

"Last night?"

Templar shook his head. "I don't know."

"Okay, Terry, where did you get to with these mobiles?"

"None of them are burners, sir. Therefore, it's fair to assume that the four phones recovered from the scene belong to the four victims. Any low-level dealer that I've ever come across uses a burner for obvious reasons. Now if you look at the board," Holt pointed up at a sketch of the crime scene, mounted on a notice board, "you'll see I've marked victims one to four, with three and four being the man and woman on the sofa. These two have exchanged many texts and phone calls in the past few months, so I think it is reasonable to assume that they are a couple. The other two victims, numbered one and two, along with this couple, only have one other number that seems to crossover between all four call logs."

"Presumably that number will be their dealer," Caslin suggested.

Holt nodded his agreement. "That would make sense. Particularly, as that specific number is registered to a burner phone and we have no record of who owns it."

"Is there any sign of that phone at the scene?" Hunter asked.

"Not so far," Holt confirmed.

"Can I see the number?" Templer asked.

"Sure." Holt passed a sheet of paper across the table to him. Templer scanned it.

"That's a number used by Fowler."

"You sure?" Caslin asked.

"Absolutely," Templer confirmed.

"Then let's get that number flagged. If it comes up on the mobile phone network, pings off of a cell tower, whatever, then I want us to know about it. I want to have you," Caslin indicated Hunter and Holt, "to chase up scenes of crime with as much detail as you can. In the meantime, Templer and I will head over to pathology and see what we can find out from Alison Taylor."

Terry Holt's phone rang and the DC answered the call. "You've got to be kidding me?" His response ensured all subsequent conversation ceased as his tone was picked up by the others. His conversation continued for another minute and then he hung up without saying another word. Turning to his laptop, he brought it out of hibernation and connected to the Internet. The others were curious, recognising his enthusiasm was born of something significant. Holt hit return and the screen before him changed and he sat back in his chair, scanning the faces of those around him. "You are not going to believe this."

CHAPTER FOUR

THE FOUR OFFICERS huddled around Terry Holt's laptop. The window he opened on the screen was small and the three of them, peering over Holt's shoulder, struggled to make out the detail of the footage.

"Can you brighten that up and enlarge it a little?" Caslin asked.

"Hold on, I'll throw it up on the projector if someone can pull down the screen," Holt said. Hunter crossed to the other side of the room and lowered the projector screen into position. Holt linked his laptop via the office Wi-Fi and moments later, the video footage was displayed for all of them to see.

"What are we looking at?" Templer asked.

"That's the house, Metcalf's place, isn't it?" Hunter asked. That became clear as the person wielding the camera panned around the room. It was night-time and there were only a few lamps on in the room, but it was quite clearly the house in Stamford Street they were present at the day before. The four victims were unconscious, perhaps already dead, and were in the same positions as they were discovered in. The camera zoomed in on each of them, although their features were obscured by selective blurring of the image before the shot panned back out and around the room.

"Any sign of Fowler?" Caslin asked Templer. The latter shook his head.

"No, not yet."

"Do you think he's holding the camera?"

"Can't say."

There didn't appear to be any audio accompanying the footage, or if there was then it was inaudible. The camera hovered over the man lying face down on the floor. A left hand came into shot. It was gloved and reached down, picking up the man's right arm at the wrist. The right hand came into view alongside the left and this hand brandished a pair of secateurs.

"Well, I guess that answers that question," Caslin said as the figure placed the victim's index finger in between the blades. At this point the graphic detail was smudged, as if a blob of Vaseline had been smeared over the screen, but an active imagination was not required to realise he had sliced through flesh and connective tissue with ease. Holt sucked air through his teeth, grimacing. He was the only one viewing the footage who was yet to see the reality of the scene. "How do you think he's filming this?"

"Looks like a head cam, to me," Holt replied. "There's no way someone is standing with the camera over this guy's shoulder filming that. He must be wearing a head cam."

The camera moved out as the man who they all assumed was the likely killer moved to the next victim, removing their index finger in the same way. There was no reaction, no grunt of pain, no response, so either the victim was already dead or, at the very least, effectively in a drug-induced coma to such an extent that they felt little or no pain.

"Where are you getting this from, Terry?" Caslin asked.

"A friend of mine works in media relations and she picked this up on the net, just now."

"Who's streaming it?" Hunter asked.

"It's on *The Post's* website," Holt stated, glancing up at her and then back to the footage. "From the timeframe, they've only just uploaded that themselves."

"Irresponsible bastards," Templer said.

"I think we found something we can agree on, at last," Caslin said. Holt split the screen and brought up the website homepage of the city's premier local newspaper. Alongside the usual headlines and links to stories was the headline story of the day. The title read *Vigilante killer strikes crack house*.

"That's a bit of a shift from their usual journalistic approach," Holt said.

"Yes, that's got tabloid written all over it," Hunter added. "Do you think Jimmy had something to do with it?"

"Let's go and find out once this has played out," Caslin said. He was hopeful that Jimmy Sullivan was not involved in the editorial decision making. His background with the London red-tops implied he had form but that was years ago.

The small group continued to watch the footage in silence as the two remaining victims, the couple seated on the sofa, had their index fingers removed as well. As the cut was made on the woman's hand, she appeared to flinch momentarily and her head lolled from one side to the other, but other than that, there was no reaction. The figure stepped back and, once again, allowed the camera to pan around the room, taking in the scene.

"Can you pause that, Terry?" Caslin asked. Holt did as he was requested and stopped the playback.

"Look at the table," Caslin said to no one in particular.

"What are we looking for?" Templer asked.

"Wait a second. Terry, press play." Holt did so, and the playback resumed, only this time everyone was focused on the coffee table in the middle of the room. The video footage blurred as the wearer of the camera appeared to look down towards a bag at their feet before kneeling and reaching inside. Drawing out their hands, they were cupping a pink and white flower, which was carefully and gently placed at the centre of the table. The person then stood up, stared down at it, focusing the camera footage directly on the flower. The cameraman's head tilted forward and they got a brief shot of his boots. They appeared to be workmen's footwear, wide, with heavy treads as the soles projected beyond the leather to either side. They were treated to one more panoramic shot of the scene before the video footage faded out into darkness. The bar creeping along the bottom of the footage indicated there was more to play out and they waited in silence, patiently. A few seconds passed before the number five faded into view. This was held in place for a few seconds more before it once again passed back to black.

"What's the significance of the five, do you think?" Hunter asked.

"How many victims were there? Four, wasn't it?" Holt asked.

"That we know of," Caslin said. He was conscious of Templer's relationship with the undercover detective. Everyone in the room was experienced enough to know that if the officer was present, then there was every likelihood that he could well be a fifth victim. "Terry, you and Hunter go back over this footage as many times as it takes and detail everything that you see. Then chase up Iain Robertson for his crime scene analysis and compare the two. I want to know if there are any differences, any inconsistencies, anything at all that stands out, no matter how large or small. Understood?"

"Will do, sir," they both said in unison.

"Templer and I will head over to *The Post* and see what we can find out."

"Ask them for all the data they have regarding the video that was sent to them," Holt said. "With a bit of luck, we might be able to track the video back to the sender. At the very least, we could see where it was uploaded from. Their tech guys will know what I'm looking for." Caslin was grateful for the latter clarification as despite his coming a long way regarding new technology in the last few years, his knowledge barely scratched the surface of the detective constable's.

THE OFFICES of where the newspaper was based were in central York. The journey from Fulford Road into the city centre took less than five minutes, largely because at this time on a Sunday morning the city was at its quietest. Pulling into the car park, at the rear of the building, there were plenty of available parking spaces. With only a handful of staff on shift this day, eighty percent of the bays were empty.

"So, who is this Jimmy that DC Holt was talking about?"

"Jimmy Sullivan. He's a journalist. Formerly, quite an established name in the national tabloids but following a few, how should we put it, high-profile errors of judgement found his way back home to Yorkshire."

"Looking to make a name for himself again, do you think?" Templer asked.

Caslin shook his head. "No longer Jimmy's style, if I had to say."

"You know him well?"

"Jimmy's a friend of mine. Believe me, if he was looking to regain his old status, then he would have had plenty of opportunities in the last few years to do so but he didn't. There will be an explanation for this."

"Career motivations can change, you know?" Caslin couldn't disagree but somehow, he didn't view Jimmy in that way, not any more, at least.

They returned to the front of the building and found the entrance door locked. Pressing the intercom button, Caslin stepped back and the two men waited. A minute passed and there was no response from within the building, so Caslin pressed the buzzer again, only this time adding two or three extra bursts for good measure. Still there was no response. Caslin cursed under his breath. A figure appeared to his left, rounding the corner and mounting steps to the front door. He eyed both the officers warily as he approached. Caslin took out his warrant card and brandished it to the young man as he moved past them, reaching for the number panel and preparing to enter his code.

"Detectives Caslin and Templer," he said, identifying them. "We need to speak to the duty editor."

The newspaper employee gave Caslin's identification only a cursory inspection and nodded briefly. "I'll let him know."

Punching in his access code, he opened the door and passed through, pulling it closed behind him and making it clear he had no intention of conversing with them any further. The detectives exchanged glances, irritation evident on both their faces. Another couple of minutes passed and there was still no movement from within the building.

"Do you think they're doing this just to annoy us?" Templer asked.

"I wouldn't be surprised." Caslin reached forward and entered five digits onto the control panel followed by the sound of the lock clicking free.

"You were paying attention."

"I always do," Caslin replied, pulling open the door and entering the building. Templer followed. They barely reached the reception desk when someone appeared from a corridor to their left. It was a familiar face. Sullivan split a broad grin as he clapped eyes on Caslin. Quickening his pace, he offered Caslin his hand and they shook warmly.

"I figured someone would be calling," Sullivan said, maintaining the grin. "I should have known it would be you."

"What are you playing at, Jimmy?" Caslin asked. "You shouldn't have run that recording without speaking to us first."

"Oh, come on, Nate," Sullivan protested. "You couldn't expect us to sit on that, could you?"

"Jimmy, we've got no idea what we're dealing with yet. It's pretty irresponsible for you to run footage of an active crime scene such as that. What were you thinking?"

Sullivan looked around him nervously, as if worried he might be overheard. "Look, we've got a new editor on board. Things are changing around here a little bit. They're not as straitlaced as they used to be. It's a pretty common story in the print industry these days. Falling advertising revenues, readership, online competition. If we're going to survive, we have to get the clicks up. That's the nature of the beast, these days."

"Well, your editor has just broadcast the scene of a multiple homicide to the world. Any chance I'll be able to get him to take the footage down?"

"You'll have to ask *her* yourself, Nate. But I have to tell you, I don't rate your chances. They gave her predecessor the boot despite his best efforts at... lowering the tone."

Sullivan led them into the interior of the building and to the elevators. He pressed the button and summoned one of them to the ground floor. They didn't have long to wait before the doors slid open and the three men stepped in. The doors closed and Sullivan directed the lift to head up to the fourth floor. Once here, he guided them off to the right and across the open plan office space that Caslin knew would be populated by the team of journalists. Being a Sunday, however, there were only a couple of people present in an office in the north-western corner of the floor.

Sullivan rapped his knuckles on the door, more out of courtesy than to announce their presence. Their approach had already been noted by the incumbents through the wall of glass that sectioned the office off from the remainder of the floor. Opening the door, Sullivan led them in.

"Claire Markham, meet Detective Inspector Caslin and..." Suddenly Sullivan realised he had not been introduced to the accompanying detective alongside Caslin and with a somewhat embarrassed flick of his eyebrows, he indicated that one of the newcomers should do the honours.

"DI Craig Templer," he announced himself.

"Pleased to meet both of you," she replied, acknowledging them in turn. Caslin took her in. She was in her fifties. Professionally attired and immaculately presented with her hair and make-up. The fact it was a Sunday with only a skeleton staff present didn't incline her towards dressing down. "What can I do for you today?"

"I want to know who sent you the video you uploaded this morning?" Caslin said flatly.

"I'm afraid I don't have the answer to that question, Inspector," she replied, smiling. "But I'll be happy to provide you with whatever we do have. Good enough?"

"We would appreciate that. Now, where did you get off putting that kind of footage online without running it past us first?"

"Since when do I need your permission?" she countered.

"This isn't social media," Caslin argued. "*The Post* has a decent reputation to uphold, a tradition that I thought even a new editor, looking to make a name for themselves, would adhere to."

"There's a reason I'm here, Inspector, and that's to make a success of this publication. The way I choose to do that is no concern of yours."

"You are aware that revealing evidence of an active crime scene could lead to a future mistrial?"

"If you can make a case for that, Inspector, then I'll be more than happy to listen to your point of view, but at this time, I would argue your point is largely one based on supposition. Now, would you like to go on the record and give us a comment as to what the motivations of the cameraman are or the significance of the number five?"

"The case is ongoing. I'm certain there will be a press release given out at some point later today. In the meantime, I'd be grateful if you would take down the footage from your website."

"Why would I do that, Inspector?"

"I don't know. Human decency. Respect for the families. Either or both."

"I think it's a little late for that."

"Why would you say that?" Templer asked. Markham looked

to her associate standing next to her, a young assistant, keen and polished, indicating for him to answer.

"The clip has already gone viral," he said, glancing at the tablet in his hand. With a few swipes of his finger, he looked up. "We have thousands of views already on our website and the clip has been downloaded and shared dozens of times. The count is going up every second. I'm afraid that even if we wanted to take down the footage, the impact will be negligible."

"It's already out there, Inspector," Markham stated. "That horse has already bolted."

"What can you tell us about the sender?" Caslin asked. Markham's associate picked up the narrative, once again.

"The clip was sent into us two hours ago. It was attached to an anonymous email which I traced back to a Google account, and before you ask, yes, I did try to trace the source. The DNS appears to be shrouded by a VPN."

Caslin rolled his eyes. Sullivan smiled. "What he's saying, Nathaniel, is the sender masked his location so we would have no idea where he was."

"He used a virtual private network," Templer confirmed for Caslin's benefit, sensing he knew more about technology than his colleague.

Markham nodded. "Apparently, the email originated in South Africa but, unless he managed to travel back in time, there's no way the sender actually filmed it, which we are assuming he did."

"Is there anything you can tell us?" Caslin asked. "Anything useful, I mean."

"Todd here, will give you everything that we have, Inspector," Markham said, indicating her assistant, who Caslin assumed was their in-house technician.

"In the future, I would appreciate you contacting us before you run the risk of compromising our investigation."

Markham smiled. It was a knowing smile. "Are you expecting another, Inspector?"

"Just call us if a similar situation arises, okay?" Caslin was haughty, irritated by her dismissal of their concerns.

"We can do that," Markham said. "Doesn't mean I won't run the footage though."

"I'd expect nothing less," Caslin said, indicating for them to leave. Sullivan held the door open and the two detectives, along with the technician, passed through it and he fell into step behind them. Caslin dropped back, placing a gentle hand on Sullivan's forearm to indicate they should hang back a little. Once confident they would not be overheard, having put a little bit of distance between themselves and the other two, Caslin addressed his friend.

"I don't expect Markham will keep her word, unless it suits her, obviously."

"Yeah, I think that's pretty astute of you," Sullivan agreed.

"If *anything* else comes in, can I count on you to bring it to me?"

Sullivan hesitated. "Aye, will do, but try and leave me out of it, would you?"

"Of course. Thanks, Jimmy."

They reached the lifts, with the plan being to take them downstairs to Todd's office, where he would put together the files containing the video footage and everything else they gathered regarding the video's origin. The doors parted and the first three walked in but Sullivan held back, remaining on the fourth floor.

"Meet for a drink later?" Sullivan asked.

Caslin nodded. "If I have time, no problem."

The doors closed and the elevator descended.

CHAPTER FIVE

"I THOUGHT Fulford Road was south of here?"

"It is," Caslin replied. "I think it would be worth stopping by pathology on the way back."

"You reckon they'll be done by now?"

"No chance of that, but we'll be able to get the steer as to whether our theory is correct regarding the contaminated supply."

"Your pathologist must be a lot more amenable than mine," Templer stated. Caslin chuckled. "The last time I tried to hurry a pathologist, I took a right kicking. Verbally speaking."

"Didn't you know, we're a lot friendlier in the north?" Caslin mocked his counterpart's southern origins.

Templer laughed. "So everyone keeps telling me."

Caslin slowed the car and flicked on his indicator, turning across the oncoming traffic in between two vehicles and accelerated into the car park. Coming to a halt, he turned off the engine and got out. Together, they approached the pathology building. Before they reached the front door, which was locked, Caslin was already on his mobile phone. The call he made was answered swiftly.

"Yeah, I'm here."

An almost inaudible buzz sounded and Caslin opened the outer door giving them access to the building. Templer followed, closing the door behind them and ensuring the lock clicked into place. He quickened his pace to catch up with Caslin, who knew his route through the building as if he were a permanent resident. Entering a stairwell, they descended to a lower floor. Templer assumed they were heading into a basement but, in reality, due to the slope of the surrounding terrain, they were merely descending to a lower level at the rear of the complex.

They arrived at Dr Taylor's pathology lab shortly after. Caslin pushed open the door and entered. Alison Taylor, York's senior pathologist, was on the far side of the room and they had to walk past two autopsy tables to join her. One of which had a cadaver covered over with a sheet whereas the second, the one closest to her desk, had the body of a deceased male. She looked up from the paperwork she was reading, smiling to Caslin before her eyes passed to the newcomer.

"Good morning, Nate." Her smile broadened. "And it's always a pleasure to see a new face."

"Alison, this is DI Craig Templer."

"Pleased to meet you," Templer said.

"Likewise."

"How far have you got, Alison?"

"Somehow, Nathaniel, I knew you would want an answer as quickly as I could get one. I've completed two of the autopsies, the male and female found side-by-side, at the scene. Plus, I rushed through the toxicological tests on all four victims and there are no prizes for guessing the results are similar for all four."

"Are we looking at poison?" Caslin asked.

"Not quite the right terminology, but the end result is the same," she confirmed. "All four had high concentrations of heroin in their blood streams, two others had traces of cocaine. The two autopsies I have concluded revealed they died of toxic shock, for want of a better phrase. You are familiar with how dealers are looking to increase the street value of their merchandise, often by cutting it with something else?"

"Back in the old days they'd cut their heroin with baking powder in order to increase the supply and therefore the profit margins, yes."

"You're right, that was old school," Dr Taylor agreed.

"These days, I think you'll find they are a little bit more advanced with what they are using," Templer said, drawing her attention towards him.

"Care to enlighten us, Craig?" she asked, interested to test his knowledge. Caslin was mildly amused.

"Suppliers are using synthetic opioids to massively increase their profit margins," Templer explained. "These synthetic drugs can be anything from fifty to one hundred times the strength of morphine, so cutting it with their heroin no longer results in an inferior product and therefore doesn't drive away the client base."

"Very good, Detective Inspector," Dr Taylor said with no hint of sarcasm. "You should keep this one around, Nate."

Caslin smiled. "You were saying, about the supply."

"Having run the blood tests and evaluated the toxicological results, I took a look at the samples that Iain Robertson supplied me with, from the scene, and I tested those alongside the blood samples. The heroin came back with two such synthetic opioids, as Craig here described, those being *Fentanyl* and *Carfentanyl*. Thousands of people each year are currently dying of overdoses related to these drugs, tens of thousands per year across the Atlantic, in the US."

"What's unusual in this scenario, is the level of synthetic opioids in this supply of heroin. Suppliers and dealers are well aware of the potency of these drugs and, I think we can all agree, they wouldn't consider it in their interests to kill off their customers. So, I would suggest that this is a case of intentional overdosing rather than accidental mixing of too much of the synthetics. Unless the person mixing got the ratio drastically wrong."

"You sound quite sure of this," Caslin said.

"Once these guys shot up with this particular batch, there was only going to be one outcome."

"What can you tell us about the effects?"

"Fentanyl overdoses can be deadly. Even at low levels the result can lead to a weakening of the muscles, dizziness, confusion, and can often leave the person suffering from extreme sleepiness. With a slightly higher dose, they can quite easily lose consciousness. Those however, are the external symptoms that we can all see."

"A video surfaced online this morning, apparently footage of these four dying, or in several cases perhaps already dead. Three of the four seem to be completely comatose but the fourth, the woman, still appeared responsive as her index finger was cut off," Caslin said.

"I'll get to the finger in a minute," Dr Taylor replied. "I'm not surprised to hear you describe that. As I said, those are the external signs. Internally is where the real damage takes place. A high dose of something such as Fentanyl lowers the body's blood pressure and leads to a profound slowing of the heartbeat. Now, when a dangerous dose is ingested, in whichever manner of choice, the heart may slow to such a pace that it almost stops beating and also, you may find the patient stops breathing altogether. Such respiratory depression can quite easily lead to hypoxia, which can cause permanent brain damage in the individual should they survive."

"In which case, how can dealers get away with cutting their heroin with the synthetic opioids?" Caslin asked.

Templer answered before the pathologist could. "Those who abuse Fentanyl regularly can build up a tolerance to it just the same as they can with any other drug."

"He's right," Dr Taylor agreed. "What the user doesn't realise though is that this tolerance may build up against the effects of pain relief or euphoria. The tolerance develops non-uniformly, leaving them at a heightened risk of experiencing overdose effects that are less impacted by their tolerance, such as respiratory depression. So, for example, any period of abstinence will see their tolerance level diminish, meaning that what was considered a tolerable dose nearly a fortnight previously could now become utterly lethal."

"So, what you're saying is, if someone is used to a supply cut with something such as Fentanyl, then as long as they continue to use, the dealer would expect them to have no ill effects but any break in that supply, or mixing of dealers, could lead to the events you're describing? Caslin said.

"That's a reasonable hypothesis, yes. And needless to say, if the user is also taking other stimulants or alcohol, benzodiazepines, in combination with heroin and Fentanyl, they can have compounding and or contradictory effects. It's a risky pastime to say the least."

"And you don't think the mix could have been accidental?"

Dr Taylor shook her head emphatically. "The levels contained within this heroin, there's no way anyone, with a healthy tolerance level or not, could have survived without an emergency medical intervention. Of that, I am absolutely certain."

"These synthetic opioids, how accessible are they?"

"Well, you can't walk into your local pharmacist and buy them over the counter, they are controlled substances. But, like any other synthetic drug, once the chemical structure is known then it can easily be replicated."

"You said easily?" Caslin asked.

"By someone with chemical knowledge, yes, but even that isn't necessarily a requirement in this day and age."

"They are readily available on the dark web." Templer advised Caslin. "Hell, I'm pretty sure you can import them from China without even accessing the dark web. You run the risk of them being picked up as they pass through customs in the UK, but things get through all the time."

"What did you find in the autopsies?" Caslin asked. Dr Taylor stepped down from the stool she was sitting on and crossed the room to the first of the autopsy tables. Both Caslin and Templer joined her and she passed him a file containing the notes made during the examination. Caslin recognised the male who was seated on the sofa.

"The first thing to note is there are no signs of a struggle, or any indication of violence whatsoever on this man's body. Therefore, I think it's safe to conclude that he was a willing participant and injected himself with the heroin. Similarly, with the woman, who I'm led to believe is probably his partner," she said glancing to Caslin, he nodded, "also exhibits no signs of forced coercion."

"They had no idea what they were taking," Templer said quietly.

"That is my conclusion," Dr Taylor said.

"What about the fingers? We've seen from the footage that they were cut off with a set of secateurs," Caslin said.

"That doesn't surprise me. If you flick through to page four, that was my guess. The damage to the remaining skin tissue, where the finger was detached, indicates a sharp blade but not of surgical grade, and also the level of pressure exerted implied a tool that magnified the force the user was able to apply."

"If you'll indulge me, please could you apply your psycho analysis skills to the removal of the fingers?"

"I'd be lying if I said I hadn't given it some thought already," Dr Taylor said.

"Would I be hopelessly simplistic to suggest the removal of the fingers is merely trophy hunting?"

"Not... hopelessly... simplistic, no," Dr Taylor replied. "However, I think we should be careful about hypothesising too much regarding this particular killer's motivations. Without more data to go on, it might steer you in the wrong direction."

"Fair enough, I promise not to make what you say the focal point of the investigation. What you think?"

"Many killers who carry out detailed schemes need to objectify their victims. This separates any level of empathy the killer may have for their victims or their associated friends and family. Mutilation goes hand in glove with objectification and allows for an unchallenged possession of the victim."

Caslin thought about the level of planning necessary to contaminate a supply and also ensure the users, in this case four people, willingly ingested the drugs and died as a result.

"You'll probably be aware of many serial killers who will often have had sex with the bodies of the victims, commonly after death, which is the ultimate form of intimacy."

Caslin nodded. "The likes of Bundy, Dahmer, they did that."

"Now, that isn't the case in this scenario but each victim has been mutilated. The act of mutilation or the act of copulation with the dead body are not in themselves acts that you would necessarily associate with someone's desire to achieve sexual satisfaction, which many believe is paramount with these killers, but they are more about control. You mentioned a video of this particular crime scene being uploaded on the Internet."

"Yes, it was sent to a local paper."

"I'm not surprised to hear that in the least. That in itself is an extension of control. Capturing the victim on video either before, during, or after the murder is a form of exerting unmitigated, absolute, and irreversible control over that person. The killer is aspiring to 'freeze time' in the still perfection that he has choreographed. The victim is motionless and defenceless. The killer is attaining their long-sought object permanence where the victim is unable to leave them."

Caslin pondered on the last point for a moment. If Alison was correct, then there was every possibility the killer suffered some past trauma from an abandonment or humiliation. That gave them an insight that could prove helpful in identifying him. At this point he was unsure of how they would do that unless he made a mistake.

As if reading his mind, she elaborated. "People who commit multiple homicides are often desperately trying to avoid a painful relationship. They may be terrified of society seeing what they are and then fear being discarded. This is most likely subconscious, resulting from an abusive upbringing or a lack of a stable parental figure in their life. This scene may lack the blood and gore that you often find with a serial killer but make no mistake, you are dealing with a very twisted individual and a very dangerous one at that."

"What are the chances that this is the result of a rival drug gang trying to take out a supplier who has overstepped the mark in their territory? Although again, I accept this is pure conjecture on our part." Caslin flicked a brief glance in Templer's direction. He knew the question was for his benefit.

"It's okay, Dr Taylor, you don't need to answer the question. I've never known a turf war to be played out in this manner," Templer said, meeting Caslin's eye and conceding ground.

"Just to be clear," Dr Taylor said, "it will be the strangest act of gang retaliation I've ever heard of."

"Do you have anything else for us?" Caslin asked.

"Only to say that both of the victims that I have studied so far were habitual drug users. Both of them frequently injected them-selves, most likely with heroin, and I also found traces of methadone in their system."

That meant to Caslin that both victims must be registered in a drug counselling programme, perhaps making it easier to identify them.

"I will continue with my examination of the remaining two victims today and I'll ensure you have the headlines of all four autopsies by first thing tomorrow. The detailed write-ups will be with you by the end of day."

Caslin's phone rang in his pocket and he excused himself,

stepping away from the other two. He saw Hunter's name flash up on the screen as he answered the call.

"Go ahead, Sarah."

"Sir, Terry Holt has double-checked the origin of the video sent to the newspaper offices. They were telling the truth. The email account is being bounced off a VPN and we've got no chance of working out the source. However, he not only sent it to the newspaper but he subsequently uploaded it to the Internet himself. Holt's doing his best to track its route back to the source but again, we suspect he is using the same software to mask his location."

"He's looking for attention."

"I agree. That's never a good sign." Hunter sounded pensive. "It usually indicates that this is just the beginning."

"There is one good thing about attention seekers though, Sarah."

"Yeah, what's that?"

"They want to be talked about. They want us to see them. Eventually, they must speak to us and that's when they come out of the shadows."

"I hear that. There's another reason I'm calling, sir. We red-flagged Fowler's mobile number. Once we loaded it into the system, we immediately got a notification that a call was made from that number to the emergency services overnight."

"A 999 call?"

"Yes. The call-handler didn't hear a voice on the other end of the line but followed standard procedure. She gave the caller time to communicate and tried to attract attention but nothing was forthcoming. Ninety-nine times out of a hundred these turn out to be accidental, or prank, calls. Made by kids, that type of thing. As per procedure, the call was passed to a colleague who initiated a call back once the line was terminated. No one answered but the location of the cell tower was logged."

"Have we tried calling the number again?"

"Yes, rings out, but the handset is still connected to the same tower east of the city."

"Do we have a location?"

"It's rural, so we can't pinpoint it but we've narrowed it down. We have a helicopter inbound and a uniform presence searching the vicinity. I'll text you the centre point. Shall we meet you there?"

"We're on our way." Turning, he caught Templer's eye. "We're on the move."

CHAPTER SIX

THEIR ROUTE TOOK them eastwards out of the city, via Heslington, before turning north and passing Dunnington and Stamford Bridge on the way to Westow, a village on the cusp of the Howardian Hills. The journey took them nearly three quarters of an hour. A few spots of rain graced the windscreen as they left pathology but now, approaching their destination, the rain was steadily falling as they circumvented the village and cut west along the line of the River Derwent.

They were on a back road linking the village to Kirkham and its ruined abbey only a couple of miles distant. The line of the road curved following the route of the river, but as they made the turn, they came across a liveried police car parked on the verge. The uniformed officer present stood out in his all-weather high visibility jacket. He flagged them down. Stooping low, the officer peered through the passenger window as Templer lowered it, identifying them. Pointing off to the left, he indicated an unmade track that headed south, parallel to the flow of the river. Shielded from the road by woodland, if you didn't know it was there then in all likelihood you would have driven past and paid it no attention whatsoever.

Caslin took the car down the track and as soon as the road

disappeared from view behind them, they reached a gated entrance to what presumably used to be a working farm. Here, they were met by another officer who pulled back the gate and ushered them through. As they passed through more police vehicles came into sight. Recognising Hunter's car, Caslin pulled up alongside. Both men got out and looked around them. The immediate vicinity saw little activity but a short distance away was a clearing surrounded on three sides by dense woodland. They could see uniformed activity through the trees. Caslin turned the collar of his coat up against the rain as it intensified. Looking to Templer, he glanced down at the younger man's footwear.

"Nice shoes."

"Thanks," Templer replied, confused.

"The woods are going to love those," Caslin said, breaking into a smile.

"Yeah," Templer agreed ruefully, eyeing the terrain around them. "Thanks again."

They set off and once they breached the tree line, the scene before them took on a macabre appearance. A blue BMW was parked in the centre of the clearing with the headlights on, illuminating everything before it. The oppressive cloud cover and ensuing rainfall, aided by the mature trees all around them, left the clearing shrouded in relative darkness despite the hour of the day. Forensics officers were endeavouring to set up a tent with which to cover the target area, but before they could do so the surrounding scene needed to be photographed and catalogued. This process couldn't be rushed but the elements were applying pressure for them to do so.

Hunter spied their arrival and crossed to greet them.

"Not seen one like this before."

Her grim expression told Caslin to brace himself. "How did you find it?"

"The aerial unit took up a grid-by-grid search pattern, extending out from the cell tower. They spotted the car from above. The lights on made it stand out. I don't think there's any doubt our guy wanted us to find it."

"What makes you say that?" Templer asked.

"You'll see." Gesturing for them to walk with her, she turned and headed towards the car.

Rounding the car, a nearly new BMW, Caslin immediately saw what Hunter was talking about. Less than fifteen feet from the front of the vehicle, he could see a human head on the floor. As they moved closer, he noted the level of damage to the face as well as the top of the skull. He thought it was a woman's head but the injuries were so severe, it was tough to tell. On the ground in front of her was a mobile phone. Caslin dropped to his haunches to inspect both it and the victim.

"That's Ben Fowler's phone," Templer said.

"You're sure?" Caslin asked over his shoulder.

"It's the model I issued him with." Caslin turned his attention to the woman. Her face was battered, with much of her features disfigured by multiple blows, lacerations and swelling. Her hair, which he presumed would be shoulder length, if he could see her shoulders, was matted with dried blood. Leaning in closer, he could see extensive damage to the skin of the scalp and was left in no doubt that she died in the most brutal and painful manner.

"I don't see any cuts to the neckline," Caslin said aloud to nobody in particular. "Presumably there's more of a body beneath?"

"That was my thought too," Iain Robertson said in his thick Glaswegian, approaching from behind. "We put a probe down and met resistance. My thinking is she's buried up to her neck."

Caslin moved aside and Robertson came past him, rustling in his white coveralls. Kneeling down, he took a small trowel in one hand, something akin to a decorator's paintbrush in the other, and gently began to loosen the soil around the neck and brush it aside. Ensuring not to taint any of the forensic evidence, within a few minutes, he was confident enough to confirm his initial suspicions. Looking up to Caslin, he nodded.

"Aye, it looks like she's all here."

"You think she was beaten before burial?" Caslin asked.

"That's possible. If you cast your eyes around at the assorted stones and rocks nearby, you'll note they don't really belong where they've fallen."

Caslin did as he was bid and checked the assorted stones. Some were larger than a tennis ball whilst others were smaller, pieces of jagged flint the size of a walnut. In some cases, they rested on fresh grass flattened beneath them and others lay atop damp moss. They were recent additions to the area. Caslin cast his eyes skyward.

"Nasty way to go, isn't it?" Robertson said flatly.

"Man, that's cold," Templer said softly.

"The mobile?" Caslin asked Robertson, with a flick of his eyes in the direction of the phone.

"Yes," Robertson said, "it's been catalogued and printed."

Caslin donned a pair of latex gloves and Hunter took out an evidence bag, bringing it over to him. Carefully, Caslin picked up the phone and placed it inside the transparent plastic bag. Sealing it, he passed it to Hunter.

"Let's get this back to Fulford Road as quickly as possible," Caslin began, "and have Terry confirm that it's Fowler's phone. Then, see if he can find where it's been and who has been in contact with it in the last forty-eight hours."

Turning his attention to the BMW, Caslin was joined by Templer. Both of them walked around the car looking for any signs of damage on both the interior as well as the exterior, looking for any indication as to how the vehicle ended up there. Even a cursory inspection revealed the car was in near perfect condition.

"Who's the car registered to?" Caslin asked, opening the driver's door.

"The DVLA has the owner recorded as a Kelly Ryan. She is a forty-two-year-old resident of York, sir, and the only recorded keeper since its first registration," Hunter said.

Caslin glanced back at the victim who was slowly and painstakingly being released from her early grave. "Does her description match the victim?"

"I believe so, sir."

"Do you think she was here meeting someone?" Templer asked, looking around and squinting against the rain.

"Iain, any sign of another vehicle?" Caslin called out. Robertson looked up, briefly pausing what he was doing. He passed the trowel and brush to a colleague and rose. Walking over to join them, he shook his head.

"We haven't found any indication of another vehicle. No tyre impressions nor evidence of a turning circle in the grass."

With the changeable weather recently, Caslin judged the ground underfoot was soft and damp. Any other vehicle would have left some kind of sign, so the vehicle was possibly left on the highway. "Have someone walk the lane just to be sure. What do we think, Craig?"

"It's out of the way. You're safe from prying eyes here. It wouldn't be a bad place for a tryst."

"Are you talking from experience?" Hunter asked, with a wry grin. That brought some much-needed lightness to the scene and all those nearby smiled, if only briefly.

"It's also a cracking place to bring someone to if you want to torture them to death," Caslin said, returning his attention to the car. Leaning into the interior he looked around. The upholstery was leather and in immaculate condition. In fact, the cabin in its entirety was a damn site cleaner than any vehicle or house he had ever owned. Templer opened the passenger door and dropped to his haunches, casting a wary eye around the interior.

"Clean. No sign of any struggle."

"Agreed."

Caslin popped the boot and both men retreated from the interior and walked to the rear. The boot space was empty. It was lined with carpet, matching the interior of the cabin, and as they rooted around, they found what they would expect the manufacturer to provide with nothing else that seemed out of place.

Caslin looked along the length of the car and caught Hunter's attention. "What else do we know about Miss Ryan?"

"She was reported missing two nights ago."

"Reported missing? By whom?"

"Her husband, Thomas," Hunter said. "He called the police a little after midnight, two days ago, stating he was concerned that his wife had failed to return home from work and wasn't answering his calls."

"Did anyone follow up?"

"Uniform called by the residence within an hour and had a word with him, but it was a little early to ring the alarm bells," Hunter said.

"Within an hour?" Templer said. "It must have been a quiet night."

"True," Caslin said, smiling. "Why was he so concerned, did he say?"

"The officers who attended reported that he felt her actions were out of character. Her husband had already contacted friends and relatives but to no avail. After visiting her place of work and finding her car missing, he rang around the local hospitals to see if she had been involved in an accident. Needless to say, she hadn't been admitted."

"We'll have to pay him a visit," Caslin said. "Once we have her out then he will need to carry out a formal identification. We'll also have to find out where she works and call in on them as well to see if she was in work yesterday. I want to start building a timeline of the hours since she was last seen alive. Start from the point of the 999 call we received last night, from this location, and work backwards from there. Do we have the recording from the call?"

"Terry Holt was looking to get that just as I was leaving to head out here," Hunter said.

"Well, this is interesting," Robertson said from within the blue tent, lifted into place to protect the crime scene from the elements while they were talking. Raising his voice so they could hear him, Robertson called the three detectives back to where the victim was buried. Moving the entrance flap aside, they came to stand behind the CSI officers, looking over his shoulder. "It looks like she's not been buried here long. The soil hasn't had a chance to compact around her and is fairly loose against the body."

The team were making fast work of clearing the surrounding soil away from the body of the victim, albeit working to ensure they maintained the integrity of the crime scene. The right-hand side of the body had been partially revealed. The loose soil assisted in the speed of their work. The shoulder, down to the waistline, was visible as the soil had been carefully removed and cleared away. The earth behind the body was still in place, keeping her upright. Presently, she had the look of a living statue being excavated by a team of archaeologists.

"What's interesting?" Caslin asked.

"Just give me a second," Robertson said under his breath. He was kneeling in front of the victim and reaching down, extending his arm and appeared to be brushing something away with smooth strokes. "Yep, I was half expecting this."

"What have you got?" Caslin was impatient.

Robertson brought himself upright and looked back over his shoulder. "Come and take a look." Caslin stepped forward and crouched down, peering into the hole. Although the left arm of the victim was still encased in soil, her left hand was now revealed as it was clasped against the right. Her wrists were bound together by a cable tie, pulled tight enough for the plastic to have broken through the skin. "I'll bet she was struggling to free herself so much that the binders cut into her. Do you see what I see?"

"The index finger?" Caslin said quietly.

"Just like back at Stamford Street. For some reason, I was expecting it," Robertson said with grim satisfaction.

"Something tells me he didn't bury her, stone her to death, then go back and dig her out in order to cut off a finger."

Robertson shook his head, "No, I doubt that very much. More likely, he cut it off before she was buried."

"And before he killed her." Caslin ran a hand across his eye and left cheek before shaking his head gently. "It might also explain why there's no sign of a struggle."

"You think he brought her here in her own car?" Robertson asked.

Caslin nodded. "If she wasn't meeting someone, I figure it's likely."

"If I can't find a trace of another vehicle present, then I'd have to agree. Once we get her out and back into the city, we'll run her clothes for carpet fibres and see if he transported her in the boot of the car. Do you see this here?" Robertson asked, directing Caslin to a point on the victim's face, near to her mouth. Caslin couldn't see what he was talking about and leaned in closer, meeting the forensic officer's eye with an unspoken query. "There, around the mouth." Robertson indicated the corner of her mouth with a sweeping arc movement of his index finger from one side to the other and back again. "You see the redness there, extending from one side of the mouth to the other and taking in the chin as well as the upper lip, below the nose? That's skin irritation, most likely caused by gaffer tape or some other restraint stuck to her mouth."

"She was gagged?"

"Yes, and then he removed it."

"To hear her scream?"

Robertson frowned and shrugged at the same time. "Perhaps the tape spoiled his presentation?"

"For us, do you mean?"

"Your guess is as good as mine, lad. Your guess is as good as mine."

CHAPTER SEVEN

DARKNESS HAD WELL and truly fallen by the time Caslin and Hunter returned to York. Bypassing the centre, they arrived in the suburbs on the south-western edge of the city. Taking a right turn off the Tadcaster Road and onto Mount Parade, Caslin found the first available parking space at the side of the road and pulled over. Eyeing the street scene, Caslin scanned the Georgian terraces. This was one of the most prestigious postcodes in York, with even a two-bedroom apartment costing significantly above the national average house price.

"She was doing well," Hunter offered, following Caslin's gaze.

"It's not a bad place to be living, certainly."

"Tell me, what do you make of Craig?"

"Templer?" Hunter nodded. He thought on it for a moment before responding. "I'll hold fire on passing judgement, if you don't mind? He's not going anywhere, that's for sure."

Caslin got out of the car and Hunter followed. Stepping up onto the pavement, he looked to her.

"Which one is it?" he asked. She pointed to the house three doors along from where they parked. The two of them walked the short distance and mounted the steep steps to the front door. Caslin reached up and took hold of the door knocker, before drawing attention to anyone inside, he glanced at her. "This never gets any easier, does it?"

"No, it doesn't."

Caslin rapped the knocker a couple of times and then released his grip, standing back to await a response. There were lights on in the interior and they didn't have to wait long before the sound of a chain being released on the inside could be heard. The panelled door swung inwards and a man stood before them. He was in his early forties, Caslin assumed, wearing suit trousers and a shirt, open at the neck with the sleeves rolled part way up along his forearms. He was slim, clean shaven and he figured this man would normally be very well presented but today his eyes appeared sunken and hollow. His stubble was perhaps a day or so old, mostly black, matching his hair, but with flecks of grey visible.

"Mr Ryan?" Caslin asked, withdrawing his warrant card from within his wallet and displaying it before him. "Detective Inspector Caslin and Detective Sergeant Hunter, based out of Fulford Road. May we come in?"

"Of course, Inspector." Thomas Ryan stepped back and gestured for them to enter. The hall was an expansive area that gave them enough room to pass by him, standing casually until he pushed the door closed. He addressed them pointedly. "Do you have news of Kelly?" The expressions on their faces conveyed the worst fears that he must have had playing through his mind. "What is it, what happened?"

"Perhaps we should sit down somewhere and have a chat," Caslin said.

"What's happened to her?" Ryan pressed, fear edging into his tone. "Have you found her?"

"We believe so, Mr Ryan," Hunter said.

"Is she... is she okay?" The change in expression on his face, as well as the shift in his body language, suggested he already knew the answer to the question. His eyes were fearful, dreading the answer.

"We are very sorry, Mr Ryan, but we believe we have found your wife. We still have to carry out more checks in order to be certain, but the person we have found matches your wife's description and was found alongside her car. At this time, we do believe it is Kelly."

"Dear God." He took a step back, bracing himself against the wall of the hallway as his legs appeared unsteady beneath him. Caslin reached out just in case the man was about to collapse, but Thomas Ryan held up a hand to indicate that wasn't necessary. Caslin retreated.

"Perhaps, we should take a seat, Mr Ryan," Hunter reiterated. He nodded and beckoned for them to follow him deeper into the house, along the hallway. The first doorway they reached was the entrance to the sitting room, located in front of the house, with a large fifteen-pane window overlooking the street outside. Ryan offered them a seat on the sofa, a large three-seater in keeping with the decor of the rest of the room. A fire was set in the hearth with logs burning, crackling away, flickering shadows cast around them as the flames danced.

"What happened to Kelly?" Ryan asked, as he seated himself facing them in a Chesterfield club chair.

"We're still trying to figure that out," Caslin said. "I'm afraid I have to inform you that it is strongly apparent that your wife was murdered." He broke down at the news, his head bowing and he wept unashamedly. Both detectives let the moment carry, reluctant to put any extra pressure on to someone so visibly upset. Often, in this type of scenario, Caslin would give the immediate relative some space in order to process such information. He could always ask his questions at a later time, however, in this situation, they needed to get the inquiry up to speed as fast as possible and he didn't feel he had the leeway on this occasion. After a few minutes, Ryan managed to compose himself and raised his head, wiping streaks of tears from his cheeks with the palm of his hand.

"What is it you would like to know?"

"When you reported your wife missing two nights ago, had you any reason to expect her not to return home after work?"

Ryan shook his head. "No, we had a dinner reservation for nine o'clock. She often works late but when I thought she was cutting it fine, I called her mobile but she didn't answer."

"What time was that?" Hunter asked, taking out a notebook and pen.

"About eight o'clock, I think. Perhaps, a little earlier. Then I called again, a little after half past. To be honest, I'm angry at myself."

"Why?" Caslin asked, intrigued.

Ryan chuckled but without any genuine humour. "I thought she was just wrapped up at work, as usual. I thought maybe she was... trying to make me angry. How self-centred is that?"

"Was that normal behaviour, by your wife, I mean?" Caslin asked in a non-accusational manner.

"Sometimes." He met Caslin's gaze. "She could be quite single-minded, could Kelly. Something that I think I taught her in our marriage."

"So, she never answered your calls... either of them, or got back to you with a text or email?" Hunter asked.

Ryan shook his head. "No."

"What did you do then?"

"I waited. At first, I just assumed she had forgotten about our plans and lost herself in her work. Once it was past ten-thirty, that's when I got really concerned and I phoned a couple of friends to see if she had dropped by with any of them, but they hadn't seen or heard from her either."

"What work does she do?" Caslin asked.

"She works for one of the national banks, here in the city."

Caslin nodded. "Doing what for them?"

"Debt management."

"And how was her work, did she talk about it much?" Caslin asked.

"Not with me, no."

"And after you phoned your friends?" Hunter asked, returning their focus to the night in question.

"I got in the car and drove to her office. It's just on the edge of the city centre. I know where she parks, although it's in an underground car park, beneath the offices, I thought I might be able to meet her in her office or something."

"And?" Hunter pressed.

"And nothing," Ryan said, shaking his head. "The entrance to the parking lot was gated and I couldn't get in. So, I went around to the entrance, buzzed the intercom and waited for a few minutes but no one came out. I figured the security guard would be there and I could ask them whether she was still at her desk."

"But no one came to speak to you?"

"No. I waited… It must have been ten minutes or so but no one came."

"What did you do then?"

"I headed home. I thought maybe we had passed each other on the road, and I half expected her to be waiting for me at the house, annoyed that I wasn't there when she got in. Obviously, she wasn't here and then I got really worried and I phoned the hospital. To see if she had been admitted in some kind of accident or something, but they had no one matching her description. Then I called you."

"Have you spoken to anybody at her place of work since that night?" Caslin asked.

"Yes, I have. At least, I tried to find out as much as I could but they weren't very helpful."

"Who wasn't?" Caslin asked.

"Her boss, colleagues." He was visibly annoyed. "I just wanted to know whether she'd been there or not."

"They wouldn't tell you?" Caslin asked, mildly surprised.

"No. They gave me some guff about data protection and whatnot." He was dismissive, irritated. "Honestly, sometimes I think this country's gone mad."

"Can you give us the address of her office?" Hunter asked and Ryan nodded that he would.

"Do you live here alone, besides you and Kelly, I mean?" Caslin asked.

"Yes, it's just the two of us."

"Is there anyone that we can call for you, Mr Ryan?" Caslin asked, worried about leaving him alone at this time.

Ryan shook his head. "No, thank you. I have people to call on, if I need to. My sister, Miche, lives nearby."

"If you are sure?" Hunter said. "It's no trouble."

"Thank you for the offer, you are very kind," he replied, "but I'll be fine. When can I see her?"

"I'm afraid we're still processing the scene," Caslin explained. "As soon as we can return her to York, we'll look to bring you down and you can see her then. It will be some time tomorrow, I imagine."

"Thank you, Inspector," Ryan said softly, his head dropping as he spoke.

Caslin took out one of his contact cards and handed it to him. Ryan accepted it gratefully and scanned the name and telephone number. "You can reach me on that mobile number at any time, Mr Ryan."

"Thank you."

"We'll see ourselves out," Caslin said, indicating for Hunter to come with him. She stood up and crossed the room to the door. As Caslin joined her, he paused and turned back. "Can you think of any reason why your wife would have driven out towards Kirkham two nights ago?"

Ryan sat back, appearing thoughtful. "I don't believe either of us know anyone who lives out that way. No, sorry. Is that where you found her?"

Caslin nodded slowly. "Yes, it is. She was in a wooded area a little way off the beaten track. It is possible that she drove out there to meet someone. At least, that's one line of inquiry. Is there anyone that she may have been meeting out there. Perhaps it is someone you might suspect she could have been meeting but were unaware of?"

Ryan met his eye. "Is that your diplomatic way of asking me if my wife was having an affair, Inspector?"

"Yes, Mr Ryan. It is."

Thomas Ryan's expression remained impassive and he didn't blink. "The honest answer to that question, Inspector, is that I really don't know what my wife might have been doing out there. Could she have been having an affair?" he said, shaking his head and breaking the eye contact. "I genuinely don't know what Kelly might have been capable of, these days."

"I appreciate your candour," Caslin said. "I have another question that you might find slightly… unpalatable at this time, but I'd appreciate an answer, nonetheless."

"If it helps you catch her killer, ask me whatever you want."

"Did your wife… did Kelly have a drug habit that you are aware of?"

"What kind of a bloody question is that, Inspector?" Ryan said, his tone turning hostile.

"A pertinent one, Mr Ryan. One that I'm afraid I have to ask."

"Why on earth would you think Kelly had a drug habit?"

"We have reason to believe that your wife's murder may be linked to another case that we are working on."

"One that involves… what… drugs?" Ryan asked.

"Yes, that's the case," Caslin replied, waiting for the answer to his question.

Ryan appeared agitated, shaking his head. He looked up at Caslin. "No, Inspector. To my knowledge, Kelly does not take drugs nor has she ever done so. Any other questions?"

"Not at this time, Mr Ryan, but thank you. I appreciate that these questions would be difficult at the best of times and truly awful at the worst. We'll be in touch tomorrow and in the meantime should you need anything, please do give me a call on that number," he said, indicating the contact card that Ryan was fiddling with his hands. "As I said, we'll see ourselves out. I'm very sorry for your loss."

The two of them left Thomas Ryan sitting in his living room and walked back into the hallway and then out into the street without further conversation. Once onto the pavement, Hunter glanced in Caslin's direction before casting her eyes back towards the house and caught sight of Ryan, standing at the window overlooking the street, watching them depart. They reached the car and Caslin hugged the side of the vehicle as oncoming traffic passed by, before opening the driver's door and getting in.

"What did you make of all that?" she asked, staring up at the now empty window. Ryan was gone.

Caslin exhaled, following her gaze. "Marriage is seldom easy."

"I'll take your word for that," Hunter said, smiling.

"One day you'll know exactly what I'm talking about, I'm sure. Interesting though. He couldn't bring himself to say it, could he?"

"He thinks she might well be having an affair."

"Or, he knows damn well that she is."

"And the office… with the whole data protection thing when he called?"

"There's definitely more going on here than he just gave us," Caslin said. "We'll stop by her office first thing in the morning and find out whether she was in work two nights ago as Ryan thought. It will certainly narrow down the timeframe from when she was last seen to when we believe she was killed."

"Or blow it wide open if she never turned up for work," Hunter added.

"It's all very interesting though, isn't it?" Caslin was thinking aloud. "Then again, most murder cases are."

CHAPTER EIGHT

THE RECEPTION FOYER was furnished with designer seating. At least, the *Le Corbusier* style they were trying to achieve was close, and may well have fooled the untrained eye, but anyone who knew how to spot the real thing would recognise these as cheaper imitations. They didn't have long to wait before a door opened on the far side of the room and a man stepped through. He was in his late 50s, balding, and bore a frown that Caslin figured was quite likely a permanent feature. The man glanced to a member of staff, seated at a desk to his left, and she indicated towards Caslin and Hunter. He crossed the foyer and smiled in greeting, the frown dispersing before their eyes.

"Mr Alexander?" Caslin asked. He nodded in reply. "I'm Detective Inspector Caslin. We spoke on the phone."

"Yes, I remember. Pleased to meet you."

"This is DS Hunter," Caslin introduced her. Hunter took the offered hand in greeting.

"Please, do come with me," Alexander said, gesturing for them to accompany him back the way he had just come. Swiping an access card against a small panel next to the door, the lock clicked and he pulled it open, allowing both of them to pass through before him.

"You are Kelly Ryan's line manager, is that right?" Caslin asked.

"Yes, I was. I still can't believe this has happened to Kelly. Such a damn shame."

"Was she popular?" Hunter asked.

"Very." Alexander was talking over his shoulder as they approached another door. He opened it and passed through, leading them into his office. Offering them both a seat in front of his desk, he closed the door, glancing somewhat nervously along the corridor as he did so, in Caslin's mind. "Although this is a large company, we have a very close-knit team. I don't wish it to sound clichéd but we are something of a family here. Kelly was integral to that."

"I understand she worked in debt management," Caslin said.

Alexander nodded. "Mortgage debt specifically, yes. Kelly managed a small team who process mortgage arrears and repossession orders."

"Busy times?"

"Always busy times, I'm afraid to say. Not quite what we faced during the last financial crash, and we manage our risk in a much more cautious way than we used to, but nonetheless, people's circumstances change or they've overreached... It's the nature of the beast that some will fall by the wayside, sadly."

"How would you describe Kelly Ryan? In terms of her ability, work ethic, standing among her colleagues," Caslin asked.

"As I said, she was very popular within the team. She has... had... a lot of friends here. Regarding her work I have absolutely no complaints. Her work ethic and performance were second to none. More often than not she was the first person through the door and the last to leave at night."

"And two nights ago, the night she went missing, her husband stated she was working late. Can you confirm this?" Hunter asked, taking notes. Caslin watched the man intently, appearing almost casual but in reality, he was weighing up every word he uttered.

"Yes," Alexander said firmly. "I understand she was one of the last to finish for the day and even spoke to one of our night shift security guards as she left the building. After your call earlier, I double checked and he confirmed that she left shortly after 8 PM."

"We would like to speak to the security guard, if you can arrange it?" Caslin said.

"Of course. Marcus was on shift last night and I spoke to him this morning and he offered to wait in case you wanted a word with him. He's ex-military. A top man."

"What about Kelly's work? Has she had any problems that you are aware of recently? Perhaps a disgruntled customer, any threats?"

Alexander shook his head emphatically. "No, nothing like that. Kelly's team is very much admin focussed. The only contact she has with people facing repossession orders or debt restructuring is done through paperwork. Her position at the bank isn't a customer facing role."

"How well do you know her?" Hunter asked. "You said your team was like a family, so, unless that's a soundbite, I'm presuming you are close to one another. Was there anything going on in her life that might appear unusual, particularly in light of what's just happened?"

Alexander drew breath, appearing uncomfortable at the question. "I'm not entirely sure what you're asking me," he said, his eyes flicking between the two of them.

"How was she within herself?" Caslin asked. "Did she say anything to you regarding her personal life or whether she was experiencing marital issues?"

"I'm not really sure that's for me to say."

"How well do you know Thomas, Kelly's husband?" Caslin asked.

"I've met him a handful of times," Alexander said. "At the occasional work do… Christmas. He's attended the staff summer barbecue once or twice. That type of event but I can't say I know him well."

"Being Kelly's line manager, presumably you fielded his call the other day, when he was trying to find out about Kelly's whereabouts."

"Yes, I did." He lowered his gaze to the desk in front of him momentarily but it was enough to pique Caslin's interest.

"He described you as not forthcoming with helpful information."

"Is that how he put it?" Alexander asked, his micro-expression giving away far more than he perhaps realised. Caslin fixed him with a stare, one that he clearly found uncomfortable. "To be honest, I don't have a lot of time for the man and at that point, I had no reason to believe that anything untoward had befallen Kelly. For all I knew, she may have…"

"May have what, Mr Alexander?" Caslin pressed.

"May have left him." The man appeared to feel awkward commenting on Kelly's personal life. "It was no secret amongst the team that Kelly had a somewhat trying marriage."

"Please could you define *a trying marriage?*"

"They were not without their problems and, quite often, Kelly was unable to leave them at the door when she pitched up to work, Inspector. God knows, anyone who's faced a marital breakup would understand how difficult that can be. Particularly when the spouse follows your member of staff into the office."

"Thomas Ryan would come here?" Hunter asked, surprised.

"Not quite, no. But he would often be chasing her, trying to pursue their… confrontations over the phone rather than allowing her the space to breathe."

"Was this behaviour recent?" Caslin asked.

"On and off for the past couple of years," Alexander explained, the forlorn expression returning. "I get the impression he's a man used to getting his own way and Kelly was no pushover, I assure you."

"I noticed you had a swipe card to get through into the back offices," Caslin said. Alexander nodded. "Do all members of staff have access cards?"

"Yes, they do."

"So, can you tell us the exact time when Kelly left the building?"

"I can do better than that, Inspector. I can tell you which door she went out of, whether she went on foot or in the car. Each access door has its own data point in our security system and the software logs not only date and time but also which point of entry or exit is used. Similarly, the underground car park has the same software and you need to swipe your access card to pass through the barrier."

"Her husband said he knew where Kelly parked and he tried to see if her car was still here on the night she disappeared."

"Well, we have extensive CCTV in the underground car park so I'm sure we will be able to tell you as much as we can. Marcus can walk you through the footage when you speak with him."

"Do you think we could do that now?" Caslin asked.

"Certainly. Please, come with me."

They stepped out of the office and turned right. Alexander led them down the corridor and into a stairwell, taking them up one floor. Entering a staff room, there was only one person present and it was obvious from his uniform that he was a member of security. He stood up as they approached, taking one last mouthful of coffee before placing the cup on the table in front of him and stepping forward.

"Mr Alexander," he said.

"Marcus, these are detectives Caslin and Hunter," Alexander said. "They want to speak to you about your conversation with Kelly two nights ago. I would be grateful if you could also walk them through our security system and give them any and all access to the camera footage that they require."

"I'd be happy to," Marcus replied, nodding a greeting to both of them and smiling, although Caslin felt it was slightly forced. Caslin and Hunter exchanged glances.

"We'll be in touch, if we need anything further from you, Mr Alexander. Feel free to carry on with your business," Caslin replied. He lingered, almost as if he was reticent to leave. Caslin judged him as curious, bordering on nosey. Turning back to the security guard, he said, "Maybe we can do this in your security office?"

"Yes, of course."

A short walk and two minutes later, Marcus unlocked the door to the security room. The space was cramped for the three of them. Marcus was a big man, easily over six feet tall and heavy set. During his time in the military, there was every possibility that much of his body mass would have been muscle. Now though, he was more flab. A number of monitors displayed split-screen footage from various points inside the building, as well as from those cameras mounted on the exterior. The footage appeared to be rotating through the predesignated routine and Caslin watched for a few seconds, taking into account the movements of staff and customers along with pedestrians passing by outside. From what he could make out there were four angles covering the underground car park.

"Tell me," Caslin began, "the car park, how do you get in and out?"

Marcus turned his attention to the footage. "There's only one entrance and exit and you have to swipe your card to raise the barrier to get in or out. It's a staff only car park."

"Did Kelly Ryan use the car park two nights ago?"

"Yes, she did. I spoke to her that evening as she was leaving work. She was just getting into the lift to take her down. When I came on shift, there were only a handful of cars parked downstairs and I recognised hers as being one of them."

"She definitely left in her car?" Hunter asked.

"I assume so," Marcus said. "But we can have a look. Just give me a second to bring up the footage." He sat down at his desk and started thundering away at the keyboard, searching for the relevant files.

"How did she seem the other night, when she left work?" Caslin asked.

Marcus glanced up, over his shoulder. "Quite normal, I must say. We didn't speak for long but she was the same as usual. Always friendly, willing to take the time and effort to speak to you. A lovely lady. Here it is."

They turned their attention to the monitor directly in front of Marcus's keyboard as he brought up the black and white footage from the night in question. Focussing on the cameras recording events in the underground car park, the screen was split four ways. They waited patiently as Marcus fast-forwarded through the footage until the time stamp hit 8 o'clock and then he pressed play. He pointed to the top right quarter of the screen, indicating that that was where they should focus. The camera was aimed at the elevators and when the time stamp read four minutes past the hour, the doors to the lift opened and a woman stepped out.

"That's Kelly," Marcus stated. They watched as she walked towards, and then beneath, the camera, disappearing from view. The security guard then pointed to the top left quadrant footage and she could be seen walking into view. She was alone in the parking level. Looking at the footage from the other three cameras, no one else appeared to be present in the car park.

"Which car is hers?" Caslin asked.

"That one there." He pointed to a BMW that was visible in the bottom left of the screen, on the lower level. Caslin now recognised the same car they'd seen in the clearing of the woods the day before. However, only the rear quarter panel of the car could be seen as a van was parked alongside, obscuring the view. They watched as she approached the vehicle. She appeared to pause as she reached the back of her car, staring at something not in the view of the camera due to the presence of the van.

"Is she talking to someone?" Hunter asked.

Caslin narrowed his eyes, trying to decipher as much as he could from the grainy footage. "It doesn't look like it." After a brief moment, she turned sideways and moved between the car and the van, disappearing from sight.

"I think the van's parked too close," Hunter suggested. "Wind that back, would you?"

"Sure," Marcus said, reaching forward and rewinding the footage. Pressing play once again, they watched and Hunter pointed out her thinking.

"You see, she turns sideways in order to squeeze down the gap between them. And look at the wheels of the van, how close they are to the edge of the bay."

"The van could be trying to avoid the support pillar on the offside," Marcus suggested, indicating the giant concrete pillar, one of many supporting the floors above.

"Whose van is that?" Caslin asked. Marcus shook his head to indicate he didn't know. "Do you have all employee vehicles on record?"

"Absolutely." The security guard paused the footage, then accessed another file and executed a search for the van's registration details. "What is that, a Transit?" he asked, trying to ascertain the make and model in order to narrow down the search. Caslin agreed. Moments later, Marcus turned to them and shook his head with a frown. "There's nothing registered to any employee."

"What about a visitor, maintenance perhaps?" Caslin asked.

"Give me a sec," Marcus said, resuming his search of the database. "No, nothing recorded that day."

"Okay, go back to the footage and roll it forward," Caslin said. They resumed playback. A couple of minutes after Kelly disappeared from view, the car reversed out of its parking bay with the rear of the BMW at the forefront of the camera footage. It then set off away from the current camera with the focus shifting to the last of the four displays, the one mounted alongside the exit. This camera was mounted on the exterior of the building and faced the nearside of the cars departing the underground car park. The BMW came into view, stopped at the barrier and an arm reached out in order to swipe the access card against the panel and the barrier was raised. The car then turned right onto the street outside and disappeared from view.

"Can you take that back a bit?" Caslin asked. "Back to where she reversed the car out of its bay." Marcus did so and once again, they watched the car's reversing lights come on as the BMW came into view. "Pause it there," Caslin said and Marcus did so. They peered at the footage.

"What are you looking for?" Hunter asked him.

"Can't see who's driving," Caslin said. "Go forward to when she leaves the car park." Marcus fast-forwarded to the point where the car came into view at the barrier and froze the frame.

"You still can't see," Hunter said. The positioning of the camera, as well as its viewing angle, made it impossible to get a shot of the face of the driver. The security guard edged the footage forward a few frames at a time but Kelly Ryan's face did not come into view. When she reached out with a pass card, Caslin tapped Marcus on the shoulder and he paused the playback.

"When she came out of the elevator, she was wearing her over-coat, wasn't she? What colour was it, grey?" Caslin asked.

"Not sure – but certainly light," Hunter agreed.

Caslin pointed at the footage frozen at the point of exit. "Unless she changed coats, she's not driving that car."

The arm extending from the driver's window was wearing a dark coloured coat and gloves. "You're right," Hunter said quietly.

Caslin placed a hand on Marcus's shoulder. "We're going to need to know the names of every single person who came in and out of the garage that day, and I want to know who was driving that van parked alongside Kelly Ryan's car."

CHAPTER NINE

CASLIN PUSHED OPEN the door to Dr Taylor's pathology lab and walked in. He held the door open as he looked across the room and realised the pathologist was still in the middle of her examination. Glancing across in his direction, she raised a hand and beckoned him to enter.

"You couldn't have timed your arrival any better, Nate," she said, as he approached. Alison Taylor lifted the splash visor that both protected her face from any bodily fluids and at the same time preserved the integrity of the body from any potential contamination. Taking a step back from the autopsy table, she smiled a greeting.

"I'm sorry," Caslin said. "I would have left my visit until later if I'd known you weren't done yet."

"I'm just finishing up, to be fair. You won't be surprised by the cause of death."

Caslin shook his head slowly, eyeing the damage to Kelly Ryan's face and head. Often, once a body was removed from the crime scene and processed through pathology, it would appear somewhat cleaner than it had done upon initial discovery. In this case, however, there was little improvement to be seen. The level of damage to her head was such that even a seasoned detective such as Caslin felt his stomach turn. "It was certainly a brutal way to go," he stated.

"You'll get no argument from me," Dr Taylor replied, removing her gloves by rolling them off over her hands and depositing them in a waste bin to await incineration. Picking up her notes from her desk she returned to where Kelly Ryan's naked body lay. Standing opposite Caslin, on the other side of the table, she flicked through her paperwork. "She suffered multiple blows to the head and face from heavy objects, with each being a different shape and size. It's quite clear to me that these injuries were sustained from a prolonged assault. The rocks and stones catalogued at the scene are your weapons."

"A medieval stoning," Caslin said, under his breath.

"So, it would seem. The victim suffered several sub-cranial haematomas, multiple lacerations and contusions, resulting in a dozen skull fractures, breaks to her jaw, nose and a dislocation of her right eye from its socket. Her right cheek also suffered several fractures that transferred almost from her ear to the nose."

Caslin let out a deep sigh. "Are there any other injuries besides having her right index finger removed?"

"You were there when Iain revealed that?"

Caslin nodded. "We're still to determine how she reached the scene, whether she was abducted and forced there or whether she went there of her own free will. We have CCTV footage of someone else driving her car away from her work place, which was also the last time she was seen alive. She's not visible in the car, so I'm leaning towards the former."

Dr Taylor scanned through her notes as she spoke. "There are two small marks, two inches apart, on the back of her neck where her head meets the shoulders. I'm inclined to think they're the result of a close contact Taser strike. That might answer part of your question."

"What about the removal of the finger?"

"That was done prior to burial. There is evidence of significant blood flow from the base of the finger that wouldn't be there had it been removed post-mortem. Her hands were clasped together and bound with a cable tie in such a way that the blood flowed over the other hand. That wouldn't have been the case were she already dead."

"Any evidence of resistance?"

"No. There are no defensive wounds or bruising that could imply she fought off an attacker at any point. The cable ties were used both on her wrists and ankles, and although there does appear to have been some damage to the skin tissue in those areas, most likely caused by her struggling to free herself, it would appear that didn't happen as much as you might think."

"What you mean by that?"

"If she spent a great deal of time struggling, I would expect there to be greater tissue degradation." She took her pen and leaned over, pointing out the areas she was referring to. "The ties have cut into her skin, most notably at the wrist but not so much at the ankles. This suggests that her legs were immobilised to a greater extent, and judging by the way she was buried in the ground, I think it suggestive that she was unconscious and awoke to find herself there. She wasn't buried standing up, her knees were bent and brought up almost to her waist."

"The killer didn't dig the hole deep enough," Caslin said. "He may not have had time or the inclination to do so."

"It's customary practice when carrying out the sentence of stoning for the victim to be buried before the act takes place. A man is buried up to his waist, whereas a woman is buried up to her shoulders," Dr Taylor explained.

"Why is that?"

"To protect her modesty, I believe," Dr Taylor said with a frown.

Caslin shook his head at the apparent irony of a desire to protect somebody's modesty alongside the barbaric brutalisation of the same body to the point of death.

"And yet it still goes on," Dr Taylor said. "But even the most religious of states tend to lean towards making the practice illegal even when turning a blind eye to its use in some regions."

"Iain Robertson said he would ask you to look further for any trace evidence. He was hopeful that you might find something for us to go on."

"Yes, indeed. I've sent her clothing to the CSI team for further analysis but I did find fibres underneath her fingernails. Iain is going to try and match those fibres either to the carpet of the floor of the car or the lining of the boot. Even a cursory check under the microscope shows me they're unlikely to be clothing fibres and more likely to come from the car."

"Is there any evidence of drug use either recreational or habitual?"

"As you asked, I did thoroughly inspect the body for any indication of needle marks and found none. I even looked for the hidden entry points for needles such as you find when someone is attempting to hide their abuse."

"Such as in between the toes, that type of thing?"

Dr Taylor nodded confirmation. "But as I said, there was nothing. I also carried out a full toxicology analysis on her system and that returned trace levels of alcohol but nothing significant. I think it's quite likely that she'd had a glass of wine at lunchtime. Or perhaps, she had ingested a smaller volume of alcohol at some point during the evening, based on the time it would have taken her body to process the alcoholic content and still be present in her system at the time of death."

"We have her leaving work shortly after eight, so what time do you judge she died?"

"Ian's liver test, taken at the scene, suggested a time between 11 o'clock and 1 AM. From my analysis, I think that's a pretty accurate timeframe and I don't think I can narrow it down any further."

Caslin did some mental arithmetic. If Kelly was abducted shortly after eight and died between eleven and one, that gave the killer a minimum of three hours to take her from the car park to where she was buried in the woods and then killed.

"Can I throw something else into your timeline to confuse things a little?"

"Sounds intriguing," Caslin said.

"Kelly Ryan had sex on the day of her death," Dr Taylor said, referring to her notes. "But I can't tell you when."

"Any indication of sexual assault?"

Alison shook her head. "There was certainly no damage in or around the vagina to imply the sex was not consensual. Likewise, there was no damage to her underwear or other clothing indicative of a forced removal. Therefore, I would conclude that it wasn't a result of a sexual assault but that doesn't mean that her killer wasn't the person who had sex with her. The method of her death, or should I say, her execution, because that's what it was, does imply a level of intimacy with the killer."

"It's a close-up crime, very brutal," Caslin agreed. "It does suggest a personal level of complexity, certainly."

"We spoke the other day about objectification and the killer's desire to have an ongoing intimate relationship with their victim."

"About them having unresolved trauma surrounding relationships?"

"That's right. The killer transfers those subconscious emotional frustrations onto their victims. In a case like this, I wouldn't be surprised for the killer to have had sex with the victim. Quite often that is post-mortem."

"That would explain no evidence of force being exerted on her," Caslin said flatly. "But then he got her dressed afterwards? That would be unusual. Did you retrieve any trace evidence that might point to who the sexual partner was?"

"Yes, I did. With the vaginal swab I've collected a strong semen sample and I anticipate a decent DNA profile will result from that. Also, I've been able to collect pubic hair that doesn't match the victim, being of a completely different hair colour, but I'll confirm that with the proper analysis. Either way, we will be able to run the profile through the database. If there isn't a match in the system, should you locate a suspect, I'm sure we will be able to rule them in or out."

Caslin was puzzled. In the two crime scenes, the killer appeared to be extremely methodical in his approach, leaving very little behind to enable him to be tracked or identified. There was every chance this was a mistake, Caslin expected him to make them but he sensed this killer was different to those he had met before.

"Do you think he won't make an error?" Dr Taylor asked, almost able to read his thoughts. "Even the most prolific of serial killers make mistakes somewhere along the line, even the most intelligent. Although, I agree, having unprotected sex with the victim would be quite an error in this day and age for one as meticulous as he seems."

"Well, let's hope it's the mistake that brings us to his door. You said you were just finishing up. Is there anything else I should know ahead of you producing your final report?"

"Oh, that's right, I almost forgot." She turned away and walked back to her desk. Plucking a fresh pair of gloves from a box on the desk, she returned to the autopsy table, dropping the visor back into place and putting on the gloves. "There was one more thing I was about to do when you arrived."

Caslin was intrigued. "Is it interesting?"

Dr Taylor met his eye as she bent over and picked up two of her instruments from a tray at the side of the body. "It looks as if there's something obstructing her airway and I was just going to remove it." With the tools of her trade in hand, Dr Taylor prised open Kelly Ryan's mouth until her jaw was slightly over an inch separated from the roof of the mouth. Caslin strained to see what might be inside but couldn't, resigning himself to watching as Alison Taylor reached into the mouth cavity with a pair of tweezers and deftly removed something from within. "Now that is certainly interesting," she said quietly.

"What is it?"

She brought the tweezers away from the mouth and placed the object in a stainless-steel bowl on the table. Caslin moved closer and inspected it. It was yellow vegetation, now tinged brown, and had the appearance of the ovule of a plant or flower. Returning to the mouth, moments later she produced several further pieces of detritus. Although degraded and decomposing, each one was a combination of pink and white, with the former most prominent on the outer edges but all were easily discernible as petals from a flower. Two minutes later, satisfied that everything present had been removed, she took off her gloves, discarded them to one side and removed her visor.

"Have you ever seen anything like that?"

Caslin flicked his eyes from the bowl to the pathologist and back again, examining the contents. "No, I can't say I ever have." Using the camera on his phone, he took a couple of shots of the petals.

Any further comment was cut off by Caslin's phone ringing.

"Sir, it's Hunter. There's been another video uploaded to the net."

"Not the bloody *Post* again?" Caslin asked, frustration creeping into his tone.

"No, not this time. This time, it's on social media and is already going viral. It's being shared like wildfire."

"What does it show?"

"Kelly Ryan's murder, sir. In graphic detail," Hunter explained. "I think this killer is definitely looking for attention."

"Well," Caslin said, casting a lingering look across the still form of Kelly Ryan, "he's certainly got mine."

CHAPTER TEN

THEY WATCHED in silence as the footage played out in front of them. ACC Broadfoot had joined the briefing at Caslin's request, so that he could see how the case was developing. The video was recorded on a mobile phone and therefore the footage was of relatively low quality. The footage was jumbled and bounced around a lot as the holder of the camera walked the scene in darkness. Only when the mobile was placed in one location and the car headlights turned on, were they able to see exactly what was going on.

In the beam of the headlights, they could make out Kelly Ryan, buried up to her neck a short distance away from the camera. Gaffer tape was visible across her mouth and it was obvious that she was conscious, if disorientated, as the first of the stones were thrown in her direction. Several missed their target but the fourth struck her. Several members of the team looked away at that point. In truth, no one wanted to be watching this footage but they all knew that even the slightest detail could provide the lead that could take them directly to her murderer. The five of them watched the grisly scene develop and listened to the gut-wrenching, terrifying sounds that were picked up through the microphone.

The video continued for what felt like an age but the time code denoted it was a little over seven minutes long. At the end, the battered, mutilated figure of Kelly Ryan slumped forward. The killer retrieved the mobile phone from its vantage point and crossed the clearing, keeping the victim firmly in shot. Standing before her, he zoomed in on Kelly's face drawing audible gasps from those watching back at Fulford Road. Then the footage faded out to be replaced by a black screen and the number two appeared. The numeral remained, dominating the screen, until it slowly faded back to black and the playback ceased.

"I've issued a press release," Broadfoot said, breaking the heavy silence. "Requesting that all media outlets do not replay this footage or use stills in their publications, on the grounds that this twisted individual is seeking media attention. The last thing we want to do is fuel his fetish any further."

"Do you think they'll listen?" Caslin asked.

Broadfoot inclined his head to one side, appearing thoughtful. "The reputable ones will but I fear the traditional media isn't going to be our problem."

"There's no chance of taking it down from the Internet, is there," DI Templer said. It was rhetorical. He was right. The video was across multiple social media platforms and had already been widely shared, with footage gaining traction in the prominent news stories of several countries abroad. Somewhere along the line, he had been entitled *The Night Stalker*. Such an emotive name would no doubt feed the imagination and potentially provide fuel to the fire of the media interest.

"What's the significance of the numbering?" Broadfoot asked, his eyes scanning the team in front of him.

"We've not got an answer for that yet, sir," Caslin replied. Their initial thoughts were disproved by the appearance of the second video release. "The number five was displayed on the first video, at the drug house. We considered that the four victims present plus the dealer who we now know is undercover officer,

Ben Fowler, would total five, but it would appear it is not as simple as that."

"You mentioned something about the flower." Broadfoot's expression was focussed, displaying no emotion as he moved to the next point he wanted to address.

"Yes, sir," Caslin replied, standing up and crossing to a whiteboard mounted on the wall. "We managed to identify the bud of the flower that was deposited in the mouth of the second victim, Kelly Ryan. It's been identified as *Nelumbo nucifera*, the *Lotus Flower*. This is significant because one of these was left at the centre of the crime scene at Stamford Street, with the four deceased victims around it. Alison Taylor found similar lodged in the mouth of Kelly Ryan."

"And the significance is?" Broadfoot asked.

Caslin indicated for Terry Holt to pick up the narrative. "This particular species of lotus is sacred to both Hindus and Buddhists. Hindus revere it, with the divinities Vishnu and Lakshmi often portrayed sitting on a pink lotus in their religious iconography. The lotus is seen as the symbol of what is divine, or immortal, as well as inhumanity and is also a symbol of divine perfection. In *Tantric* and *Yogic* traditions, the lotus symbolises the potential of an individual to harness the flow of energy moving through the *chakras*. Whereas, in Buddhism, the lotus represents purity of the body, speech and the mind. It's a representation of purity floating above the dirty waters of material attachment and physical desire."

"Are we looking at some kind of religious fundamentalist here?" Broadfoot's expression remained unchanged but his tone was edged with concern.

"It's too early to reach for any conclusion like that, sir," Caslin argued. "We are still trying to make sense of this but the flower is somehow symbolic." He indicated for Holt to continue.

"The lotus flower has references in several religions of Southeast Asia, India, China and right the way through even to Christianity. All parts of the flower are edible and the seeds have often been used in Chinese herbal medicine. They still are today and the by-products of the production process are widely consumed in Asia, throughout the Americas and Oceania. That's largely due to the high content of physiologically active substances. The use of the plant and its seeds dates back 3000 years."

"We can't say for sure how this ties in but somewhere along the line, one or more of these belief systems must come into play," Caslin said.

"Right, I need to make a statement to the press." Broadfoot stood up, he was tense, Caslin could tell. "This has suddenly become far higher profile than the deaths of a handful of junkies. I will need some answers on this, and I'm going to need them soon."

"We'll keep at it, sir," Caslin replied.

Broadfoot excused himself and as he passed out of the room, a uniformed sergeant poked his head around the door frame, immediately taken aback by the senior officer stepping in front of him. He addressed Broadfoot politely, who nodded in acknowledgement but continued on his way without another word.

"Caslin," the sergeant said, grabbing his attention. "You have a visitor downstairs."

"Who is it?"

"Michelle Cates."

Caslin flicked his eyebrows in Hunter's direction to signify the name meant nothing to him. "See if you can figure out where that video was uploaded from and also, if we can get anything from the footage that might indicate who this guy is." In response to a question that he knew was about to be asked, he added, "I know it's a long shot. I reckon he's covered his tracks again but you never know."

Leaving the team to get on with their tasks, Caslin made his way downstairs to the front office. Passing through the secure door into the foyer, he looked around. There were two people standing at the counter speaking to the civilian clerk, Simon, and they paid him no attention whatsoever. An elderly man was seated in the corner. His eyes were drawn to a woman who noted his arrival. Catching him scanning the people present, she stood up and tentatively approached him.

"Inspector Caslin?" she asked, raising her eyebrows in a way that belied her uncertainty.

"Yes, I am," he replied. She smiled and something about her demeanour lightened the darkness that this case found him wading through. Although certain they had never met, he felt a warmth towards her, a familiarity, but where that stemmed from, he had no idea. She was attractive to him, instantly he brought himself upright and almost as quickly he realised the impact of her impact on him. A flush of red crossed over him. That was unsettling. "I don't believe we've met." He was hopeful that he was right, the fear of embarrassment leapt into his mind.

She shook her head, broadening her smile. For a moment, he was lost as he took in her appearance and then remembered where he was. "I was hoping I could speak with you, Inspector," she said. "I'm Michelle Cates. My brother is Thomas Ryan."

Caslin felt a slight stab in his chest as he was brought back to reality with a bump. "Oh... I see. Of course, please come this way." He led her to the family room on the edge of the reception. Knocking on the door just in case it was occupied, he waited until there was no response and then opened it. As expected, there was no one inside and he held the door open for her.

Pulling out a chair, he offered it to her and she sat down. Caslin went to the other side of the table and took a seat opposite.

"What can I do for you, Mrs Cates?"

"Miss Cates." She corrected him before waving away his apology just as he started to utter it. "I'm worried about Thomas," she said. "About his state of mind. He told me about your conversation with him and, although I don't doubt he misconstrued some of the narrative. I'm concerned about the impression he may have left you with."

"Concerned? In what way?" Caslin was confused.

"Thomas and Kelly had their problems." She lowered her

voice as if she was betraying a confidence. "Neither of them is without fault but... Thomas would never harm Kelly. He loves her. Probably too much for either of them, if the truth be known."

"What do you mean by that?"

"I don't wish to... I'm in an awkward position here, Inspector." Her head dropped as she spoke. "I wouldn't like to betray a confidence and if I do, it will leave me in something of a predicament in the relationship with my brother."

"Your sister-in-law is dead, Miss Cates. She's been murdered and if there's anything you think I should know, then you ought to tell me."

She raised her head and met Caslin's gaze. "The confidence isn't the issue, really," she replied. Caslin sensed her reticence. "You see, Kelly and I were close. She was immensely supportive during the breakup of my marriage and I've tried my hardest to reciprocate in the last year or two."

Caslin nodded in a manner designed to put her at ease. At the same time, he observed her wringing her hands across the table, noting the absence of a wedding ring. "Please, go on."

"I think there's a possibility that Kelly was having an affair." She glanced up and away from Caslin, flicking her eyes nervously around the room as if to merely voice the suggestion was tantamount to betrayal. "In fact, I'm almost certain of it."

"Did Kelly talk about this with you?"

After a moment, she nodded slowly. "Yes, she mentioned it."

Caslin understood her situation. If Thomas was unaware, although clearly, he had his suspicions, then his sister knowing but not telling him would damage the trust in their relationship. "Did she tell you who the affair was with?"

Michelle Cates shook her head. "No, she never gave me any details. I don't even know how serious it was. It may have just been a casual thing and could have ended by now. I don't know."

"What did she tell you about him?"

"Nothing much. Just that it was a lot of fun and she hadn't felt so alive in years."

"Did your brother know?"

She shook her head. "Probably sounds strange, doesn't it? That I knew my sister-in-law was cheating on my brother but I didn't tell him."

"A little." Caslin was honest.

"I love my brother, Inspector. I also accept that he can be… difficult to live with."

"Difficult, how?"

"They are both… strong characters. They each like to have their own way and there was always an undercurrent of a power struggle within their relationship from day one." She shook her head slowly. "They're both career minded people and to get as far as they both have, you need to have a degree of single-mindedness, to be fair."

"You said they had problems?"

"Thomas has always been fixated on two things in his life. First, he wanted to have a successful career, which he has certainly achieved. Secondly, he wanted a family. Unfortunately, he sees that as something of a failure in his life."

"They couldn't have children or Kelly didn't want them?"

"No, not at all. She wanted a family just as much as he did but you're right, she couldn't have children. It was a source of intense friction between them. Almost constant. They tried IVF but that failed and then they discussed adoption but neither of them could agree on a path forward. As much as I hate to say it, Thomas was… perhaps too hard on Kelly and that's why I have so much sympathy for her… as I did for her."

Caslin could understand how much pressure that situation could place a couple under. The years of trying for a baby, followed by the medical tests, experimentation, all ending up with nothing for their efforts aside from the mental anguish of accepting what they desired was not achievable. A sense of hollow loss, all that remained. "Forgive me for asking this, Miss Cates."

"Please, call me Michelle."

"Forgive me. Was your brother ever violent towards Kelly?"

"No, never!" She was emphatic and apparently unfazed about him asking the question. "Thomas is an awkward bugger but he is not violent, never has been."

"I'm sorry, I had to ask."

"That's okay, Inspector. I understand."

"As far as you're aware, was Kelly ever a recreational drug user or in and around people who moved in those circles?"

Michelle Cates laughed. He liked the sound of it. "Kelly worked in the banking sector. I should imagine that recreational drug use was rife among many of her colleagues, but as for Kelly, no. Not as far as I'm aware and believe me, I would be aware."

"Did she have any hobbies that you are aware of? I'm thinking that with a highly pressurised job, if she were to be having extra-marital relations then it would most likely be either with someone sharing a mutual interest or a colleague."

"No, Kelly didn't really have hobbies. She wasn't sporty and didn't really mix with people outside of those she worked with. So, I would expect you to have the most joy looking there."

Caslin took out one of his contact cards and passed it across the table to her. She took it willingly and read the details. "If you need anything, my contact numbers are on there and even if I'm not available when you call, I will call you back. Likewise, if you think of anything else that you feel I ought to know, then I'd appreciate you being just as candid with me as you've been today."

"I will, thank you," she replied, smiling and standing up. Caslin followed suit. Moving across to the door, he grasped the handle to open it and see her out. Assessing her body language as she put on her coat and picked up her handbag, Caslin thought it looked as if a great weight had been lifted by her revelations.

"At some point, your brother might need to know this information," Caslin said almost apologetically.

She nodded. "I'll be the one who tells him. I'm very much

afraid that he will hate me for it, and some might argue that would be justifiably so."

"Perhaps," Caslin said. "But he will need people around him who care in the coming months. He'll come around."

"Thank you for taking the time to see me, Inspector," Michelle replied, placing an affectionate hand on his forearm. "I appreciate it."

"I meant what I said. Please call me if you need to."

She smiled again and Caslin opened the door. Leaving without another word, Caslin watched as Michelle Cates crossed the reception foyer and stepped out into the steady rainfall outside. She glanced back over her shoulder. If she noticed his attention, then she didn't offer a reaction, merely fastening her coat and descending the steps towards the car park.

Caslin watched her for a moment longer before heading back upstairs, all the while considering how in this job, he met people he liked in the most random of circumstances.

CHAPTER ELEVEN

ENTERING THE OPS ROOM, Caslin summoned the team together for a briefing. They were diligently gathering and filtering all the relevant data from the previous twenty-four hours in an attempt to build a timeline, not only for the movements of Kelly Ryan but also trying to find a crossover with the deaths at Stamford Street.

"Terry, talk to me about Kelly Ryan's place of work," Caslin instructed him.

"Security has been very helpful. They've sent us all of the CCTV footage from Kelly's last day at work, recording everything in the underground car park along with the footage from the cameras showing who entered and left the building on foot."

"Did you go over the abduction again?" Caslin asked.

"We did. Craig and I reviewed it together," Holt referred to DI Templer.

"However, we came to the same conclusion as you did," Templer said. "You can't make out the actual abduction because the van parked alongside her car obscures the camera footage. My guess would be he was waiting inside the van, parked it so close to her car in order for it to be a distraction. When she squeezes down between the two vehicles, he slides open the side door grabs her, pulls her into the van and immobilises her in some way."

"Alison Taylor believes she was stunned with a Taser," Caslin said.

"That figures." Templer nodded his agreement. "For him to have incapacitated her, bundled her into the car and out of sight before reversing out as quickly as he did in the footage, she must have been rendered unconscious in pretty quick time."

"It's quite a brazen attack," Hunter stated. "I mean, it's one thing to hit someone in a public car park with multiple entrance and exit points, but to do so in a controlled space on private property is risky."

"I'd hazard a guess, he had already worked out where the security camera was but that covers the abduction," Caslin said. "You're right, it is a risky move on his part. He still needed to enter the car park in the van. Have you made any headway with that?"

Holt nodded. "The transit van enters the car park at half past seven, driving around slowly before pulling in alongside Ryan's car." Templer tapped away at his keyboard and then gestured towards the projector screen. Seconds later, footage from the camera mounted at the entrance appeared.

"Here it is arriving," Templer stated. The van turned off of the main road and pulled up at the barriers. Despite the camera mounted above and giving a direct shot of the interior cabin, the driver inside was still masked in shadow. The driver was dressed all in black with not only a heavy overcoat and gloves but his face and head were covered with a balaclava.

"Damn it," Caslin muttered under his breath.

"Yeah, he certainly knew about the cameras," Templer agreed with Caslin's sentiment.

"What about the index?"

"No joy there. He switched the plates. These belong to a Vauxhall Corsa, registered in Plymouth. Forensics have been through it. The interior is wiped clean, so no use to us there." Caslin was disappointed but that would be an obvious error for the abductor to make. "But this is where it does get interesting." Templer pointed back to the footage as the driver lowered his window and reached out to press something against the security panel. Withdrawing it, the barrier lifted and he was able to drive forward, down the ramp and into the car park.

"He had an access card," Caslin said.

"It gets better than that," Holt said excitedly. "You will note the time stamp on the camera when the van entered, 7:31 PM. We were able to balance that timeframe with the recorded entries of people entering and exiting the building and we know whose access card was used."

"Excellent," Caslin said. "Who was it?"

"That's where the puzzle gets more complicated," Templer said. "The driver of the van used Kelly Ryan's access card."

That information threw Caslin for a moment. "Have you checked whether she reported hers lost or stolen?"

Holt shook his head. "I spoke with her boss, Simon Alexander, and he said there was no record of her reporting the loss of her card. He went so far as to check with security as well as the department who issue new or replacement cards, and they confirmed that nothing had been reported missing."

"What's more," Templer continued, "we checked whether Kelly used her own card that day and she did, entering the building just after 8 o'clock in the morning. In this scenario, if Kelly's card wasn't stolen or lost, then we must be looking at someone who has cloned her card in the days, weeks, or months leading up to her abduction."

"Then we have another line of inquiry," Caslin said. The killer must either be known to her or else she had some kind of contact with her abductor recently. They couldn't rule out the possibility that she may have been having a sexual relationship with someone, possibly even her killer. Alison Taylor told him Kelly Ryan had sexual intercourse with somebody on the day of her death and the revelation of an extramarital relationship in the recent past, confirmed by Michelle Cates, tempted him to think they were one and the same person. "We need to get into this woman's life and find out where she's been going as well as who she's been seeing. Did you have any luck tracing the second upload?"

"No. He used the same virtual private network to hide his location," Holt said. "This guy is pretty good at covering his tracks."

"It's easier to do when you're faceless and hiding behind technological barriers," Caslin stated, "but once you start factoring in building relationships with people or coming into contact with them it becomes a damn sight harder to maintain your anonymity. Somehow, if the bank's data is correct, he got close enough to Kelly Ryan to not only get access to her card but also to clone it and put it back without her being any the wiser as far as we know."

"Unless of course, the killer also works at the bank," Hunter suggested. "A bank insider could possibly get hold of her access card or necessary details in order to produce a copy, and there's every possibility no one would realise."

Caslin thought on it. There was a logic to that theory but how that factored into the murders at the drug house in Stamford Street, he couldn't figure. "Let's keep an open mind on that. Go back to Simon Alexander and produce a list of employees with as much information as we can get from him. Then, start working through the names and try and see how they interact with Kelly, her personal and professional life. Make sure we expand the list beyond just her team but include anyone who would have the capability or access to the data required. This includes our helpful security guard."

"I'll get on it," Hunter said.

"Terry," Caslin turned to the DC. "I want you to go through Kelly Ryan's personal digital footprint. Mobile phones, emails, financials and see if anything stands out."

"Are we looking for anything specific, sir?"

"Look for anything abnormal but bear in mind she's been

having something of a casual fling somewhere along the line. That may still be ongoing or it may have fizzled out, we don't really know. But if we're looking for someone who had close enough access to her possessions to bypass the security at the bank, it's fair to assume that someone participating in an adulterous affair would fit the bill. She's managed to keep this from a husband for quite some time despite his obvious suspicions. The links may not be obvious but they will be there. Don't underestimate her ability to conceal what she's been up to."

"Our killer's decided that these junkies and Kelly Ryan's death should be tied together," Templer said as Hunter and Holt set about their new tasks, leaving the two senior detectives alone. "By making a call to the emergency services from the scene of Kelly Ryan's murder, on Fowler's phone, he guaranteed that we would not only find her pretty quickly but also there would be a direct link between the two crime scenes."

"How did you find out about the house in Stamford Street?" Caslin asked. "Did you have someone with eyes on Fowler?"

Templer shook his head. "No, Fowler was pretty much a kite. You know, we didn't have any string attached to him. It was far too risky, hence why he had to be so careful about when he recorded anyone covertly. To have a permanent watch on him… now, there's no way that would have flown."

"Did he miss a check in?"

"No, we hadn't been out of contact that long. The call came in to North Yorkshire's tip line and obviously we have the address flagged, so it came straight down the network to us."

"Who called in the tip?"

"It was anonymous. If I recall correctly, they said they thought a burglary was in progress and that the residents were home with young children."

"Clever boy," Caslin said quietly. "That would ensure an immediate response with regard to the safety of the family. He's no doubt disguised his voice but let's get a hold of the recording and run it through some analysis just in case it reveals anything."

"Will do. He wanted them to be found," Templer said quietly. "This guy is crazy."

"I don't doubt that but I think there's more to it," Caslin said sitting forward and forming a tent with his fingers beneath his chin. "Tell me, how many serial killers have you investigated? It's not a trick question, I'm curious."

"None. This is my first."

"In my experience, most serial killers kill because they can't control their urge to do so but in every case I've come across, it was the urge to kill that either gave them the thrill or at the very least satisfied their desire, if only for a short while. This guy is different in that he wants us to see what he's doing. He wants us to know what he's getting away with and is trying to send us a message."

"How do you know?"

"The flower. The Lotus," Caslin said pulling the file towards him containing the crime scene photographs. He leafed through the folder and took out the relevant shots depicting the lotus flower on the coffee table at the drug house, in Stamford Street, and also the pictures from Alison Taylor's pathology lab that he photographed before leaving that morning. "He's placed these at both scenes which is another way of tying the two together. This, plus the numbering and the videos, is telling us something."

"It tells us this guy's a crazy son of a bitch," Templer stated, scanning the pictures in front of them.

"Calculating, dangerous son of a bitch," Caslin added. "And I'm telling you now there will be more to come. This guy is two or three moves ahead of us and unless we catch up fast, the body count is only going to increase."

"Presume, just for a moment, that he doesn't know Kelly Ryan. For instance, he's not her lover," Templer argued. "How we can get to him if there is no direct link. Don't get me wrong, I think every line of inquiry we're pursuing is legitimate but if this guy's as calculating as we think then we need to draw him out."

"I'm open to suggestions as to how we do that."

"He wants our attention?" Templer asked. Caslin nodded his agreement. "Well, if he wants our attention, then maybe we should give it to him. He sent the first video to the press to get the story out. The second, he uploaded himself because he knew everybody was going to be looking for it. Now he's got the eyes of the country, if not the world, focussed on him but he's achieved it on his terms. How about we put the spotlight on him through our lens rather than his?"

"Yeah, what are you talking about?"

"He's probably revelling in this *Night Stalker* name the press has saddled him with, it's kind of catchy. How about we get something out in the media that he might not like? Perhaps you could have a word with your friend, the one who works at *The Post*?"

Caslin sat back in his chair allowing Templer's suggestion to filter through his mind. "You mean play to his narcissism?"

"Exactly," Templer said, grinning. "But just imagine how he'll react if we don't talk about his genius and creativity and merely point out what a sad loser he is? We have to make him angry. It may well poke a reaction. I'll wager he won't be able to resist pushing back."

"Risky strategy. The reaction is unpredictable. It could be strong and escalate matters."

"He's already killed five people with an undercover officer unaccounted for. How much worse can it get?" Templer countered. "Besides, the reaction might lead to a mistake."

"An interesting idea," Caslin said, mulling it over. "You have experience of this sort of approach?"

"I read criminology for my Masters Degree," Templer explained. "Believe me, it's a sound strategy."

"Who do you think we should use to bait him? After all, that's what you're suggesting we do."

"I think you should do it."

"You're probably better qualified," Caslin argued, willing to defer to his colleague's wider knowledge and experience of psychology.

"We're looking to rile him. I hardly know you, Caslin, but I've not met anyone more naturally gifted at getting up someone's nose than you." Caslin was about to object but noted Hunter stifling a grin in the background, whereas Terry Holt erupted into laughter.

"Thanks very much... team," Caslin replied, shaking his head and splitting a grin of his own.

"You've got to admit, he has nailed you in two days," Hunter said, returning her eyes to the computer screen in front of her.

"Comments like that will not get you a pay rise, Sergeant," he replied. "I meant to ask, where did we get to in running down the victims from Stamford Street? Anyone revealing connections to either Ryan or your investigation and Detective Fowler?"

"No, as far as we've been able to ascertain, they were all customers. None of them are known elements of the network Fowler infiltrated. They all have criminal records in one form or another. Petty crimes – shoplifting, theft, burglary and a couple of convictions for fraud. Nothing high level. We're still running down known associates but we'll need to draw some manpower as it's a lot of ground to cover."

"I'll have a word with Broadfoot, extra resources won't be an issue," Caslin replied.

"Are you going to run it by him?" Templer asked.

"Our plan to flush him out?" Caslin clarified. Templer nodded. He shook his head. "Broadfoot's far too cautious to approve that. Better that we do it and I justify it afterwards."

"Yeah, somehow I figured you'd say something like that."

CHAPTER TWELVE

THE TWO CAMERAS were making him feel self-conscious. Despite the recording having already taken almost half an hour, Caslin hadn't settled in to the process at all. That didn't surprise him. Many years ago, he had had his brush with fame among the media circles. Initially, the attention had massaged his already exaggerated ego but when the attention spiralled into notoriety, as the case went bad, what had once left him with a sense of achievement, now tasted bitter. Since that day, Caslin chose to defer the spotlight, allowing it to pass on to colleagues whilst he took a backseat and got on with his job. Attention was neither sought nor desired. However, on this occasion, he had to put himself back at the centre of the media scrum, but at least it wasn't for anything so trivial as vanity or kudos. This time, he was trying to entrap a dangerous and brutal killer.

"What type of person are you dealing with here?" Jimmy Sullivan asked. This was the portion of the interview that the entire event was engineered to bring them to. Previously, they skirted around the investigation, the set up regarding the number of officers involved as well as the details of each crime scene, the most gruesome of which were not up for discussion. The format was well agreed in advance between the investigative team and the editorial team of the paper. The subject matter, the line of questioning, down to the very detail of the tone of the interview, had been well choreographed to reach this point, ensuring as much as possible that the interview didn't appear a total concoction. After all, the exchange had to be realistic for two reasons, not least to guarantee the newspaper's willingness to take part but also, perhaps more importantly, in order to fulfil the entire object of the exercise and draw their killer out of the shadows.

"This person wants to be seen as something special," Caslin said flatly, turning his head and speaking directly to camera. "He has the nagging desire to be recognised, to be seen as some kind of macabre genius. Perhaps even to be revered at the same time as being feared."

"Is this how you see him?"

"No," Caslin stated emphatically, shaking his head, his lips parting into a half-smile. "This man is none of these things. My experience, along with the psychological assessment of several experts that I've discussed the case with, leads me to the certainty that what we are dealing with is a very warped individual indeed. Now, we are not sure what life events would have led him to become so twisted but it's most likely we're looking for an inadequate person who is of below-average or limited intelligence."

"And where do you think he fits into society?" Sullivan asked.

"I should imagine he's one of two types of people. Either he's drifted from one job to the next and never managed to stick at anything past the point where he was found wanting by those around him," Caslin suggested. "Or he's one of these guys, we've all met them, who spend a lifetime in one role, barely ever managing to be promoted but at the same time irritating all of their work colleagues by suggesting everything would run a lot better if only he was put in charge, fostering a grievance against all those who move up the chain."

"Yes, we all know those," Sullivan said with a chuckle. "So, you see in this quite a weak character?"

"Weak? I would say so, yes. Regarding his character, he may

well be someone his friends, if he has any, and neighbours think they can trust but scratch the surface and you will almost certainly find an individual who you wouldn't want to spend more than ten minutes in the company of, standing alongside the staff room coffee machine."

"What about his personality?"

Caslin shook his head. "A distinct lack of charisma, would be my guess and believe me, I've been in this job long enough to know the type of person I'm looking for."

"I know you won't be able to give us exact details regarding an active case, Inspector Caslin," Sullivan said, following the script. "But how close are you to putting a name to this killer?"

Caslin shifted his gaze towards the camera off to his right, once again, staring straight at the lens. "I can assure you and everyone watching that we have active lines of inquiry and we are not far off. The net is tightening and this killer will be off the streets soon enough, I give you my word."

"That almost sounds like a promise, Inspector."

Caslin held his line of sight in the direction of the camera. "We're closer than he thinks. He is arrogant, narcissistic and thinks he's got the better of us. The truth is, he couldn't be more wrong."

Sullivan wrapped up the interview there and then, and the cameras stopped recording. Unhooking the microphone clipped to his shirt, Caslin drew the cable out and passed the equipment to the sound engineer who accepted gratefully. Having made the decision to try and draw a reaction from the killer, at the suggestion of Sullivan's editor, they went for more than just an interview to be published in the following day's paper. By recording the exchange on camera, they would be able to put it up almost immediately on the paper's website giving maximum opportunity for it to be widely distributed.

"I think that went well," Sullivan said smiling. Despite the interview being something of a ruse, it was still a fact that the paper was obtaining a significant scoop. Once the case played out, their role in catching the killer would give them another angle for them to write about in the copy, not to mention the attention and focus that would be brought the paper's way by airing the interview in the first place. A raising of the publication's profile would have the knock-on effect of higher advertising revenues, so from a purely economic point of view, the paper couldn't lose.

"Let's hope it has the desired effect," Caslin said, watching the dismantling of the equipment and it being packed away. "You missed your calling, Jimmy. I could see you hosting *Question Time* or perhaps some regional news programme on an obscure cable channel, in the early hours of the morning."

"High praise indeed," Sullivan replied broadening his smile into a grin. "You never made that pint the other day. How about later?"

Caslin shook his head. "I'll see how it goes with all this." He waved his hand in a circular motion, indicating the cameras. "But I doubt it."

"Okay but you know where I'll be if you change your mind."

Opening the door to the media room of Fulford Road Station, usually set aside for large press conferences, Caslin was met by Craig Templer. He was present during the interview but upon receipt of a phone call stepped out of the room.

"That was going well as I left," he said to Caslin, falling into step alongside him.

"I thought so."

"Broadfoot got wind of it," Templer said. "He wants a word with you upstairs."

"Is he putting the brakes on it?"

"Not sure. I imagine if he had already made up his mind, he would have shut it down immediately," Templer argued. "The fact that he wants to see you... got to be a good sign."

MINUTES LATER, Caslin approached Broadfoot's office. His personal assistant smiled as he approached, picking up the receiver on the desk before her. Presumably she was calling through to announce his anticipated arrival and by the time he reached the desk she was already ushering him through. Entering the office, ACC Broadfoot was standing behind his desk with his back to the door and looking out of the window. From his vantage point on the top floor, the view across the centre of York was striking. The overcast skies of the previous days had cleared that afternoon and now the sun was setting, bathing the city in soft yellow light. Caslin reached the centre of the room, coming before his superior's desk. He waited.

Broadfoot took a deep breath but remained where he stood, transfixed on the view. "This is a very dangerous approach you are taking, Nathaniel."

"It's a calculated risk, I'll grant you."

"An approach that could well blow up in our face," Broadfoot said, turning to face him. His expression was controlled and his tone measured, but the underlying concern was clear to see.

"I know this isn't standard procedure, sir," Caslin said. Broadfoot inclined his head in agreement. "But this case is different. This killer is different. If we going to end this before it gets bloodier, then we need to get ahead of him rather than be where we are."

"We've been here before though, Nathaniel," Broadfoot countered. "This is not the first serial killer you've investigated."

"No, sir, you're right but the others have always lived in the shadows. They didn't seek the limelight, they didn't want to be known. They satisfied their urges and then moved on. This guy wants the opposite. He wants everyone talking about him and he wants us to be fearful of him... and I believe, he craves our respect. This interview is all about drawing him out."

"You're goading him," Broadfoot said. Caslin didn't disagree.

"Yes, I am. Absolutely," he replied. "This is someone who is randomly picking his victims off the street as and when the opportunity arises. He's planning this, meticulously. No matter how intelligent they are, these types of killers will always make a mistake at some point, but I don't want us to pick up his mistake in two, three... four years' time and catch him then. I want to force him into making a mistake now."

Broadfoot crossed his arms in front of him and brought his left hand up to his chin, stroking it whilst thinking through Caslin's logic. "In that case, I'll make a call and let's see if we can broaden your message."

Caslin left the office as Broadfoot reached out to his own high profile media contacts. Any prospect of meeting Jimmy Sullivan for a pint at Lendal's was forgotten as an interview for the evening television news was hastily arranged.

LEAVING THE TELEVISION STUDIO, Caslin had lost all track of the time. The completely unfamiliar environment of visiting the make-up department, the green room as well as discussions with various producers and other members of the studio team, whose roles Caslin could only guess at, had taken their toll. Entering the building in the fading sunlight of the late afternoon, he now emerged into the artificially lit city centre, under the cover of darkness. He considered going for a late-night drink but in all honesty, fatigue was catching up with him. Deciding to skip the nightcap, he set off for his apartment in Kleiser's Court.

Feeling his phone vibrating in his pocket, his first thought was that the traffic noise was drowning out the ringing but then he remembered the production team had asked him to silence his phone just in case it rang whilst he was on air. Reaching into his pocket, he drew it out and glanced at the screen. The number was displayed but was not one he recognised.

"DI Caslin," he announced.

"Hello, Inspector," a female voice said. It was one that

sounded familiar to him but he couldn't place it. "It's Michelle Cates."

"Miss Cates," Caslin acknowledged her, surprised to find her calling him. "What can I do for you?"

"I'm sorry to trouble you, Inspector, particularly so late," she said, sounding genuinely apologetic. "But you did say to call if I needed to."

"And I meant it. How can I help?"

"You're probably going to think I'm mad," she said. "But I saw you on the television and what you were saying about... the man who... killed Kelly and I'm... frightened."

"I appreciate why you would be but—"

"No, you don't understand, Inspector." She interrupted him. Whereas her tone initially was contrite, now it switched to assertive. It was as if she had something burning inside of her that she wanted to get out. "Earlier, I thought there was someone outside my house. In the garden. It's a secure space. The boundary wall is five feet high and for someone to be there, they would... they can't just walk in. It wasn't just me, my daughter saw him too. What if it's him?"

"Did you call the police?" Caslin asked, concerned. He had no reason to doubt what she had seen and under the circumstances, her anxiety levels were justifiably high.

"I did, yes and the operator advised me they would send a patrol car through the area as soon as they could but in the meantime, we should stay in the house and keep the doors and windows locked."

Caslin checked the time. Responding to a possible prowler wouldn't be considered a high priority if there were more pressing incidents, particularly if the threat was considered vague. "Okay, Miss Cates," Caslin said reassuringly, "I'm going to make a call and have a uniformed car come to your address as soon as possible. I want you to follow the operator's advice and stay in the house. Can you give me the address please?" She told him where she lived with her daughter and he realised he was only a short walk away. The address was only a minor detour from his route home. He looked at his watch. "I'm actually nearby. So, I could also stop by myself, if that's okay?"

"Thank you, Inspector. That's very kind. If it's not too much trouble?" Her reply sounded genuine, both surprised and relieved in equal measure.

"I'll be with you in about ten minutes," he said, reassuring her, "and please, try not to worry."

CHAPTER THIRTEEN

I𝐓 𝐰𝐚𝐬 𝐩𝐫𝐨𝐛𝐚𝐛𝐥𝐲 𝐜𝐥𝐨𝐬𝐞𝐫 to fifteen minutes by the time Caslin mounted the steps to the home of Michelle Cates. Taking hold of the door knocker he rapped it twice and waited. Looking over his shoulder behind him, the river Ouse flowed past only a stone's throw away. The residence was one of the Georgian townhouses, built on the quayside, and directly opposite the old merchant warehouses on the river bank opposite. These had long since been converted into prestigious residential apartments but the exteriors still tipped their hat to their industrial heritage.

He didn't have long to wait before the door opened and he was met by a rather agitated Michelle Cates. "Thank you for coming so quickly." She opened the door wider and invited him in. "I'm starting to think my paranoia got the better of me and I'm wasting your time."

"It's no trouble, honestly," Caslin said, smiling. "The old saying of better to be safe than sorry still applies."

She led him further into the house and through into an open-plan kitchen and dining area. The original building was tall and narrow, being made up of four storeys including the basement area, which was at the level of the quay. The residential floors were elevated in order to mitigate the damage in the event of the river bursting its banks which did happen from time-to-time, flooding parts of the city centre. The room they were in now was a modern addition of contemporary glass and aluminium construction in stark juxtaposition to the traditional building materials.

"I was sure I saw someone out there," Michelle said, indicating the garden beyond the curtain wall of glass. Caslin moved past her and approached the door. Much of the garden was shrouded in darkness due to the established foliage and the presence of centuries-old trees. The interior lighting also made it difficult to make out the details outside. The property was an end terrace. Beyond the gable end were the *Tower Gardens*, named after the nearby *Clifford Tower*, a medieval tourist attraction. The light pollution from the city centre did help a little. The orange glow of the street lighting penetrated part of the garden. He eyed the locking mechanism and glanced back to her. "Yes, it's locked," she said in response to the look he gave her.

"I'll have a look around." Caslin opened the door. Immediately, the sounds of the city at night could be heard, the traffic passing by and the occasional shout. "Lock the door behind me, just in case." She nodded and approached as he stepped out into the darkness. The door closed behind him, the sound of the lock engaging as Michelle did as he requested. Looking around, there was nothing that jumped out at him that was untoward. The boundary wall was brick, solid and well maintained as far as he could see. Walking forward, his eyes began to adjust to their surroundings and he listened acutely in order to try to distinguish between the night-time sounds of the city and anything that might be close by.

Aware that the mind could play tricks in the darkness, Caslin tried to tune out the natural response of seeing danger in every shadow and the rustle of the wind through every branch. Locating the gated access to the garden at the rear of the property, Caslin found it secured with a slide bolt. There was no evidence that it had been open recently but when he tested it, he found it moved with ease. Located at the top, it was conceivable that if someone lifted themselves up onto the wall alongside it, they could have reached over and unlocked the gate from the outside. Similarly, although the wall was solid it was topped with curved brick, an attractive detail but hardly a deterrent or barrier to someone seeking entry.

The cultivated borders were a mixture of small and large plants. Moving some of the larger ones aside with his arm, Caslin found he could step through and place himself between the boundary wall and the bushes. Moving around the garden, he found several vantage points where he could stand quite comfortably, giving him an unobstructed view towards the house, confident that he wouldn't be seen by those within. The third of these locations, he thought would be the most likely place that a would-be prowler, or burglar, might observe from. Caslin's torch was in the boot of his car, so he took out his phone and activated the torch, illuminating the surrounding area.

Searching for footprints left in the mud or signs of recently broken branches in the surrounding plants, Caslin spied three cigarette butts at his feet. Dropping to his haunches, he eyed them more closely. Having been a heavy smoker for many years previously, he thought they looked as if they'd been thrown there recently. Discarded cigarette butts, exposed to the elements for a significant period of time, took on a different appearance. Taking a tissue out of his pocket, Caslin picked one up, examining it in the palm of his hand. Bringing his light to bear, he thought it could have been recently smoked. Discarding the butt to the floor, he put the tissue back in his coat pocket.

With one last glance towards the house, he watched Michelle inside her kitchen busying herself tidying up. Although he found nothing to indicate she was in immediate danger, he was perturbed by his own thoughts and feelings. Had she imagined it? Despite the acknowledgement of the tricks his senses might be playing, his instinct suggested he shouldn't dismiss her concerns. Brushing aside the bushes in front of him, he stepped back out onto the lawn and returned to the house. Upon reaching the door,

Michelle noticed and crossed over to unlock it, allowing him to come inside.

"Did you find anything?" Something in her tone told him she was fearful of the answer.

"No, there was nothing for you to be worried about," he said, smiling. Her shoulders dropped as relief washed over her. "Tell me, do you smoke?"

She shook her head, momentarily thrown by such a random question. "No, I don't. Never have done. Why?"

"Do you have a gardener? Someone who takes care of the landscaping?"

"My mother used to. This was her house. After my marriage broke up, we moved here. Partly out of necessity but also to help take care of my mother. I have to admit, since she passed away, I've been less inclined to do things with the garden. Plus, it's expensive and… well… I don't have the same income that she did, if you know what I mean?"

"I'm sorry to hear that. I lost my father quite recently too."

"I'm sorry, had he been ill?"

"No, it came about quite quickly." Caslin immediately sought to change the direction of the conversation.

"My mother was ill for a very long time," Michelle said, her expression one of profound sadness. "She suffered with Alzheimer's and developed a host of other illnesses that wore her down over a number of years. She was tough, though. Never one to give in and she never let anything get on top of her. Sometimes I wish I was much more like her."

"It must have been hard."

"It was, particularly after the divorce. My mother was very much of the opinion that marriage was for life, no matter what. Despite… I'm sorry, Inspector, I'm sure you don't want to hear all this."

If the truth were known, Caslin found her company enjoyable, even though the two occasions he had spent with her were professionally related. He felt like he had known her for years. Forcing his mind back to the matter in hand, he asked, "I was just wondering if the gardener smoked or whether anybody else has been in the garden recently who does?"

Michelle shook her head. "No, not that I'm aware of."

"It's okay," Caslin said. "Probably somebody walking past in the street and throwing their butts over the wall."

"Mummy." A child's voice came from behind them. Both of them turned and Caslin saw a young girl, perhaps no older than ten years of age, roughly the same as his own daughter, Lizzie, standing in the doorway. She was dressed in her pyjamas and rubbed furiously at her eyes, indicative of having recently woken. Michelle crossed the kitchen and knelt down before the girl, placing both hands on her upper arms reassuringly.

"Did you wake up, darling?" she asked softly, smiling. The girl nodded.

"Who's that man?" She pointed at Caslin.

"That's a friend of Mummy's." Michelle glanced in Caslin's direction.

"What's his name?"

Michelle flicked her eyes from Caslin to her daughter and back again. Caslin came a little nearer and also knelt, so they met at her eye level. "My name is Nathaniel. My friends call me Nate," he said smiling.

The little girl eyed him warily, as if assessing his trustworthiness. "I'm Carly," she said. Seemingly, he had passed her initial test.

"Well, I'm very pleased to meet you, Carly," he replied, holding out his hand. She glanced at it and then back at him before reaching out and they briefly shook hands.

"And I think we should get you back to bed, shouldn't we, young lady," Michelle said. The child put up no resistance and with her mother's reassuring hand on her shoulder, she turned and happily set off back towards her bedroom. Michelle looked over his shoulder at Caslin and smiled, silently mouthing the words *thank you*.

Walking back across the kitchen, Caslin returned his gaze to the garden. There was every possibility Michelle Cates and her daughter had seen tricks of light and shadow, their minds filling the gaps in detail with the worst possible scenario. With what happened to Kelly so fresh in their thoughts, it would be completely understandable. However, equally there was every possibility that it wasn't paranoia and someone was there, watching. Glancing at the counter alongside him, Caslin noticed his contact card lying next to a mobile phone. Picking it up, he noticed some hand-written words on the reverse and he flipped it in his hand. On the back someone had added – *a decent man* – in blue ink. He considered what a strange twist of fate had brought him here, not that he believed much in the hand of fate.

The silence was broken by a knock on the front door. Caslin walked into the hallway with the knowledge that Michelle would most likely not be down for a few minutes yet. Opening the door, two uniformed officers were surprised to find him standing in front of them.

"It's okay," Caslin said. "I've walked the perimeter and there's no sign of an intruder. At least, not now. Are you two on shift or are you clocking off at midnight?"

"We're on six-to-two," the first officer advised him, glancing to his colleague. Caslin thought his name was Atkinson but he couldn't be sure.

"In that case, I want you to swing by here as much as you can during the remainder of your shift. Can you do that?"

"Yes, sir. We can. Is something going on we should know about?"

"The residents are relatives of a recent murder victim, this so-called *Night Stalker*." He hated using the media name attributed to the case but it was how the killer was referred to by almost everyone outside of his team. "There is a woman and young child living here alone, so a reassuring uniformed presence would be appreciated."

"Of course."

"And if there is anything out of the ordinary, I want you to contact me directly and I don't care what time of night it is."

"What about when we finish?"

"I'll make a call and have someone put it out on the wire," Caslin said, advising them that he would ensure a uniformed presence periodically throughout the night.

He bid them good night and closed the door. Turning around, Michelle descended the stairs towards him. "Thank you, Inspector."

"That's okay. I have a daughter of a similar age and I know it can be a little unsettling to find a stranger in the house unexpectedly."

"For that too, but also for what you just did with those officers." Caslin didn't realise she had overheard the conversation.

"It's just as a precaution. I wouldn't want you to be unduly alarmed."

"No, I'm not. Not now anyway." She came to stand next to him. "You're a good man, Inspector."

"Please, Miss Cates, you can call me Nathaniel... or Nate, if you prefer?"

"Are we friends now, Nate?" She smiled, playfully.

Caslin's cheeks flushed and suddenly he felt incredibly self-conscious. In a desperate act to recover his composure, he checked the time on his watch. "I should probably be off, Miss Cates," he said despite wanting to do anything but. Michelle appeared disappointed at the suggestion.

"You should call me Michelle. I remember my teachers always called me *miss*, and I didn't care for it much then, either."

"You prefer Michelle, or Miche?" he asked. Her eyes narrowed and he thought perhaps he was over familiar, misjudging the situation. She appeared to notice.

"My ex-husband always called me *Miche*. Not a fan." She shook her head and Caslin thought he needed to recover.

"I'm sorry. Your brother, Thomas, also—"

"That figures. He cottoned on to how much I hate it and does it for fun. I guess it kinda stuck with him. Thank you for coming out."

"Happy to do so, and you have my number." Caslin words felt hollow and sorely inadequate. Not for the first time when he figured he had a good thing going with a woman, he'd found a way to douse water on the flames. "Just in case."

"Just in case," she replied, the smile broadening. Caslin turned and unlocked the front door. Stepping out into the night, he looked over his shoulder as Michelle placed a hand on the door ready to close it once he had left. He shot her an awkward half-smile, worried that she would see through the brittle mask that shrouded his attraction to her. Without another word, he descended the steps and upon reaching the quayside, looked back up and saw her still standing in the doorway watching him walk away. The briefest flicker of excitement passed through him as he considered the prospect that the attraction might not be one-sided after all. The door closed.

Taking the next right, he walked uphill towards the city centre in the direction of his apartment. His mobile rang and such was his preoccupation with his thoughts regarding Michelle Cates, he didn't bother to look at the screen as he answered the call.

"You've been doing the rounds in the news rooms, I see." Caslin didn't recognise the voice but something about the tone made him stop, feeling the need to focus his attention fully on the call.

"Who is this?"

"You don't rate me at all, do you?"

"Should I?"

"You think you've got me all figured out." The caller was irritated, his tone hostile. "But the truth is you have no idea what I'm trying to achieve… but you will, I promise you."

Caslin briefly considered whether this was a crank but something told him this caller was genuine. "Why don't you enlighten me? If you're so sure I don't understand you."

"You're the same as everybody else, Inspector Caslin. You

want all the answers to every question handed to you, spoon fed, but the reality is the answers will only come if you work for them."

"And what exactly should I do in order for that to happen?"

"Don't worry. I'm here as your guide, to educate. Soon enough, you will come to understand."

The accent was broad Yorkshire. He was local. "How about we meet and you can tell me all about it?"

"You genuinely believe I am stupid." The caller's tone was turning aggressive, his anger rising despite the controlled manner in which he spoke.

"I think you have real problems that you need help with. You're going to get caught."

"I believe I have options, Inspector."

"You do. Several," Caslin agreed. "Your best is to come to me. If you have a message to get out, then I can help with that. There's no need for anyone else to die."

"I disagree. The path to the light must be cleansed prior to the journey. We are all the same when it boils down to it, Inspector."

"You've lost me."

"Death is the way of the world and killing is a part of that, whether it's animals for food, insects at bedtime or the *worst kind* of people. At least I'm honest about it."

"You're murdering people. That's not the same," Caslin countered.

"It's exactly the same! If able to or given the chance, you'd all do it too. The real difference is I'm willing to embrace my desires so I can show you the path. Whereas the rest of you live in denial." His tone switched to contemptuous. Caslin's stance was getting under his skin.

"I think you went wrong somewhere along the line," Caslin said. "Lost your way."

"Like I said, Inspector," he countered, his tone now exuding the calm, measured delivery of earlier in the call. "You will understand. I assure you."

"I understand you're a whacko," Caslin said coldly. There was a sound at the other end of the line, in the background, Caslin strained to work out what it might be but it wasn't distinctive enough.

"Please don't fall back on cheap insults. You do yourself and your intelligence a disservice." His voice sounded somewhat laboured, as if he was doing something physical whilst speaking on the phone. The conversation seemed to have become a distraction to the caller. "I've left you something, Inspector Caslin. Please don't wait too long to find it because things go off when you leave them out."

The voice chuckled and the line went dead.

Immediately, Caslin double checked the call had disconnected. Then he hit the speed dial connecting him straight to the control room. Identifying himself, he instructed the operator. "I received a call on this number and I want you to run an immediate trace. Forward the ticket to my investigation team. Flag it as a high priority, please."

Hanging up on the call, he touched the mobile to his lips, striking a thoughtful pose. As desired, they had instigated a response but what that meant, he was still unsure.

CHAPTER FOURTEEN

The Fishergate area lay beyond the city walls to the south-east of York. Taking the turn onto Cemetery Road, Caslin kept an eye out for the entrance. It was a short stretch of road and the old stone Gatehouse appeared on the right-hand side. A police car was parked at the entrance and the uniformed officer, recognising Caslin, waved him through and indicated for him to follow the road bearing off to his right, disappearing through the trees.

"It seems somehow fitting in a poetic kind of way, don't you think?" DI Templer spoke quietly, sitting in the passenger seat. Caslin glanced across at his colleague but didn't respond. Templer had fallen quiet since they received the call first thing in the morning, with the report reaching them shortly after seven o'clock. It was obvious what was going through the young man's mind. There were no words of comfort that Caslin could offer him despite having personal, very painful experience of losing colleagues during an investigation.

The gravel lined road opened out before the chapel. There was enough room for multiple vehicles to park. Caslin pulled up alongside Hunter's car. Getting out, he looked back at the imposing neo-classical inspired chapel, constructed by the Victorians well over a century earlier. Templer joined him and both men looked around trying to locate the crime scene. York Cemetery was spread over twenty-four acres of land and consisted of well-maintained paths, terraces and gardens amidst mature tree-lined surroundings. It was easy, surrounded by such greenery, to forget how close to the city they were.

An officer appeared on the path running directly from the centre of the chapel, stretching for several hundred yards with various branches off it. The two detectives headed that way and were greeted by the constable as they passed. Having checked with him, they took the next right turn and the crime scene appeared almost immediately. The path ran in a straight line but soon split, moving off to the left and the right, forming a circular walk. To each side of the path were headstones, many of them from a bygone era with names and dates largely unreadable due to the erosion of the stone. They took neither branch, continuing on.

The sounds of conversation carried to them now as they approached their destination. The path split once again to form yet another circular walk, only smaller and set within the larger. However, at the centre of this inner circle, they found the team already hard at work. The threat of rain was absent this morning with the clear skies of the previous afternoon carrying through the night. This brought dense fog to the Vale of York and the low sun was yet to make any headway in burning it off. The air felt damp, cold and the body hanging from the tree at the centre of the circle capped the scene off as dark and foreboding.

Caslin stepped forward but Templer hesitated. Caslin noticed and turned, placing a reassuring hand on the younger man's shoulder.

"Come on, let's see if it's him." Caslin addressed Templer's worst fears for the first time since they left Fulford Road. The two of them moved closer. They came to within ten feet of the body and Caslin watched as Craig Templer visibly deflated, exhaling deeply.

"It's not him." The sense of relief was obvious in his expression, let alone his tone. "It's not Fowler."

"We've not found an ID yet," Hunter said, rising from her kneeling position a short distance away. "We started searching from here and have people fanning out just to see if anything has been discarded."

Caslin looked up at the victim. He was a middle-aged white man, perhaps in his early to mid-forties. He was dressed for the weather in jeans, trainers and a thick overcoat. Looking at his face, despite the swelling and purple complexion, expected in a hanging, Caslin couldn't see any indicators to suggest he had been involved in an altercation.

"Any idea how he got here, to the cemetery, I mean?" Caslin asked.

"There were no cars left overnight or present this morning," Hunter confirmed. "There's a funeral here at ten, and the staff were coming in to make the preparations. They found him."

Caslin moved around the body, maintaining his distance so as not to risk contamination of the ground beneath, just in case there was any trace evidence that may be disturbed. Narrowing his focus, he paid close attention to the victim's hands looking for any cuts, scrapes or bruising that might indicate he had fought with an attacker. Again, he was surprised to find nothing other than what had become a signature – the apparent ritual removal of the victim's right index finger.

"No sign of a struggle," Caslin said aloud.

"Not even around the neck," Iain Robertson said, coming to join them. Caslin hadn't noticed he was there yet.

"Good morning, Iain. Say that again, please."

"Look around the neck. Although, I know you don't have the best view or the aid of a stepladder, like I did. I don't doubt Alison Taylor will be better placed to confirm it but I reckon there wasn't much of a struggle to get him into the noose," Robertson explained. "Further to that, the abrasion around the neck is almost exactly where the rope is now, which means there was very little movement from the ligature during suspension."

"Meaning?" Templer asked.

"That's indicative of the noose being securely tightened prior to suspension," Robertson said.

"Suggesting there was no struggle?" Caslin asked. "Any possibility of this being a post-mortem hanging?"

Robertson dismissed the notion. "I don't believe so, no. We've detailed the surrounding area thoroughly and there is no evidence of a body being dragged here. Judging from the victim's height and estimated weight, I would expect to see some if he were. I agree that would explain how the noose could have been fixed in place so securely, but if you look where the rope is situated." He pointed to where the rope looped over the branch of the tree above. "In a post-mortem hanging, the noose is secured and the rope thrown over and then the victim is pulled into the air before tying it off. That leaves a very obvious sign of wear, particularly with this thick, fibrous rope. Whereas, in a suicidal hanging, the wear pattern runs the opposite way as the weight of the victim stretches the rope in a downward motion." With a closed fist, he drew his hand down in a sharp motion, enacting the passage of the rope. "There's no doubt in my mind."

"No signs of a fight?" Caslin asked, seeking confirmation.

"As you rightly pointed out, no scratches or abrasions on his knuckles or extremities. The fingernails are intact and don't appear to have anything beneath them, skin, blood or suchlike. Nothing to indicate there was any form of conflict. Likewise, his clothing has no mud visible on it nor any signs of scuffs, scratches or tears."

"You're describing it as if this man went voluntarily to his death," Templer said, sounding surprised.

"I'll give you the science, you can figure out the psychology," Robertson said with a wry smile. "You may find what's on the ground before him very interesting."

In front of the hanging body lay a smart phone alongside a

carrier bag. The latter appeared empty and it was weighed down with a forensic number marker, presumably to stop it from blowing away in the wind. Alongside the bag were bundles of cash, stacked neatly alongside one other. Next to these, and in front of the phone, was a blooming lotus flower, the diameter of which was approximately an adult hand-span.

"Once Iain's CSI team had photographed everything in situ, we took the money from the bag and placed it there," Hunter said.

"How were they found?" Caslin asked.

"The phone and flower were as you see them now, with the money inside the bag alongside."

Caslin knelt and focussed his attention on the mobile phone. The handset appeared to be connected to a social media page, although without picking it up and scrolling through it, he was unsure of the significance. Hunter appeared to anticipate his next question and she crossed to where the CSI officers had deposited the majority of their kit, returning with a tablet in hand. Caslin stood and she activated the screen before passing it to him.

Caslin's first thought had been correct and it was indeed a social media page. Hunter had searched for the page, looking it up online with her device.

"The account is open to the public," she advised him. "Everyone can view it."

Glancing up at the victim's face and then back at the screen, Caslin judged it to be logged into the victim's profile page, or at least a profile page using this man's photograph. "Andrew Connelly," Caslin read aloud, largely for Templer's benefit, angling the screen in his direction.

Scrolling down the page, he saw multiple comments posted from the account on the previous day. Looking at roughly when they were posted, he did a quick bit of mental arithmetic and figured the entries ceased around the same time as he had visited Michelle Cates's house on the previous night. Each of the posts from the account were shocking and repulsive. In fact, they would be deemed inappropriate and offensive to any right-minded person. Some were provocative whilst others were downright graphic and vulgar in their content. Every single one of them were photographs, or stills from video footage, featuring what were quite clearly underage children alongside a man who he recognised as the victim, Andrew Connelly.

Continuing to work through each of the posts, there were too many for him to keep count. Caslin judged there were multiple victims. Even when the faces of the children were distorted, presumably to hamper their identification, he was still able to spot racial backgrounds, genders and rough age groups. Similarly, there appeared to be shots of Connelly appearing far more youthful. He had been an active child abuser for many years. Caslin took his eyes off the images and passed the tablet back to Hunter, meeting her eye and casting a glance skyward. His stomach turned, as it always did when forced to face this subject matter. A few moments passed before anyone chose to speak.

"Is it his phone, do we know?" Templer asked.

"No, it's the same phone he called you from last night," Hunter said. "What's more, it's Kelly Ryan's."

Caslin released a controlled exhale, returning his attention to the evidence before him. Dropping to his haunches, he cast his eye across the bundles of cash. They were a mixture of mostly ten and twenty-pound notes, along with three bundles of fifties. They were freshly issued and came sealed with a band of wraparound paper. Upon closer inspection each band was initialled.

"These were drawn across the counter of a bank and recently too, I should imagine," Caslin said. "Has anyone counted it yet?"

"£2860," Hunter confirmed.

"That's a random figure." Caslin was surprised.

"We counted it three times just to be sure," Hunter replied. "But you're right, it is an odd sum."

"Does it look like any has been removed?" Templer asked.

Hunter shook her head. "The amount has been noted and initialled, by the cashier, I should imagine. The odd total is recorded on a transactional slip that was in the bag along with the money. You're right, it was withdrawn yesterday from a bank here in the town."

"Right, as soon as the doors open, I want you in there finding out who withdrew it, when and why, as well as any other details you can come by. CCTV footage, the lot," Caslin instructed. Hunter nodded.

"Was the transaction slip time stamped?"

"It was printed at two-thirty-five, yesterday afternoon," Hunter confirmed.

"We found a wallet," Terry Holt said, appearing from an adjoining path. He approached brandishing a transparent evidence bag containing a black leather wallet.

Coming over to them, he opened the bag and took out the wallet. Hunter passed Caslin a pair of forensic gloves. He donned them before taking the offered wallet. Opening it up, the first thing he found was a photocard driving licence bearing the name of Andrew Connelly. The residential address was within York's city walls. Opening up the sections revealed no further cash, only debit and credit cards in the same name. There was a small dogeared photograph of a woman and a young girl. The picture didn't seem particularly old, merely ragged as a result of being kept in a wallet. Caslin flashed the image to Hunter, whose gaze lowered to the ground and she gave an almost unnoticeable shake of the head.

"Wife and daughter?" Caslin suggested.

"Most likely," Templer agreed.

"This gets better." Caslin pulled a business card from among the credit cards. Reading the information on the front, he slowly shook his head.

"What is it?" Hunter asked.

"He works for a community trust," Caslin said flatly. "Aimed at providing access to extracurricular activities for underprivi-leged children."

Murmurings of outrage and disgust emanated from everyone present as they processed the magnitude of that revelation.

"There's your suicidal motivation, right there," Robertson stated.

"What about the money?" Holt asked. "Why did he have it and why was it left?"

"Let's not jump to any conclusions until we've had a chance to process the scene," Caslin said. "Terry, once you're not needed here, I want you to have a sweep of the area and pull any footage that you can from traffic cams, private CCTV, dash cam footage from taxis, buses, anything you can think of. I want to try and catch Connelly's arrival here last night as well as anyone who he could have been meeting. In the meantime, Hunter and I will go to the registered address on his driving licence. Maybe his wife can help us with his movements yesterday."

"What can I do?" Templer asked.

"I'm presuming we haven't found Connelly's phone?" Iain Robertson glanced in his direction and shook his head. "The number is on his business card. I want you to get hold of the records to find out who he's been speaking to and get it flagged on the network. If I'm right, then the killer has it and is no doubt planning his next move. In all likelihood, the next time the phone is active will be when there's another victim to be found. However, if it pops up before that, we need to be ready to move on the location."

"I should imagine he'll be uploading another video soon as well," Templer said, "so I'll follow that through at the same time."

"Can you also contact Child Protection and bring someone in to follow up on the footage that's been posted on his social media account? We will need to start identifying these kids. They might still be vulnerable and need to be brought into safety or... let's just find out who they are." Caslin paused, taking a moment to collect his thoughts. Everyone felt revulsion but his own children came to mind. "I doubt any of us is going to shed a tear over Andrew Connelly's death, but let's do our jobs and try to put it to the back of our minds what he may have been up to. Some of these kids might still be in danger and I dare say, they all need us focussed right now. And what's more, remember who we are dealing with. Put aside whether you think Connelly had this coming or not. Our killer is acting on his own motivations. We have judges and juries to decide on punishment. This man doesn't get to choose, no matter how abhorrent his target."

CHAPTER FIFTEEN

PULLING UP AT THE ADDRESS, a rather unassuming 1960s semi-detached property in the Foxwoods suburb to the south-west of York, Caslin looked around as Hunter turned the key in the ignition. This wasn't an area he was familiar with, being one covered by officers based at the Acomb Road station. However, it was a leafy residential suburb with wide streets and a variety of green areas suitable for young and growing families.

"I think it's that one over there." Hunter indicated a house with a small driveway, neatly manicured garden and white weather boarding lining the exterior of the upper floor. Getting out of the car, Caslin pushed the door closed and scanned the driveway. A dark green hatchback was parked there and beyond that, at the entrance to the garage, a children's bicycle was propped against the wall. Walking up the path they both noticed movement as a figure passed the front door, a blur of motion through the obscured glass panel to the left.

Caslin reached up and pressed the button to the doorbell, hearing it chime in the interior. They only had to wait a few moments before someone came to answer the call. They were met by a woman in her thirties. She smiled warmly, assessing the callers, appearing almost ready to dismiss whatever it was they were about to say. That was until Caslin identified himself and showed her his warrant card.

She was genuinely taken aback at their presence, as most people were when the police came calling. "I'm so sorry. We get a lot of cold callers... They are usually nice enough people but it does become tiresome."

"Mrs Connelly?" Caslin asked. She nodded. "Do you think we could speak inside?"

"Yes, of course." She stepped back, beckoning for them to come inside but at the same time her expression changed from welcoming to fearful. "Has something happened to Rebecca?"

"Rebecca is your daughter?" Hunter asked. The woman nodded and Hunter responded quickly. "I'm sure she's fine. We're not here about your daughter."

Hunter closed the door and they were led from the hall into the living room. The Connolly's home was immaculately presented, aside from what appeared to be the remnants of breakfast still present on the dining table.

"I'm sorry, you have to forgive the mess. I wasn't expecting company. I figured I'd have everything put away by the time my husband gets home from work."

Caslin dismissed her concerns with a wave of the hand as she gestured for them to sit down. "That's okay, Mrs Connelly. I'm afraid we have some rather distressing news for you."

"It's Andy, isn't it?"

"Andrew Connolly is your husband, is that right?"

"Yes, he is," she confirmed. "Has he got himself into some kind of trouble with speeding again? I told him you'd throw the book at him if he didn't slow down."

"I'm very sorry to have to tell you this, Mrs Connolly," Caslin interrupted, "but we believe your husband has passed away." He delivered the news as gently as he could in a matter-of-fact tone. In his experience, that was the best way. She looked at him with an expression that questioned the validity of his statement.

"I... I don't understand."

"Your husband's body was found this morning, here in York," Caslin explained.

She shook her head emphatically. "No, there must be some kind of mistake. Andy travelled to Leeds yesterday, for work."

"We will have to carry out an identification in order to be sure but I am in no doubt that this is your husband." At that moment, her head sank into her hands, the realisation hitting home.

"How?" She uttered the word almost inaudibly.

"We are only at the early stages of the investigation but it would appear that your husband committed suicide." She broke down at that point and Caslin glanced across the room, meeting Hunter's eye and he could tell she didn't necessarily agree with his casting her husband's death purely as a suicide. There would be a time to share the complexities of how her husband died but there was a logic to Caslin's approach. Until he knew otherwise, he would consider Andrew Connolly's widow as both a potential witness and a suspect in his deviant behaviour. Whether she was a willing participant or turned a blind eye to her husband's activities, Caslin intended to find out. Equally, there was the possibility she was totally unaware and, in that case, he sought to spare her the graphic details.

They allowed her a few minutes more for the news to sink in and then, when she had regained her composure, she lifted her head to meet Caslin's gaze. Tears lined her cheeks.

"When was the last time you saw or spoke with your husband?"

"Yesterday," she said glancing up and to the left. "Shortly after lunchtime, I think. He called me from work."

"Did he seem out of sorts?"

She appeared thoughtful. "He wasn't his usual self, I must say. He was distracted but nothing he said… made me think anything was wrong."

"What did he say?"

"That something had come up and he had to travel to Leeds to sort it out. He told me not to worry and that he didn't know when he'd be back, but I shouldn't wait up. If it got too late and he was too tired, he would just stay over and drive back today." She flicked her eyes between the two detectives. "I wasn't expecting him back until after work this evening."

"What kind of work did your husband do, Mrs Connelly?" Hunter asked.

"He works for a charitable trust," she explained. "They work within the community providing extracurricular activities and developmental opportunities for underprivileged and vulnerable children. That can be anything from confidence building weekends away to daily after-school clubs. Not all working parents can provide wraparound care. He is very passionate about it."

Caslin shot Hunter a look. One that didn't go unnoticed. He turned back to Mrs Connolly. "Has your husband ever suffered from any form of mental illness or struggled with depression in the past?"

"No, not at all," she said. "I don't understand how he could have done this. Are you sure there hasn't been a mistake?"

Caslin shook his head. "I don't believe so, Mrs Connelly. Tell me, your husband was found with a rather large sum of money on his person. Does this ring any bells with you?"

She seemed rather confused at that suggestion. "How large?"

"Somewhere in the region of three thousand pounds."

"Where on earth did he find that kind of money?" She was visibly stunned at the amount.

"It seems it was withdrawn from the bank yesterday afternoon," Caslin stated. "Did your husband have access to the bank account of the business he worked with, or is it possible he withdrew it from a personal account?"

"I know for certain he doesn't have any involvement with the finances at the trust," she said, frowning. "And we have a joint account for the house but we don't have any savings or anything like that."

"Do you think we could have a look at your most recent bank

statement, if you have it to hand? That way, we can check whether it's from your bank or from somebody else's account."

"Yes, of course. I keep the statements over here." She stood up on unsteady feet. Caslin went to offer her physical support but she waved him away, walking across the room to the nearby bookcase. Taking down a lever arch folder, she returned and placed it on the coffee table in front of her.

Opening the folder, she flicked through the dividing sections separating credit cards and utility statements. Reaching the section where they kept the bank statements, she passed the folder over to Caslin. Hunter got up from her seat by the front window and came to join him, peering over his shoulder.

"That's the same bank as recorded on the withdrawal slip," Hunter confirmed.

"Mrs Connelly," Caslin said, looking over to her whilst tracing his finger across the bank statement in front of him, the previous month to the current one, "there appears to be several cash withdrawals this month and last. Here, on the first, and again on the fifteenth of each month to the value of £700. Can you tell me what these were for?"

She leaned over and he pointed out the transactions and from the look on her face it was quite obvious she was unaware of the withdrawals. "I... I don't understand," she said, flustered. Flicking back to the previous month's statement, they found the same withdrawals were made at similar intervals. The woman was becoming increasingly agitated, the pace in which she was turning the pages threatened to tear the statements such was her aggression.

Caslin placed his hand over hers. It shook as she withdrew it. "Do you have any knowledge of these withdrawals?" he asked.

She shook her head slowly. "No, we don't have... things have been tight for a while. Andy told me not to worry and that he was working on something and that things would get better."

"Did your husband have any expensive habits?" Hunter asked.

Mrs Connelly looked across with an inquisitive expression on her face. "I don't understand what you mean."

"Was he a regular gambler? Did he frequent the bookies?"

She shook her head. "No, nothing like that. Andy is a very conservative man. He likes things to be as they should be. Besides, how could he show his face in front of the congregation every Sunday if he held such vices?"

"What do you think he was taking the money for?" Caslin asked.

"I've no idea." She shook her head.

"Has your husband made reference to anything unusual recently?" Caslin asked. "Either something happening at work or someone new coming into his life that may have caused him concern."

"Not that he's mentioned." She looked away, thinking hard. "Come to think of it, he has been distant recently but, what with the finances, I thought he was just suffering from a bit of stress."

"Do you work, Mrs Connolly?" Caslin was curious. With money tight and a child in school, there was always the possibility for a second income.

"No! I used to before we were married but afterwards, Andy didn't want me to. I suggested I could go back to work but he wouldn't hear of it." Suddenly, her mouth fell open, tears welling. "Whatever will I tell my daughter? Inspector, I must go to the school and pick her up."

"I know this is difficult, Mrs Connelly, but we need to speak with you about another matter first. We will contact the school on your behalf and have them take Rebecca out of class, just in case word gets out before we can bring her home," Caslin said. She nodded and Caslin indicated for Hunter to step out of the room and make the call.

"What else is it, Inspector?"

"Was your husband active on social media?"

"A little, yes. Personally, I find it all nonsense and an incredible waste of time but Andy said it was important he had an account so that he could stay in touch with Rebecca."

"How much time did he spend on social media then?"

She smiled as she thought about the answer to the question. "Well, that was his argument but secretly I think he really enjoyed it. He was always sharing jokes with Rebecca and her friends, as well as the kids from the centre. I didn't think it did any harm. Why do you ask?"

Hunter returned from the kitchen. She smiled as she sat down. "I've spoken to the Head at your daughter's school and she's going to take Rebecca to her office and wait there."

"Thank you," Mrs Connolly said, breathing a sigh of relief.

"Would you say that Andy spent rather a lot of time inter-acting with the kids by social media then?" Caslin flicked a glance in Hunter's direction, thereby bringing her up to speed with what they were discussing.

"Sometimes I did tell him that he should let them get on with their own lives without an old man jumping in all the time," Mrs Connolly said, chuckling. "That said, the kids seem to like having him around. That might be because he was always bringing them things."

"What type of things?"

"Magazines, sweets, chocolates. Nothing too extravagant," she explained. "What's this got to do with anything?"

The detectives both held impassive expressions. She appeared to find them unnerving. "Mrs Connolly, we have an active social media account that appears to show your husband in… compromising situations with children," Caslin said flatly.

"Compromising?" Her eyes narrowed as she spoke. "In what way?"

"I'm afraid there's no easy way to tell you this but your husband was abusing them."

Mrs Connolly's mouth fell open, eyes wide. She shook her head emphatically. "No! That can't be right. You've made a mistake!"

"There are pictures... many, many pictures," Caslin said, meeting her eye. "There is no doubt."

She broke down as those words sank in. Her entire body shaking as she wept uncontrollably. Eyes closed tightly, her lips curled in such a fashion as to indicate a person wrought with suffering and pain. After a few moments the sobbing subsided and she regained a measure of composure, mumbling almost inaudibly, "My Rebecca."

"We don't know." It was an honest reply. Caslin couldn't sugar coat the facts but nor did he want to speculate. "Did you ever have any inclination about your husband's behaviour around or towards the children?" It was a harsh but a necessary question. At this point, they did not know whether Connelly's widow could somehow be complicit in the apparent systematic abuse of the children. Until they did, either way, they would tread carefully as no one could be given an easy ride.

She shook her head again, staring into Caslin's eyes, hers shot through with red and brimming with tears. "Never. How could I as a mother?"

"I appreciate this is very difficult for you," Caslin said, adopting a conciliatory tone, "but it is very important for us to ask. Looking back, was there anything unusual in his behaviour? Not necessarily recently."

"I find this all fanciful. Andy has never... he wasn't particularly interested in... the physical aspects of a relationship. If you know what I mean?" She said the last quietly, almost wishing the words not to be heard. Caslin encouraged her to continue. "Once we had Rebecca, he lost interest in that type of thing. For a long time, I thought it must have been me." She reached for a box of tissues, wiping the tears from her cheeks and blowing her nose. "I guess it wasn't me, after all."

Caslin glanced toward Hunter and drew her attention. "Perhaps, I should make us all a cup of tea. If that's okay with you?" He looked to their host, not wanting to take liberties but he had an ulterior motive. She said that was okay and he got up.

Hunter's eyes followed. Once he was sure he wouldn't be seen, he pointed two fingers towards his eyes and then angled them away, signifying he intended to have a look around. Hunter acknowledged with the briefest incline of her head, a movement that would mean nothing to anyone who didn't witness the exchange.

Caslin entered the kitchen, pulling the door to. Looking around, he found the kettle and filled it to its maximum with water, setting it to boil. Knowing that would give him a few minutes' grace, he entered the hallway through another door so as not to be seen from those in the living room. Risking a glance into the living room, he saw that Hunter had moved into his seat and Mrs Connelly was now looking in the opposite direction to where he stood. Quickly crossing the gap, he crept up the stairs treading as lightly as he could.

There were three bedrooms and a bathroom off the landing. One bedroom, to the front of the house, was very small and little more than a box room. This was utilised as something of a home office or study and Caslin quickly leafed through some of the paperwork, but nothing particularly caught his eye. Everything was neatly arranged, ordered. The sign of a controlling personality. There was a laptop and as soon as the warrant came through, he would ensure that got back to Holt. Framed photographs adorned the walls. The majority of them were shots of Connolly alongside various children, boys and girls, of different ages. Some appear to have been taken on camping trips, hill walking or on sporting occasions. With each face that Caslin examined, that same familiar churning of his stomach returned.

The next bedroom he entered was Rebecca's. It was much the same as his daughter, Lizzie's, was at home. The two girls must have been a similar age and a flash of anger rose inside Caslin as he considered the prospect of someone like Connolly targeting his own daughter. The anger subsided as he thought about the man's widow. If she was as innocent as she seemed, he considered what she would be feeling at this moment. Leaving the room largely untouched, he briefly cast an eye over the master bedroom. Everything was tidy, clean and well presented. He wondered whether Andrew Connelly's desire for everything to be just right extended to controlling his entire family's movements and behaviours?

Returning downstairs, he entered the living room, not bothering with making the tea. He figured she was so shocked by their news that his ruse to snoop around wouldn't be discovered. "Mrs Connelly." She looked up at him. Although her face was tear-stained, she appeared calmer now. "We're going to have a few officers come by and go through your husband's possessions. In the meantime, we will arrange for a couple of plain clothes officers to take you to the school and pick up your daughter. Perhaps, it might be best for the two of you to stay away from the house for a while. Is there anyone you know that you can visit with for a couple of days? I'm afraid once the press get a hold of this, they will come calling. And they will be persistent."

"Yes, I have family nearby. We could probably stay with them. Should I call them?"

"Please do. We will also need to take a formal statement from you in due course."

Caslin beckoned Hunter to step out into the hall with him as Mrs Connelly reached for the telephone. "There's a home office upstairs devoted to Connelly's favoured pastime of mixing with the children. There's also a computer and I imagine we'll find an awful lot more on the hard drive. Get Terry on it quickly as possible."

"Where are you going to be, sir?"

"I don't doubt the video will be uploaded within the next couple of hours, so I'm going to go over to his workplace and find out as much as I can before everything hits the fan."

CHAPTER SIXTEEN

CASLIN PULLED open the left hand door and entered. He was in a short, squat rectangular building fashioned from a mixture of prefabricated concrete panels and an old corrugated roof that was most likely full of asbestos. He judged it was once a commercial unit, thrown up at some point in the sixties and approaching the end of its useful life. Nobody was present at the reception desk, little more than a table with a signing-in book and a scattering of information leaflets, home printed by the look of them. Sound carried from beyond another set of double doors in front of him and he migrated towards it.

Pushing open the door, Caslin found himself in one large room that stretched almost to the rear boundary but signs at the far end indicated there were toilets and changing facilities through the doors. In one corner there was a boxing ring with what appeared to be netting hanging around the exterior. Off to his right were various pieces of gym apparatus and on the walls behind these were photographs of gymnasts in action. Moving closer, Caslin noted that many of the shots were taken in this very building.

"Can I help you?" A voice came from behind. Caslin was startled having not heard anyone approach. There was another door to his left and they must have come from there. He smiled and took out his identification.

The man paid it a cursory inspection as Caslin identified himself. "Is this your place?"

"Aye, I'm Tommy Banner," he said, smiling warmly. He was a stocky individual, tattooed and balding. "At least, I look after the day-to-day running of the centre."

"You provide services for disadvantaged kids, is that right?"

"Yes, we do. We're not limited to those from less well-off backgrounds, you understand. We also help where we can with vulnerable children, providing somewhere for the kids to go if the parents are working. Not many have a steady nine-to-five these days."

"You say working with vulnerable children. The local authority must be involved somewhere along the line."

"Oh, yes," Banner agreed. "This centre is part funded by the local council. We would need them on board to be able to do what we do."

"Where does the rest of the funding come from then?"

"Much of it comes from a local church group, whereas the remainder comes from donations or fundraising activities we take on ourselves. The children are often a large part of that; we try to arrange as many family days as we can. Doing so really brings the community together."

"I see. How long have you been going?"

"These past four years." The man exuded pride, obviously pleased with their accomplishment. "Funding is becoming an issue, though. Between you and me, I'm not entirely sure how much longer we can keep going."

"I'm sorry to hear that." Caslin couldn't help but think the revelations surrounding Connolly's activities would kill off any future source of local authority funding, let alone the black mark in the eyes of the general public.

"It's not the first time we've been in this situation. We'll work something out," Banner said with confidence. "I'm sure you're not here at this time of the morning to ask me about charitable funding. How can I help you, Inspector?"

"I'm afraid I have some bad news about one of your colleagues; Andrew Connolly."

"Andy? What's he been up to?"

"I'm sorry to have to tell you that Mr Connolly was found dead this morning."

Banner appeared visibly shocked. "When, how?"

"He was found early this morning," Caslin informed him, deliberately withholding any further detail. "The circumstances surrounding his death are still under investigation. What can you tell me about him? He worked here full time, is that correct?"

"Yes, he was one of three paid members of staff," Banner said, still trying to take in the news.

"There are only three of you?"

"Three paid staff, yes. The remainder are made up of part-time volunteers who agree to help out for a set time period, perhaps two months at a time. In reality, it tends not to work that way as people stay on or provide more hours as and when they are available. People are very generous. You only have to spend a little time here with the children to see the positive impact that you can have in their lives," Banner replied, a measure of the pride returning amid the sadness. "Forgive me, I think I need to sit down."

"That's okay." Caslin indicated towards a handful of circular tables behind them. They walked over and both men pulled out a chair. Caslin noticed the door that Banner had walked out of led to a kitchen.

"I can't believe Andy's gone." Banner shook his head.

"Has he been with you long?"

"He was one of the first to volunteer when I opened this place. He quickly made his presence known and I saw the value in having him around and so, when things really got going and I needed full-time staff, it was a no-brainer to take him on."

"And what do you know of him, personally?"

"I didn't really socialise with him outside of work." His tone was very matter-of-fact, genuine. Banner took on a thoughtful expression. "To be honest, this place is everything to me and I don't really do much else. It's come to dominate my life. My wife keeps the books and ensures everything ticks over financially. That leaves me to do what I do best, keeping the children out of mischief."

"Tell me, did Andy ever have access to the finances here?"

Banner appeared surprised at the question and scratched the stubble of his face, shaking his head. "No, not at all. Why do you ask?"

"I spoke with his wife this morning and there's some odd activity in their account. She was at a loss to explain what was going on. We're just trying to build a picture."

"Oh, I see. I only ever met his wife on two occasions... I think that's right, yes. June, isn't it? Or Jane. You know, I'm not sure now." Banner looked to the ceiling, struggling to remember. "He brought his wife and daughter, Becky, I remember her, lovely girl, to a couple of our family days over the summer last year. They seemed like a nice family. They must be devastated."

"How close was Andy to the children?"

"Oh, he was marvellous with them," Banner said, expressing true delight with one of his team. "To see how Andy could take some of those children under his wing and really look out for them was something to behold. He was great with the group as a whole, but he was truly gifted at spotting those that needed something more, you know? Andy was always willing to go the extra yard. Sometimes I wonder where he got his passion and motivation from."

Caslin nodded but didn't say what was going through his mind. "*Jane Connelly* was under the impression that her husband was required to travel to Leeds yesterday, for work."

"No. That's not the case at all. I don't understand where she got that idea." Banner was genuinely baffled. "I mean, we do have an affiliation with a similar project in Leeds and we often carry out joint trips and events. It allows for a sharing of the costs, but there was no reason for Andy to travel there yesterday. Not anything that I'm aware of."

"And you would know?"

"Yes! Of course, I would know."

"Were you here yesterday?" Caslin asked. Banner nodded that he was. "What about Andrew?"

"Yes, he was here too. Until lunchtime anyway."

"He left?"

Banner nodded. "He was supposed to be working a full shift and I was going to take the afternoon off but all of a sudden, Andy said something had come up and he had to go."

"Did he say what?" Caslin took out his pocketbook and a pen.

"No, he didn't. He said he had to shoot off for a little bit and then he'd come back but he never showed." The recollection triggered a display of irritation but it soon passed. "I assumed it was something to do with *Jane*, or maybe Becky, so I didn't get too upset about it."

"What made you think that?"

"Well, he was fine in the morning but then around midday he took a phone call. After that he was somewhat agitated and left shortly after. That's why I figured he'd had a call from home or the school and had to rush off."

"Anything like that ever happen before?" Banner thought about it and then shook his head. "Presumably, you keep records on all the children who attend here or pass through?"

"Of course, yes. We would anyway but the local authority demand it and we have good links with the local social workers."

"I'm going to send some officers down here at some point today, Mr Banner, and I would appreciate it if you could help them gather that information as soon as possible, along with a list of the other paid staff and your volunteers."

Banner appeared taken aback and it dawned on him that there was something going on he was unaware of. "This is unusual. Is there a problem?"

"I've no doubt this will be hitting the media in due course, but there are aspects to Andrew Connolly's life that you are going to find unpalatable, to say the least." Caslin watched the man for a reaction, however small. "Everyone who works here or has volunteered, either in the past or the present, will need to be interviewed by my team and I dare say you'll be spending more time with child services in the coming days and weeks. All the children who passed through your centre will need to be assessed."

"Are you saying... Andy..." The penny dropped. "That can't be?"

"This is your worst fear coming to pass, I assure you," Caslin said flatly, "and I take no pleasure in telling you."

"THE LATEST VIDEO IS UP." Holt called to Caslin as he entered the ops room. Taking off his coat, he hung it on the back of his chair before sitting down.

"Can you put it up for me?" Caslin pointed at the projection screen. Holt tapped away on his keyboard and moments later the projector fired up and the footage started to roll. Both Hunter and Templer turned away from what they were doing, all eyes on the screen. Details were difficult to make out as the footage was shot at night and there was very little external light to help. The previous night was overcast and despite the cemetery being on the edge of a populated suburb, the sheer scale of the site, as well as the mature trees, protected the area from the encroaching light pollution. To the east, past the cemetery's boundary, there lay an equally large area devoted to allotments.

The video was filmed on Connelly's mobile phone and was evidently hand held. The footage was unstable, adding to their difficulty in making out the detail. The picture dropped in and out of focus frequently as the holder moved around.

"There doesn't appear to be any confrontation between the two of them," Templer said. The camera angle zoomed out, widening the picture. The only sounds that could be identified came from traffic in the distance and the occasional snap or rustle of booted feet treading on the vegetation beneath their feet or the wind whistling through the branches overhead.

A momentary break in the clouds allowed shafts of silver moonlight to illuminate the scene. At that point, the person operating the camera zoomed in on the recognisable figure of Andrew Connolly placing his head through a noose. The image blurred as the cameraman approached, the mobile angled to the ground. They had to conclude he was tightening the rope at the nape of Connolly's neck. Stepping away, the camera came back up focussing on Connelly as he mounted a stepladder. Turning gingerly at the top, he looked directly at the camera. He was sobbing, his bottom lip quivered. Again, the cameraman moved around to the rear and the picture went black but sounds still emanated, sounds they struggled to interpret but the footage was still recording.

"What do you think he's doing now?" Hunter asked.

"He's taking up the slack of the rope," Caslin replied. The mobile was retrieved and the holder panned back to Connolly, sweeping back around to the front, viewing the victim's face. There were a few more seconds where both men stared at each other. Connelly mouthed the words *I'm sorry*. He seemed paralysed with fear. The watching detectives waited patiently for Connolly to step off but he remained where he was. The footage wobbled. Caslin could imagine the holder either encouraging him to step off or growing frustrated at the delay. Seconds later, there was movement as the camera surged forward, losing all focus. There was a panicked scream and the sound of a thud accompanied by the rattle of metal. The team looked at one another.

"Did he just kick the stepladder over?" Holt asked. No one replied.

The footage came back into focus, held once again by a steady hand. Heavy breathing could be heard. Connolly was swinging from left to right. Caslin was transfixed whereas the other three looked away. The footage held steady as Connelly struggled for breath, his face contorted in a mixture of pain and sheer terror. Caslin was grateful for the darkness that masked the final moments of the man's life.

Minutes passed before the camera panned down from the body to the ground, moving closer in order to film the carrier bag as well as its contents. Even in this light, the cash was visible. The angle of the camera changed to reveal the lotus flower held in the palm of a gloved hand. This was then placed on the ground, next to the bag before the footage returned to the form of Andrew Connelly, suspended from the tree. No longer was he gasping for breath, no struggling, no clawing at the rope or fighting for life. The footage paused and then faded to black. The number three appeared for the remainder of the video before playback ceased.

"What is it with the money?" Holt asked.

Caslin exhaled deeply. "Hunter and I saw repeated withdrawals from Connelly's bank account over the past few months. Always the same dates, always the same sum. Jane, Connelly's wife, was unaware of any reason for this cash to be withdrawn. My theory is that somehow our killer found out what Connelly has been getting up to and was bleeding him dry."

"Blackmail?"

"I think so, yes." Caslin looked back at the screen, the number three still visible. "He is meticulous. We know he plans these events in great detail. They aren't random or opportunistic attacks. For him to know what Connelly has been getting up to, he must have been around him for some time. If we go back through the Connelly's accounts and see when Andrew started making these withdrawals it might give us an idea how long the killer has been targeting him."

"But if he's been blackmailing him, why did he leave the money? There's nearly three grand there," Holt argued. "Do you think Connelly didn't turn up with enough?"

"He doesn't care about the money," Caslin countered. "He may have needed it before but for some reason, he doesn't need it now. Last night wasn't about money." Caslin played through the scenario in his mind. The killer arranged to meet Connelly, either demanding a larger payoff or perhaps he suggested this would be the final one. Regardless, he drew him to the cemetery to carry out his ruthless power play. "This was all about control. It was a pre-planned exercise in manipulation designed to torment his victim and drive him to suicide. Who knows what was said to Connelly in the build-up to last night but when he got there, he was presented with the reality of his darkest secrets going public. Then, he offered him a way out."

"Suicide." Templer rubbed at his face. "And when Connelly didn't look like he was going to take it, the killer booted him off the ladder and stood there watching him die."

"And not forgetting he also filmed it so the rest of us wouldn't miss out," Caslin added.

"Why didn't he film the removal of the finger this time?" Templer made a valid point.

"Although he does it to every victim, and has done in the past, I don't think that's part of his message to us."

"Then why does he do it?" Templer asked.

"That's an act for him," Caslin replied, "and him alone."

CHAPTER SEVENTEEN

"I PULLED every bit of CCTV from any camera surrounding the entrance to the cemetery or covering the approach road," Holt said. "There's only one vehicular access as well as the pedestrian gate. There isn't a lot to go on but I did find this footage produced by a security camera located on the exterior of a building opposite. The system is high quality, so I'm pleased with the clarity of the picture."

"That's good news, Terry." Caslin placed an approving hand on his shoulder.

"Yeah, don't get carried away though," Holt replied. "It doesn't give us much to run with." Holt brought up footage and Caslin's eyes narrowed as he concentrated. The picture was black and white, predominantly covering the foreground in the immediate vicinity of the building the camera was mounted on. However, at the top of the shot could clearly be seen the imposing wrought-iron gates of the entrance to the Victorian cemetery.

After a few moments, a car passed by and Holt dismissed it with a casual wave of the hand to imply it was nonsignificant. Instead, he pointed to a pedestrian. Appearing from out of shot to the left, they watched as a man approached the cemetery's gate, stopping and glancing around him in every direction before entering.

"I know it's hard to tell from this distance but he looks nervous to me," Caslin said aloud.

"And that was before he realised he was walking to his death," Holt added. They knew it was Andrew Connolly, it was obvious, not only because the clothing matched but he looked in the camera's direction. The resolution was such that they could identify him.

"Is that time stamp correct?" Caslin asked.

"I'll check but if it's out then I don't think it's by much, judging from the volume of traffic passing by in the footage I've seen," Holt stated.

"This puts him arriving at around 8:30," Caslin said. "I received a call from his tormentor around an hour later. Whether Connolly was alive at that point, I don't know but during the call he appeared distracted. While he was talking to me, I reckon he was at this particular crime scene. Any sign of our mysterious suspect?"

Holt shook his head. "I've been through the footage for an hour and a half prior to Connolly's arrival and through to two hours after the estimated time of death, and there's no sign of him."

"I didn't see Connolly carrying his own stepladder. Did the killer fly it in with a drone?"

"Yeah, along with himself." Holt was despondent.

The adjoining allotments offered the perfect opportunity to both arrive and depart unobserved. The CSI team, assisted by a large uniformed contingent, carried out a fingertip search in the immediate vicinity of the scene. A stepladder was found inside the groundskeepers' lock-up.

"I don't suppose there's any chance that they've been able to lift any prints?" Caslin asked.

"They picked up multiples from the lock-up as well as documenting the equipment stored within just in case he was careless.

However, he was wearing gloves in the video, so I don't think we should get our hopes up," Hunter said.

"He's going to slip up somewhere along the line, they always do," Caslin replied. "What about the bank footage? Any joy there?"

"We went through it, sir," Hunter said. "Connolly is seen on an exterior camera approaching the bank in broad daylight, alone. He enters and fills out a withdrawal slip and takes it to the teller. They have a brief discussion and she counts out the money for him, putting it into an envelope, and he leaves."

"What about the member of staff, did you speak with them?"

"We did, yes," Holt said. "With that sum of money, it's borderline as to whether they fall back on their protocols or not. However, she did ask what he wanted the money for?" When a customer withdraws a large sum of cash, standard procedure is to look for signs they may be acting under duress. "Nothing in his demeanour, or what he said, indicated that Connolly was under any pressure. Therefore, she allowed the withdrawal to take place. Admittedly, both the teller and her line manager said they tend to pay closer attention to pensioners than they do to customers like him. He didn't exhibit any of the signs to trigger their concerns."

Caslin sighed. With the payments always being in cash, there was no electronic path between Connolly and his presumed blackmailer. However, it did leave them with an avenue to investigate. If he was right, then Connolly had a relationship with the killer. That wasn't to suggest they knew each other, although they couldn't dismiss the possibility. "They've had conversations and unless Connolly was leaving envelopes stuffed with cash in agreed random places, then there is every possibility they physically met on more than one occasion. This means that their paths have crossed and if we can pinpoint Connolly's movements, either through his phone, places he frequented or his ritual habits, then maybe we can determine where these meetings took place. I know that's a long shot, before anyone says it."

"How did he know what Connolly was up to?" Hunter asked.

"The same way he got your phone number, I expect, sir. I mean, he's tech savvy. He's been able to mask his domain every time he's been online to upload a video, and he got hold of your number in order to call you the other night. Perhaps he's also hacked Connolly's social media."

"I don't doubt his tech skills," Caslin agreed but they were missing something. "He still needed to get on to Connolly in the first place before moving on to hacking his account. Paedophiles like Connolly don't tend to operate in isolation. They may carry out systematic abuse alone but often they have the urge to share that experience with others, whether in online chat rooms or across the dark web for instance."

"You think they met in an online chat room?" Hunter asked, inclining her head in such a way to indicate she saw it as a possibility.

"It's not beyond the realm of possibility that he went looking online for someone like Connolly, then narrowed it down locally once he integrated himself deeper into the community," Caslin suggested. "Again, that suits his style to spend time methodically researching his targets."

"Or it could be simpler than that." Templer spoke up from the other side of the room. The three of them turned to look at him inquisitively. "It could just as easily be a relative of one of his victims who found out and decided to set themselves up as judge, jury and executioner. Let's not forget we are also considering the same scenario as a possibility with the victims of the poisoning in Stamford Street. This could all be some disaffected member of their own community."

"Where would Kelly Ryan fit into that?" Caslin asked. "Not that your logic isn't sound."

Templer shook his head. "I don't have an answer for that. We need to know more about her life."

Caslin's mobile rang and he glanced at the screen. Although he hadn't saved the number, he recognised it was Michelle Cates. A brief flicker of excitement tugged at his chest and he excused himself from the group, answering the call on the way into his office.

"Michelle." Closing the door behind him, he faced away from those in the room in a primitive attempt to avoid anyone picking up on his pleasure at receiving the call.

"Nate, I'm sorry to call you," she said hastily, flustered.

"That's okay." Fearful for a moment there had been another unwanted visitor at her home, he tried to reassure her. "Is something wrong?"

"I know this probably has nothing to do with you but what with everything that's been going on recently…" Her voice cracked as she spoke.

"It's okay, Michelle. What's on your mind?"

"Carly is home from school. She's quite upset. One of her friends… she was pulled out of class today and left early. It turns out her father killed himself."

"Yes, I'm aware of the case and the circumstances are under investigation."

Michelle's voice raised in pitch and she started to ramble almost incoherently. "They're saying on the news… and all over social media, that he was abusing kids… Carly is… she's been to this place where he works. She knows Becky. She's been to this girl's home! Nathaniel, I bloody sent her there. Do you know what I've… what if…?"

"Michelle, I need you to take a breath," Caslin said. "I know this is difficult. I have children myself and the thoughts running through your head must be awful, but I'll tell you this, I was at the centre earlier today speaking with the management. Now, I shouldn't really be speaking about it but we are investigating."

"My little girl," Michelle said, bursting into tears at the prospect of every parent's worst nightmare coming true.

"I know this is hard," Caslin repeated, trying his best to be upbeat. "There are hundreds of children who have passed through the centre at different times. The probability of your daughter being a... one of those affected is very slim. Try to hold on to that."

"I know you've no reason to, Nathaniel," she said, "but could you come around... later... if you have time?"

Caslin knew he shouldn't because that could compromise his objectivity in the case but, at the same time, he was confident he could navigate a safe path and besides, he wanted to. "I'll stop by this evening on my way home." He looked over his shoulder, worried he would be overheard despite standing alone in his office. Hunter caught his eye but looked away as soon as he clocked her observing him.

"Thank you." Michelle sounded relieved. "I'll see you then."

Caslin hung up on the call, touched the handset to his lips and smiled. He could certainly have reassured her over the phone but the prospect of seeing her again was too appealing. The excitement of the anticipation of their next meeting rose within him.

Leaving his office, Templer beckoned him over.

"I've been putting some thought into this numbering sequence that appears at the end of each video," he explained.

"What have you come up with?"

"The motivation cannot simply be focussed on his craving for attention. Were that the case, then he wouldn't be going to such great detail in staging each scene."

"You're talking about leaving the lotus flowers as well as the numbering, aren't you?"

Templer nodded. "He's sending us a message. Not only us, but the wider world in general. If your primary objective is to have all eyes on you, then his actions have succeeded but, in that scenario, you wouldn't be leaving the money behind at Stamford Street nor the carrier bag stuffed with cash, let alone staging the flowers. He has a greater purpose."

"Terry looked into the flowers earlier," Caslin said.

"Yes, he did," Templer agreed, "but he was looking specifically at the lotus flower, which is widely used across the world in the iconography and belief systems of multiple religions. Focussing on the numbers and tying them to a religious belief narrows the focus significantly."

Caslin thought on it for a few moments. "You're going down the line of *The Ten Commandments* or *The Five Pillars* of Islam, right?"

Templer nodded to indicate they were thinking along the same path. "Right. Although, every religion seems to have a list of rules, guidelines that practitioners should live their life by. In fact, many of the regions have multiple lists. From *The Ten Commandments* to the *Seven Deadly Sins* through to Judaism's *613 Commandments*, whoever has the time to memorise all of those, I don't know. Anyway, specifically cross-referencing the numbering with the added emphasis of the lotus flower I've tied it to Buddhism."

"Isn't Buddhism considered to be the most peaceful of the dominant faiths?" Caslin countered.

"Don't all religions classify themselves as religions of peace?" Templer argued. From the disdain with which he made the comment, Caslin figured he was far from a religious man. "The reason I focussed on Buddhist practice is because of how prominently the lotus flower is connected with it in western society. If you had asked me before Terry did his research, then I would have thought of this one first because I didn't know it had any significance in other religions."

"Okay, you've got my attention," Caslin said, indicating for him to continue and pulling up a chair.

"Well, the first thing I came to was *The Four Noble Truths*. They focus specifically on suffering, the truth of suffering, the causes, the end of suffering as well as the path that leads to the end. These are described as the essence of the Buddha's teachings."

"I can already see a flaw in this," Caslin said. "The video recording at Stamford Street..."

"Finished with the displaying of the number five. Yes, I know," Templer interrupted him. "However, as I said previously, religions often have several numbered lists in which to adhere to during your life. Buddhism is no different. Beyond *The Four Noble truths* there are *The Five Precepts*."

"Precepts?" Caslin asked. "Like rules?"

"Not so much rules. More like guidelines. Buddhism doesn't set out rules or commandments. They are commitments that all followers of the Buddha's teachings try to adhere to. In their simplest interpretations they could fit with our three crime scenes so far."

"I'm not so keen on the *so far* part of what you just said," Caslin replied, indicating for him to continue. He waved to Hunter and beckoned her to join them. She did so, bringing Terry Holt with her. Caslin had a sense that DI Templer was onto something.

"As I said, we have to look at these very loosely because, as I understand it, the precepts are actually very detailed and go far deeper than the first few lines of a headline search on the Internet. However, go with me on this," Templer said, as the others sat down. "The murders at the drug den on Stamford Street were documented with the number five. The Fifth Precept, simplistically, asks for people to refrain from the taking of intoxicating substances because they cloud the mind. That ranges from alcohol through to recreational drugs, even gambling if it's a habitual action, so I think it's quite easy to see how that ties in."

"The precepts are a moral code, as I recall," Hunter said. "I remember seeing a documentary about them a while back."

"The third precept focuses on refraining from sexual misconduct," Templer continued. "As I say, it does go far deeper but I think we can all agree that Andrew Connelly's behaviour certainly ticks that box. My understanding is that the teachings reflect sexual relations within marriage as the acceptable moral path. Molesting children would certainly fall foul of that guideline."

"What about Kelly Ryan?" Caslin asked. "There's some indication that she was having a relationship beyond the confines of her marriage."

"But the number two was assigned to her, wasn't it?" Holt asked.

"That's right, it was," Templer confirmed. "The second is often thought to be referring to stealing but I've done a little bit of reading around it and a better interpretation would be to define it as *taking what is not freely given*. That's not exactly the same thing."

"What was it her line manager said her team did?" Caslin asked.

"They worked on debt management." Templer was growing in stature as the outline of his theory developed. "The administration of repossession orders when clients couldn't meet their mortgage repayments was part of their role. Very few people willingly want to be evicted from their homes."

Caslin considered their next step. "Terry, I want you to go back to Kelly's line manager, at the bank, and pull up a list of all the repossession cases she's been working on recently. Add to that list any she has underway where the clients haven't been evicted yet."

"Yes, sir," Holt said, making a note. "How far back do you want me to go?"

"Six to twelve months. Perhaps further if there are a significant number," Caslin said. "He may have been planning this for some time, so we have no idea when he first conceived of the idea. While you're there, I want you to revisit her colleagues. Apparently, Kelly Ryan didn't have many interests outside of her work. Therefore, it stands to reason if she mentioned who she was sleeping with on the quiet, they will be the ones who she spoke to about it."

"We've already interviewed them, sir," Hunter stated, with a shake of the head. "They didn't offer us anything."

"If Kelly was involved with a senior member of the staff, they may have felt threatened. Give them a further nudge and apply a bit of pressure. You might get a favourable response."

"Will do, sir," Holt said.

"I'll come with you," Hunter said.

Caslin then exchanged glances with Templer. His logic was sound. "You said there are five in total? That leaves us two more."

"There are Five Precepts, sure. If I'm right, then we still have the first and the fourth to come."

"And they are?" Caslin asked.

"The *precept of truthfulness* and then there's the big one, the first. The one considered more important than any other, covering *the harming of living things*."

"There's no irony there then," Caslin countered with intended sarcasm.

CHAPTER EIGHTEEN

CASLIN LOOKED AT THE CLOCK. It was late afternoon and a thought occurred to him. Standing up and moving away from the table, he left the others still discussing Templar's theory. Retrieving his coat, he slipped it on and headed for the door. Catching Hunter's eye as he passed her, he replied to the unasked question.

"I'm just popping out for a bit."

"Okay, what shall I say if anyone asks for you?"

"Tell them I've gone out," Caslin replied, not looking back. Making his way along the corridor, he carried out a brief Internet search and was pleased to find his idea bearing fruit. The address was on the edge of the centre, just beyond the city walls, although he had no recollection of this particular building despite driving past on countless occasions.

Leaving the station and setting off for his car, Caslin was pleased that the threat of rainfall appeared to have passed. There was a strong breeze and despite clear skies and warm sunshine, it still felt colder than perhaps it should have been at this time of year. Starting the car, he turned right out of the car park and onto the Fulford Road leading into York. The traffic on the ring road was building as he drove the short distance to his destination. Not quite sure which building he was looking for, Caslin scanned the street scene as he approached. There was a large intersection where several routes converged, either passing in or out of the city itself or continuing to circumvent it. Waiting at these traffic lights, Caslin saw what he was looking for.

The sequence of the lights went from red through to green and Caslin imposed his lane change on an unsuspecting motorist, drawing an angry blast of a car horn. York was one of those cities where people unfamiliar with the location often fell afoul of incorrect lane choice as the route was not always clear. On this occasion, Caslin's destination was a building much the same as any other on the street, nothing stood out to differentiate it from the surrounding ones apart from signage that, unsurprisingly, was low key. Pulling across the traffic, he mounted the pavement and parked the car at the front of the building. There was limited space but he left it there, nonetheless. Another driver sounded a blast of their car horn and Caslin pretended not to notice, despite it being undoubtedly aimed at him.

The building was a detached residential address, the likes of which were, these days, more often than not converted into commercial premises rather than occupied as domestic homes. Such properties were large, expensive to own and run, and because of their proximity to the city usually came with very little outside space. The combination of these factors made them unviable, as well as undesirable, as family homes in the modern era.

Caslin rang the bell but then realised the door was unlocked, with the latch open, and he entered. The interior was clean and well presented, white painted walls with the original pattern tiles laid out on the floor before him. There was a small table to the left with an abundance of leaflets set in holders. He cast an eye over them. The sound of creaking treads announced someone coming down the stairs. Caslin turned to see the approach of a short man, probably in his mid-sixties. He was bald from forehead to crown and unlike many with the same growth pattern, he chose not to keep the sides and back of his head close cropped. White hair bulged out in a horseshoe around his head. Aside from that, he wore jeans and an ivory knitted jumper, one that his late father would have described as a cricketer's offering. Caslin was surprised. The approaching man noticed the reaction, drawing a wide and genuine smile.

"What were you expecting?" He spoke in a broad Yorkshire accent.

"Is it that obvious?" Caslin returned the smile.

"You can always tell the newcomers who are here for the first time. I think many people expect to find us all shaven headed, walking around in orange robes, chanting and tapping cymbals."

Caslin laughed. "I have to admit the thought did occur."

"I'm Chen Tao, one of the teachers here at the centre." He introduced himself, offering Caslin his hand.

"Detective Inspector Caslin."

"Now it's my turn to look surprised." Chen Tao raised his eyebrows. "What can I do for you, Inspector, is this a professional call?"

"I'm afraid so, yes. I'm not very aware of your traditions and I was hoping you could fill in some gaps to my knowledge regarding Buddhism, as well as the motivations of those people who follow it."

The smile returned. "Now there's a challenge. I'm certainly willing to try. Please, do come through."

Chen Tao led them further into the building. They bypassed the original drawing room and through to what would have been the dining room but had now been substantially increased in size with a large extension to the rear. The room was now a meeting hall with perhaps two-dozen chairs stacked along one side. Collapsed trestle tables were neatly ordered against the opposite wall.

"How many people attend here?" Caslin was impressed by the scale. With no idea of the group's popularity, he was impressed by the potential numbers they could accommodate.

"We have a diverse group. We run evening classes for those who are exploring the *Dharma* - the teachings of the Buddha –

along with meditation classes, yoga sessions and various other community-focussed evenings. We can have anything up to thirty people present for those but when we have a guest speaker, then that number can swell into the hundreds. In those case we often have to book somewhere else. The centre is too small."

"That's impressive," Caslin said, not intending to sound as surprised as he appeared.

"We also run weekend retreats here."

"Places for people to come to... recharge?"

"That is dependent on the nature of the retreat," Chen Tao explained. "There is a different focus for each but all are beneficial either for spiritual development or reinforcement."

"Presumably you've seen an uptake in numbers with mindfulness so much in the public consciousness these days?"

Chen Tao laughed. "It has certainly become fashionable, hasn't it? Mindfulness is a part of what we do but I would argue it has been practised for thousands of years, not only in the last decade."

Caslin was apologetic. "I'm sorry, I didn't mean to offend you."

"No offence is taken, I assure you. Secular mindfulness is useful but, and I don't wish to appear dismissive, it will only take you so far. Nevertheless, it would be fair to say the centre has grown in the last few years which we are all very pleased with."

"You refer to it as a centre rather than a temple?"

"A temple has certain connotations, particularly in western society. We welcome people from all faiths and backgrounds, no matter whether they are Christian, Muslim, or of any other denomination. Even committed atheists attend here. We are here to help guide people along their spiritual path and their progression is largely by their own will. Practising from a centre is far more appropriate. Is there anything specific that you are interested in because your enquiry is rather broad?"

"I'm very interested in the *Five Precepts*."

"Ahh… the ethics. Fascinating subject, even for those who have studied them for years."

"Ethics?" Caslin asked.

"The precepts form the basis of Buddhist doctrine for both lay and monastic followers," Chen Tao explained. "In their most basic form they are principles that we aspire to live by that will aid us along our path to enlightenment. The ultimate goal of any Buddhist."

"I'm led to believe they are guidelines, things that we should refrain from doing. Bad things, for want of a better phrase," Caslin said.

Chen Tao shook his head indicating that he disagreed. "They are a set of guidelines but are often misconstrued in the way you describe, Inspector. I think that's a hangover from western society where previous generations have been raised along religious paths and their… dogma… has transposed itself."

"I don't understand."

"For instance, if you talk about *The Ten Commandments*, then they are rigid and are not open to any form of interpretation. *Thou shalt not kill,* for example, is quite explicit but the precepts are not solely focussed on the negative because everything in our existence is about balance. Let me explain with an example." He lifted a chair from a stack, offering it to Caslin before retrieving one for himself. "The fourth precept covers the *principle of truthfulness*. In its negative form, we are expected to refrain from *false speech* which can obviously be interpreted as lying, but also extends to gossiping. However, there is also a positive form of this principle. That being we should work towards a more truthful communication. In doing so, we *purify our speech* which also purifies our mind."

"I see." Caslin thought about it. "So, there is a positive and negative aspect to each of the precepts?"

"Absolutely. In this case we could define truthfulness as *a courageous respect for reality*, even when acknowledging and facing up to the truth goes against what we see as our self-centred goals, or when it might cause us our greatest discomfort."

"That's interesting. Most of us don't really get past the headlines."

"Many don't. The precepts are not simple guidelines, they are not soundbites used to adjust your frame of reference or perception of the world around you. They are guidelines set out in order to help you develop the qualities that you will need on your path. They are about straightforwardness, integrity and challenging yourself to understand how your views and reactions are shaped by not only your own actions but also how your perception of the world around you forms what you are and see."

"They are about developing you, helping you to…"

"Without wishing to confuse you, Inspector." Chen Tao politely held up a hand, interrupting him. "I think you would find that the Buddha would most likely point out that there is no *you* to speak of, for we are all linked within this universe, but I understand that may be one step too far in the confines of this conversation." He smiled. It was clear he wasn't being dismissive but genuinely attempting to help Caslin to understand.

"And this is all geared towards achieving enlightenment?"

"We all hope to achieve enlightenment, but to do so in one lifetime I believe is unlikely. It is quite possible that before a person can obtain enlightenment, they may well pass through several lifetimes beforehand."

"Can I deduce from what you're saying that there is no punishment within Buddhism for failure to follow these guidelines?"

"As Buddhists, we must adhere to the laws of the land in which we live. There can be no opt out from society's rule of law but you are correct, punishment is not part of our tradition. I'm sure you'll be aware of the concept of karma?" He inclined his head in Caslin's direction. Caslin nodded that he was. "I should imagine, not wishing to leap to judgement, that your knowledge of the concept of karma is also slightly skewed."

"Karma is a case of what goes around comes around, isn't it?"

"In essence, in its simplest form, that has become a commonly held view. However, karma is upheld as the consequence of your behaviour, be it positive or negative. Karma is the action that we do and it is the *vipaka* that is the ripening of that karmic action, or the consequence that we then experience. And again, people tend to view this blend of action and consequence in isolation whereas, in reality, what we are all doing is gathering karma throughout this life, the previous one, as well as our future lives and it will ripen at different times along the path."

"So, forgive the colourful language, but if someone is a total bastard in this life then there is every possibility that the consequence may only strike them in the next?"

Chen Tao shrugged. "That is possible, yes."

"In which case, what is there to deter someone in this lifetime from carrying out horrendous acts of violence?"

"Eventually, if a person follows the Dharma, they will come to realise the pain and suffering they inflict on others will revisit them at some point. But, in a direct answer to your question, I think there is nothing within Buddhism, or outside of it for that matter, that can ensure someone will think along the lines you describe. Tell me, does the threat of capital punishment deter a man from taking another's life?"

"No, I don't believe it does."

"Therefore, the concept of punishment as a deterrent is a fallacy."

"For the most part, I would have to agree," Caslin said, nodding. "I'm sure many others wouldn't."

"I don't doubt that, Inspector."

"But the law is clear. Prison sentences are both a deterrent and an opportunity for rehabilitation," Caslin argued.

"To my knowledge, the rehabilitation programmes that exist within the prison reform structure have mixed success rates," Chen Tao responded. Caslin didn't disagree. "However, the only thing that will truly rescue these people from their negative path is the Dharma."

"Only if they are prepared to learn," Caslin countered.

Chen Tao smiled. "For that, we all need an open mind as a starting point. May I ask, what is the nature of the case that you are investigating?"

"You'll understand that I can't openly discuss an ongoing investigation, but we have a working theory that someone is using the precepts as a moral justification for carrying out awful attacks on people," Caslin said, choosing his words carefully.

"Are you talking about this *Night Stalker*, who is all over the news?"

"And here's me thinking I was being cryptic." Caslin smiled, drawing one from the man next to him. "There is the distinct possibility that he is mentally unstable or is something of an extreme radical when it comes to his belief system. Somehow, I can't see a true practitioner of Buddhism allowing himself to persecute others in such a violent and grotesque way."

Chen Tao waved the index finger of his right hand from side to side dismissing Caslin's comment. "Only if that were true, Inspector. Unfortunately, not all followers of Buddhism walk the same path. Just as there are offshoots of other religious orders who follow their own doctrine, there are those who interpret the Buddhist canon in ways that many of us do not find agreeable."

Caslin was intrigued as he had always considered Buddhism to be the one religion devoted purely to spiritual development. Sitting forward in his chair, he encouraged the teacher to elaborate. "Please, go on."

"There is an ethno-nationalist branch of the *Theravada* sect, the most conservative of the traditions and commonly practised in Thailand, Laos and Cambodia as well as in Sri Lanka. They believe a peaceful and calm state of mind cannot exist until all practitioners of the Muslim faith have been eradicated."

Caslin's mouth dropped open. "To the extent of acts of violence?"

"*Extreme* acts of violence." He took on a melancholy look. "This is how we come to see the persecution of the *Rohingya* in Myanmar for example. Sri Lanka, in response to the changes brought under the British colonial rule of the late nineteenth and early twentieth centuries, saw the rise of modern *Sinhalese Buddhist Nationalism*, fuelling an incredible level of violence and hatred in its name. They targeted any who were perceived as antagonistic towards Buddhism. By the way, that included fellow Buddhists of Tamil descent."

"So how did they square that circle with their Buddhist teachings?" Caslin was genuinely surprised. The conversation highlighted his own ignorance of world events. Until this point, he always thought his knowledge was extensive but he knew little of this. He felt a degree of embarrassment.

"Sinhalese nationalism was rooted in local myths denoting them as a religiously chosen people, racially pure, and of special progeny. The *Dravidian Tamils* were regarded as inferior. Any minority unwilling to support the newly created ethnocentric system was an open target. Sadly, it doesn't take much for those who are creative and possess destructive beliefs to commit terrible acts in their name."

"Have you ever come across anyone espousing such beliefs here in the UK, or York, for that matter?" Caslin asked.

Chen Tao shook his head. "Many come to the centre who are perhaps not ready to walk the path or demonstrate what we refer to as *unskilled behaviour*, but no one with attitudes that come even close to those I've described."

Caslin glanced at the clock on the wall and then double checked by looking at his watch. It was late in the day. "Thank you for your time." He stood, offering his hand.

Chen Tao took it. "I hope I was of some help, Inspector. We have a meeting in around half an hour. You'd be more than welcome to join us and participate in the discussion. You may even find it eye opening."

"Perhaps another time but I am afraid I have a prior engagement."

"You're welcome any time."

Caslin turned and began to walk away before pausing and looking back over his shoulder. "This may seem like an odd question…" Chen Tao was open to another question. "Is there anything you've ever come across within Buddhism regarding the mutilation of a person's body?"

Chen Tao was perplexed but he thought it for a moment. "There are stories, myths, one might say." He indicated for Caslin to wait as he crossed the room, kneeling before a cupboard and opening the door. Inside were several shelves crammed with books, some old and some new. Scanning along the spines, Caslin watched as he sought the one he was looking for. Plucking it from the second shelf from the top, he pushed the door to. Returning to Caslin, he handed him the book.

Caslin scanned the cover. It was heavy and well worn, with the pages taking on a dark brown colour such was the book's age. "This is… meaty," he said, not wishing to sound ungrateful.

Chen Tao laughed. "That is a brief history of the past 2000 years and the development of Buddhism within that timeframe. There are many tales documented within it that have been recanted in one form or another. Feel free to borrow it and read it at your leisure. You never know, you may find what you're looking for in there."

"Thank you. I'll get this back to you." Caslin held the book up, nodding appreciatively. "Tell me, what comes after the *Fifth Precept*?"

"For those who pass on to become *Mitras*, or who go on to be fully ordained, there are further precepts to study but they are more monastic undertakings for those post-ordination. More related to religious ceremony and spiritual retreats than daily life. For example, a vow of celibacy or abstaining from food on certain religious days. In terms of living guidelines, we have *The Noble*

Eight-fold Path but these are unrelated to the precepts. There truly is much scope for further development."

"Are most people aware of this? The way the precepts change, I mean."

Chen Tao smiled. "Lay persons… probably not. There is little call for lay Buddhists to adhere to these stricter precepts."

"Thank you again." Caslin silently pondered the last as he set off for the exit. *Where would their killer go when he reached the fifth?*

CHAPTER NINETEEN

MOUNTING the steps to the Cates's residence, Caslin reached for the door knocker and suddenly felt self-conscious. Logically, there was no reason for him to be nervous but nevertheless, he considered his outward appearance momentarily before dismissing the doubts. A warm flush passed up the back of his neck. He rapped the door three times and stepped back to wait. Soon after, the door opened and he was greeted with Michelle's broad smile although she too, appeared slightly bashful as their eyes met. She wore her hair down, adorned in minimal make-up and jewellery and cut an attractive and classy figure in a two-piece red trouser suit and cream blouse.

"Please, Nathaniel, come in." Standing to one side, she welcomed him in. "I hope you didn't mind me calling you?"

Caslin shook his head enthusiastically. "No, not at all. You can call me Nate, if you prefer."

Michelle Cates appeared taken aback. "Sorry, I meant earlier this afternoon, when I phoned."

Caslin felt his cheeks flush red with embarrassment. "Sorry, my mistake." He flicked his eyes away from hers.

"No, I'm sorry... I am addressing you personally, aren't I? I shouldn't presume—"

"No, no, it's not an issue, I'm quite happy with it," Caslin replied, attempting to stave off the growing awkwardness of their exchange but only seeming to add to it further. He stopped talking and looked down at the floor. Taking a deep breath, he brought his head up and met her eye once again. She smiled again whilst closing the door. It was a relief for him to see and he returned it. Michelle visibly relaxed and he thought she might be experiencing similar feelings to his own. At least he hoped so.

"Shall we start again?"

"Perhaps that would be a good idea," Caslin replied, broadening his smile into a grin.

"Have you brought some light reading?"

Momentarily confused, Caslin stood open-mouthed before realising he was holding the book given him by Chen Tao. "Oh, this." He laughed. "Someone leant it to me and I've not been home yet."

Inclining her head in order to read the spine, Caslin offered the book up to make it easier. "Interesting choice of subject matter. I get the impression you're a man of many surprises. I was just about to have something to eat." She gestured for him to follow her towards the kitchen. He glanced at his watch. "Yes, I know it's late. Carly had netball training earlier this evening and it always sets us back."

Glancing around, looking for somewhere to place the book, he chose an occasional table adjacent to a coat stand. The last thing he wanted was to have this tome next to them while they ate. The history of Buddhism wasn't likely to sell him as an exciting date. "Is Carly around?"

"What with the events at school today and then training, on top of everything else we are dealing with at the moment, she's absolutely shattered. She's already in bed. I checked on her earlier and she's out for the count."

"How is your brother, Thomas?" Caslin asked as they entered the kitchen.

Michelle glanced over her shoulder towards him, offering him a stool at the breakfast bar. "Are you asking out of courtesy or in a professional capacity?"

Caslin was unsure how to interpret her response. If he were more familiar with her personality, he would no doubt be able to judge the seriousness in her tone. "I'm off duty." The reply was ambivalent.

Michelle's ability to read him was finer tuned than his regarding her. "I'm just kidding, Nate. Relax. To be honest, I'm not sure how Thomas is coping. I think it's always a struggle when you lose someone close to you but to do so under these circumstances, I've no idea how he's feeling. I try to at least speak with him daily since... but he's not a man who likes anyone to make a fuss. I don't really know what to do for the best."

"As long as he knows you're there for him if he asks."

"I floated the possibility of him moving in with us for a while. The house is big enough, after all." She raised her eyes heaven-ward, angling her head in a reflective pose. "But I'm not sure he's even come to terms with our mother's passing yet, and this place is so full of memories," she said, her eyes tracking around the room before settling on Caslin.

"He didn't go for it then?"

Michelle shook her head. "Are you hungry? You never said." Caslin had to admit his mouth was watering at the smell of the food simmering on the stove. "It's nothing exciting, just a puttanesca that I threw together. There's plenty to go around."

"Thank you. That would be lovely. Is there anything I can do," he asked, looking past her and across to a casual dining table at the end of the contemporary glass addition.

"You could set two places at the table." She pointed in the direction he was looking. Taking off her jacket and hanging it up alongside the doorway to the hall, she gestured to a cabinet behind him. "You'll find cutlery and everything else you need in those drawers to your right."

Ten minutes later, Caslin pulled out a chair for himself along with another for his host, as she came to the table with two bowls of steaming pasta. Michelle encouraged him to sit down while she walked to the fridge and returned with a block of Parmesan cheese, picking up a bottle of red wine along the way. She brandished both, one in each hand, and smiled. Caslin nodded appreciatively and looked around for a bottle opener.

"You did say you were off duty," she said, indicating a dark hardwood sideboard behind him. "In the top drawer." Caslin searched where instructed, turning back with a bottle opener in hand and set about cracking the seal and removing the cork. Michelle retrieved two large glasses from a nearby shelf, setting them down alongside each other on the table. The bottle was opened and Caslin lifted it, angling it slightly towards the light in order to read the label. He was impressed at the quality of her taste. "Is it to your satisfaction?" Her tone was playful.

"You can't go far wrong with a *Grand Vin*."

"You like your wine?" she asked, finely grating the cheese over their food without asking him if he wanted any. He didn't mind. The more the better.

There was once a time when he was laughably picky when it came to decisions on which wine best accompanied a given meal but these days, he would judge his younger self to be pretentious. However, he chose not to share the self-deprecating thought. "I appreciate the finer things in life," he said, glancing from the label towards his company. The comment sounded much like something his younger self would have said and he regretted saying it. She didn't appear to notice. "Should I let it breathe?"

"It hasn't breathed in twelve years, so let's not worry about that now," Michelle replied with a half-smile. Caslin laughed and poured each of them half a glass.

"You said earlier you were worried about Carly," Caslin said, re-taking his seat and picking up both a fork and a spoon before setting about his meal. She nodded. "Have you noticed any change in her behaviour recently?"

Michelle thought on it for a moment, picking up her glass and tasting the wine once she'd finished her mouthful of food. Placing the glass back down on the table, she kept a hold of the stem between thumb and forefinger gently turning the glass where it sat. "Nothing that I've found unusual. She has been a little quiet since Kelly…"

"What about your relationship with her? Do you get on well?"

Michelle bobbed her head. "Yes, we are very open with each other, always have been."

"You said Carly knows Andrew Connolly's daughter?"

"They share classes at school. Not to mention they play in some of the same sports teams which is how she wound up at the centre he works at. It's not easy being a single mum, working and trying to open the door to as many experiences for your daughter as you can," she said, taking on a reflective expression.

"Yes, I know where you're coming from."

"You have children, don't you?" Caslin nodded. Usually, he would try to keep conversation regarding his children to a minimum, not wishing to expose his disjointed personal life. "Do they live with you?"

"No, they live with their mother but I understand the restrictions children place on your time, particularly when you're doing everything alone."

"I wasn't suggesting you were humouring me." She reached across the table and gently touched the back of his hand. "You just have the look, you know?"

Caslin inclined his head to one side, frowning. "*The look?*"

"Yes. The look of a man who probably throws everything he has into his work in order to mask his loneliness."

Caslin was taken aback at both her assessment of him as well as her candid nature. "You are… direct."

Michelle was immediately apologetic. "I'm sorry, I didn't mean to offend you, I just… I often find I'm good at reading people. If I'm way off the mark—"

Caslin smiled and shook his head. "To be honest, I think you're right on the money." A strange emotion passed through him. On the one hand, her critique could be taken as a slight but truthfully, she had read him very well indeed. He raised his glass, tilting it in her direction and raised it to his lips.

"I'm also experienced in relationship failure. Carly wasn't exactly an immaculate conception."

Caslin laughed. "Divorced?"

"Separated." She raised her own glass to her lips, taking on a faraway look. "For now, at least…"

"Having a difficult time?" Caslin asked before seeing the change in Michelle's expression and quickly adding, "Sorry, not really any of my business."

"No, don't worry. We had our problems. We married young… that seems like such a long time ago now." She shook her head, smiling ruefully. "My Mother fell ill and Daniel lost his job with the council and couldn't find work. Then his mother died suddenly. It was a shocking time for all of us. I had to return to work to try and make ends meet. It was one thing after another. Eventually something had to give." She took another drink, almost finishing her glass. Caslin thought she was hitting it pretty hard. He'd been there. "Now we have all of this… and Carly…"

"Hey, if you're half as good at reading your own daughter as you are me, then I should imagine you've got nothing to worry about."

"It would be easier if I knew what I was watching out for."

Caslin sipped his wine before answering, savouring the after-taste on his tongue. He approved of her choice. "Any frequent bouts of aggression. Withdrawing into herself and wanting to be alone or making excuses as to why she can't take part in physical activity because she doesn't want to get undressed in front of others." Caslin was thinking aloud. "Has she become obsessive or suffered from anxiety at all?"

Michelle shook her head. "No, nothing like that. Carly's very confident and outward looking. She can't wait to try new things, a lot like her mother in that respect."

Caslin felt there was more behind her expression, her smile. He hoped so. "How has she been in general, regarding her eating and sleeping patterns? Does she skip school or experiment with alcohol, hang out with friends who take drugs? That kind of thing."

"No, certainly not." Her response implied the very notion was laughable.

"Then, in that case, I should imagine you have very little to worry about."

"But she's been around that man," Michelle replied. The warm smile switched to be replaced by a stern look. "I can't know for sure, can I?"

"Paedophiles like Connelly are clever," Caslin explained. "They will put themselves in positions of responsibility and trust around children. They gravitate to those roles. It's almost as if they are drawn to certain professions. They systematically work out, for want of a better word, who their best targets are. They may have access to a hundred children and from that group they will know which ones to target. These will be the most vulnerable or the most damaged… the ones they think will be the easiest to manipulate and therefore ensure it remains secret. That might be a very small percentage of those who they are in contact with over-all. From what you've told me, Carly doesn't fit the profile. I think you can be very confident."

"What about the unlucky ones?"

Caslin took a deep breath and sipped his wine. "We are working to identify them and get them into safety if we can."

"Those poor children."

"I know."

"It's almost hard to judge someone for killing him, isn't it?" Michelle said, catching Caslin off guard. She noticed his reaction. "Not that I'm condoning it."

"I know what you mean," Caslin said, choosing his words carefully, "but let's not forget why we have the rule of law in the first place, precisely to stop people exercising their own forms of vigilante justice. Connelly may very well be beneath our contempt or our sympathy, but not every case is likely to be as cut and dried." Immediately, Caslin regretted his last comment, remembering Kelly Ryan's death at the hands of the same murderer. "Forgive me, that was insensitive."

Michelle reached across the table again and took a firm grip on Caslin's hand this time, meeting his eye. "That's okay, honestly. You're right of course."

Conversation moved onto lighter subjects as they enjoyed the remainder of their meal. For a short time, both of them slipped into a level of comfort neither would claim to have recent experience of. For Caslin, it was a snapshot of what life used to be like before a succession of terrible personal life-choices steered his path in an entirely different direction. An hour passed that felt like mere moments. The sound of a little girl calling out from upstairs carried to them, breaking through their laughter.

"That's Carly," Michelle said, placing her glass on the table and rising. "I'll just go and check on her." Caslin watched her leave the room. The sway of her hips caught his imagination and when she glanced back over her shoulder, she realised it too. Michelle smiled and he felt his face reddening for the second time that evening.

Caslin took his wine and came to stand before the bi-fold doors overlooking the garden. Casting his thoughts back to the last time he was there, investigating the potential prowler, he was pleased there was no reoccurrence of the intruder. The stepping up of patrols in the area returned no further sightings and he was left to wonder whether Michelle had been right that evening – her paranoia placing figures in the shadows where there were none to be seen. If not for the cigarette butts, he'd found, he would think so too. Staring out into the darkness, unable to see anything because of the interior light, he felt the hair on the back of his neck standing, the sense that someone was watching him.

Unlocking the first of the doors, he opened it and stepped out onto the patio. The sounds of the city at night came to him. The evening was cool with a gentle breeze. His eyes slowly adjusted to the light and he scanned the perimeter, watching the branches of the trees swaying gently to and fro. His mobile rang and Caslin withdrew it from his pocket, answering without looking at the caller.

"Sir," Hunter said, "I'm sorry to call you so late but we have another victim."

Caslin was deflated. "So soon? Are you sure it's one for us?"

"I'm afraid so but this one's different," she replied. "We're on *Bishophill Senior*. Are you at home?"

Caslin glanced back into the kitchen to see Michelle returning from upstairs. She saw he was on the phone and set about clearing away the dishes. "No, I'm somewhere else. I'm in the city though. I'll meet you there shortly."

With one last look around, the feeling of being watched had left him. Returning inside, he closed the door behind him, securing the lock. Slipping the mobile back into his pocket, he smiled as Michelle came over to him. She poured herself more wine from the bottle and offered him a top up.

Pursing his lips, he shook his head. "I'd love to but something has come up," he said, regret edging into his tone. "I have to go."

"Always on duty after all?" she replied, raising her glass in his direction.

"I'm sorry."

"That's okay." She was smiling as she spoke but without conviction. "It's not like we're on a date, is it?"

"Perhaps another time?"

"A date?" she countered. This time, he was unfazed, confident even.

"I would like that."

Putting her glass on the counter, she walked with him to the front door. Releasing the latch, she opened the door, leaning against it, cradling the edge against her shoulder where her arm met her chest. Caslin paused at the threshold, turning to her, unsure of how he should behave. Michelle read his indecision and moved in his direction. He mirrored her movement and they met. Her lips felt smooth, soft to the touch, and he felt a wave of excitement that matched his anticipation as they kissed. Withdrawing, she followed and he responded, reaching around her waist and drawing her to him. Michelle arched her back and pressed into him. The embrace lasted for a few moments longer before he released his grip and she lowered herself, moving away from his lips but remaining close.

"I'll be seeing you, Nate Caslin," she said in a sultry whisper, one final flirtation for him to take with him into the night.

"You will," Caslin replied, fumbling his response. She touched his forearm as he moved off, her eyes directing him to his left and the book he'd placed there earlier. "Thanks."

Bidding her goodnight, he descended the steps to the street below. Glancing back up, he saw her watching him walk away. Turning, he walked backwards for a few steps, smiling and offering her a wave, indicating she should go inside. Michelle returned it, closing the door, and Caslin resumed his course, walking tall, his smile widening with every step.

Bishophill Senior was on the opposite bank of the river Ouse, barely a ten-minute walk from his current location if he crossed the Skeldergate Bridge. For the first time in years, Caslin felt a motivation for something beyond his immediate family's needs and the requirement of his caseload. He was already looking forward to seeing her again.

CHAPTER TWENTY

BY THE TIME Caslin reached the scene, a uniformed presence had already taped off both ends of the road, securing it from passers-by as well as traffic. A constable lifted the tape allowing Caslin to slip underneath. Eyeing Hunter's car, he opened the passenger door and dropped the book on the passenger seat before approaching the small group gathered nearby. Both DS Hunter and Craig Templer were present. Templer greeted him.

"Caslin, this is an interesting turn of events," he said, indicating over his shoulder at the body of a young man lying at Hunter's feet where the road met the pavement. She left her inspection of the deceased and came to join them. Local residents were coming together at the edge of the cordon in an attempt to make sense of the commotion as well as, no doubt, feeding their growing morbid curiosity.

"Apparently, he ran out into the middle of the road without looking and was clocked by that car," Hunter informed Caslin, pointing at a white hatchback. The car had subsequently mounted the pavement and struck a lamppost but, by the look of the damage, Caslin presumed the impact had happened at a relatively low speed.

"We have the driver?" Caslin asked.

Hunter nodded. "She's over there." Caslin looked to his right, seeing a female figure sitting in a liveried police car. "We've had a word, breathalysed her, but not taken her statement yet. She's negative on the blood alcohol content."

Caslin turned his attention to the body and the other detectives parted to make room for him to approach. The man lay in an unnatural position. Caslin assumed at least one of his legs and an arm were broken, judging by the angle in which they lay. Whether that was a result of the impact of the car or of hitting the tarmac or the kerb, he couldn't be sure. The man's eyes were open and his face bore a look of shock, an expression frozen in time. Had he been fully clothed, then Caslin would have described the victim as slim but naked as he was, his frame was skeletal and emaciated rather than slender.

Leaning in closer, Caslin took in his features. The eyes appeared hollow, sunken, his skin tone was pale with dark rings hanging under the eyes. The skin across his cheekbones and jaw was depressed and scanning the length of his body, Caslin noted the lack of muscle definition from head to foot. Shifting slightly to his left and stooping, he angled his head to get a better look at the underside of the man's arms. There were multiple needle points, scars and scabs that were indicative of a heavy drug user. Hunter saw him make the observation and dropped to her haunches alongside him.

"The other arm is the same." She pointed to the left arm.

"Do you think he was high?"

DI Templer answered the question. "The car that hit him had a dash cam mounted."

"Have you reviewed the footage?" Caslin asked, over his shoulder.

"Yes, but only on the camera itself so detail is a little hard to make out bearing in mind the view is only illuminated by the street lighting. He comes into the picture running from the left, from Fairfax Street. As I say, it's hard to tell but his run looked erratic to me. He charges out into the street and to be fair to the driver, there wasn't a lot she could do."

Caslin looked up the road, towards the car embedded in the lamppost. "She swerved but clipped him on the way through before being forcibly stopped over there." Hunter concurred. Turning his attention back to the dead man, Caslin found it hard to judge how old he was but figured him to be in his late thirties or early forties, but the physical shape he was in made him appear a lot older. "No chance of any ID then."

"He looks familiar though," Hunter said, flicking her eyes from Caslin to the body. "I know him from somewhere but I just can't place him."

Caslin also returned his gaze to the deceased. "Do you think you've nicked him before? Can't say I recognise him at all. Could he be a junkie that you've come across in another case?"

Hunter shook her head. "Not sure but it'll come to me."

"Take his prints."

"Now?"

Caslin focussed on the missing index finger of the right hand. "Yes, do it. I know we'll get cleaner prints when Alison carries out the autopsy but our killer is ramping things up at an alarming rate. If we can get ahead on the identification, then all the better."

"It's strange for it to go down this way," Templer said, looking in both directions up and down the street. Caslin glanced at him with a querying look. "I mean, the other killings have all been methodically planned and controlled whereas this," Templer indicated the surrounding area with a swirl of his left hand, "is about as uncontrolled as it could be."

"I know what you mean," Caslin agreed. Every previous crime scene was well-managed. This was in stark contrast. "The index finger has already been removed, but at previous scenes it's looked like he did it near to or shortly after death."

"Maybe this one escaped?" Templer suggested, re-evaluating the scene. They were standing in an established residential location on the edge of the city centre. Lines of terraced houses were present on both sides of the street as well as those in the adjacent roads. It was a pleasant and unassuming area.

"If so," Caslin began, following Templer's lead in scanning the nearby properties, "then he can't have come far dressed like this. He must have been close."

"I'll round up some bodies and start going door-to-door," Templer said. Caslin agreed. If the dead man fled his captor at the point of his planned murder, then the killer may still be in a nearby property. Templer took out his radio and contacted the control room to request as many bodies as he could to assist them. Caslin returned to where Hunter was, still standing alongside the dead man. She glanced in his direction and held her gaze. He noticed. Something about her expression troubled him.

"Been anywhere nice this evening?" she asked.

"How do you mean? I had dinner."

"Looks like she was good company." Hunter's face split into a half-smile and she tapped her lower lip. Caslin got the message and wiped across his mouth with the back of his hand. Even with only the benefit of the street lighting, he recognised the lipstick residue.

"Thanks," he said, running his tongue around his lips in an involuntary motion.

"Is she nice?"

Caslin smiled, looking away and feeling sheepish. "Another time, Sarah. Another time."

"Sorry to have disturbed you," Hunter said, smiling playfully with a flick of her eyebrows.

Caslin ignored her amusement at his obvious discomfort and turned the attention back to the body.

"IF YOU KNOW HIM, then his prints will most likely be in the system."

"Give me a sec, I might have it," she said, taking out her

mobile phone and connecting to the Internet. Waiting patiently, Caslin scanned the watching members of the public. The thought occurred to him that if the killer were nearby, he might not be able to deny himself the thrill of mingling with the faceless crowd and observing his handiwork. It wouldn't be the first time. "Take a look at this, sir."

Caslin tore himself away from observing the watchers and came alongside her. She angled the screen of the phone in his direction and he cocked his head, taking in the picture. "That looks like him."

"I'd say so," Hunter agreed, looking from the deceased to the photograph on her mobile and back again. "He was in much better shape when this was taken though."

"Probably why you didn't recognise him. I still don't know him. Should I?"

"I never met him but I remember the case," Hunter explained. "You'll have heard of it."

"Remind me."

"Alex Moretti, or Alessandro, if I remember right," Hunter said. "He was the GP accused of assisting a number of his patients in their suicides."

"Ah… yes. Now I remember," Caslin said excitedly, narrowing his eyes as he sought to recall the detail of the case. "No charges were ever brought though."

Hunter shook her head. "No, the *General Medical Council* investigated and ruled there was not enough evidence against him for him to face being struck off."

Caslin nodded. "And the police inquiry found similar, so the CPS ditched it. When was this?"

"Beginning of last year, or the end of the year before," Hunter suggested with uncertainty. "Give me a second and I'll read the article here."

"Yeah, you can always believe what you read on the Internet," Caslin said with intended sarcasm. "Any sign of a lotus flower yet?"

"No, nothing, which feeds into Craig's theory that he escaped his captor."

"Do I need to run a PNC check for his home address or are your journalistic talents able to find them on the net?"

"Lower Priory Street," Hunter said, glancing up from her phone. Pointing towards nearby Fairfax Street. "Barely a hundred yards away." Caslin looked in that direction and called for Templer to join them. Instructing a uniformed officer to ensure nobody went near the victim, the three detectives set off.

Breaking into a trot, Templer put in a request for confirmation of Moretti's home address with the control room. The media article reported the street where he was known to live but not the house number. Reaching the end of the road, directly opposite was the grass bank running the length of the city walls, encircling their location. Lower Priory Street ran off both to the left and the right of them and they pulled up just as Templer's radio crackled into life.

Looking to the nearby houses, Templer directed them to their left.

"This way," he said, taking the lead. They ran the short distance to Moretti's house, a Victorian end of terrace with an alleyway to one side, giving access to the rear of the adjacent houses on Fairfax Street. There was a larger property attached on the other side. The only entrance to the latter was around the next corner. Unusually, Moretti's house was effectively a standalone building with no other property overlooking it.

The front door opened straight onto the street. Caslin eyed the above windows. The interior was shrouded by closed curtains and no light emanated from within.

"There must be a back door or window," Caslin said, indicating for DI Templer to head down the alley and the detective turned. Seconds later, he disappeared from sight, running into the darkness. "We'll go through the front."

"Should we wait for assistance?" Hunter asked.

For all they knew, the killer could still be inside with an undercover detective held captive. The last thing Caslin wanted was for a drawn-out hostage situation to develop. "No, if he still here let's take him by surprise."

"Let's do it," Hunter replied confidently.

Caslin hammered his fist on the door. Hunter kept her eye on the curtains for a signal that someone was inside. Meeting Caslin's look, she inclined her head towards the door. Caslin took three steps back, inhaled a deep breath, and launched himself forward raising a booted foot and applying as much force as he could against the door, aiming as close to the latch plate as he could. The first attempt was a failure but he stepped back and redoubled his efforts. The second kick saw the wood of the door jamb splinter and he forced the lock to detach. With one final surge, he struck the door and it flew inwards at pace, swiftly followed by the two detectives, Caslin in the vanguard.

"Police!" he shouted without response. They were in a narrow, unlit hallway. One door was set to their right. The stairs to the upper floor were in front of them and along the corridor lay the kitchen. The sound of breaking glass came from the rear of the building. Reaching the first door, Caslin pushed it open with his left hand and chanced a look inside. The sitting room was empty apart from a sofa and a few pieces of standalone furniture. DI Templer appeared at the threshold to the kitchen. He stopped there and waited.

Caslin pointed to the dining room and Templer nodded, kicking the door open, the two of them piled in. This room was also empty. Templer crossed to the far side, drawing back the curtain and looking out into a paved courtyard to the rear. The nearby street lighting barely stretched to cover the area but the glow of the orange light illuminated a small pond in one corner. The remainder of the courtyard was paved in concrete slabs. Caslin flicked the nearest light switch but nothing happened. They remained in the dark. The two men returned to the hall and joined Hunter as she slowly climbed the stairs to the first floor.

Activating the torch on her mobile phone, she cast an eerie

blue light up the stairwell. All three tuned their senses, preparing for anything that might come at them from the darkness. The air was stale. The smell stung their noses. There were three doors off the landing and the first was open, leading to a bathroom above the kitchen. This had a pitched roof with a small skylight set into it, providing the only source of natural light. The bathroom was cramped and empty. The two remaining doors were to separate bedrooms, one at the front overlooking the street and another to the rear. The landing doubled back from the stairs, almost to the front of the house. Anyone in the front facing room would need to get past them to escape.

Mouthing a silent three count, Hunter shoved open the first door to the rear bedroom and both she and Templer entered. Caslin waited on the landing with one eye on the remaining bedroom. Seconds later, they reappeared with a shake of the head. Together, they approached the last room and repeated the procedure. This time Hunter opened the door and Caslin passed through first.

As they found with the previous rooms, this one was also empty. Caslin leaned against one of the walls while Hunter located the light switch, flicking it on had the same effect as downstairs.

"Maybe they've tripped?" she said, scanning the room by the light of her mobile.

Templer stood at the doorway and glanced around. "I'll have a look for the fuse box downstairs."

Caslin turned his attention to the room he was in. There was a double bed set against the far wall. The mattress was covered with a sheet but there were no pillows or duvet. There was the overbearing smell of urine and excrement. The sheet was heavily soiled and apparently lay unchanged for quite some time. The headboard, as well as the foot of the bed, was crafted from wood and lined with upright slats. Attached by chains at all four corners were manacles you might expect to find in the bedroom of a

BDSM enthusiast. At the centre of the mattress lay a blooming lotus flower, white petals fading to pink on their exterior.

"He left us his calling card," Caslin said.

"Whether Moretti escaped or was released, the killer can't have been gone long," Hunter concluded.

Caslin stood, glancing in the direction of the bedroom window, overlooking the front. His eye line carried to the stone walls of the city and the often-trod tourist path along it. Barely fifty yards away was a gated exit leading beyond the medieval walls. "Once out of the centre, he'll be in the wind."

"We should pull the CCTV in the area and see if we get lucky," Hunter said. Caslin nodded.

Returning his focus to the bed, he moved closer and inspected the restraints. These were hard-core, not the playful fur-lined variety couples might use to experiment with. These were manufactured from cold hard metal. Although difficult to judge in the available light, Caslin observed a dark smudge on the rim to one of them. He frowned, an expression that didn't go unnoticed. "Blood," he said quietly, answering Hunter's unasked question.

"Probably straining to get free."

"Judging by the state of the sheet and the smell, I'd say he was chained here for weeks."

"Or even months," Hunter added, drawing his attention towards the corner of the room where she was standing. Caslin crossed over, looking past her to see. There was a wicker waste bin. Piled to the point of overflow were transparent pouches. Caslin knelt alongside, separating them with a pen that he took from his pocket. "Drip bags by the look of them."

Caslin looked up at her over his shoulder, noting the IV stand in the far corner of the room. He had missed it before. "That will explain some of the needle marks then."

Hunter opened a freestanding wardrobe, nestled into the alcove to the right of the chimney breast. "And that's not all." She tapped Caslin on the shoulder. Cardboard boxes were stacked atop one another inside. On the shelves above these were intravenous bags, still full of liquid. The shipping labels stuck to the exterior of the boxes were marked with logogram writing, suggesting they had been imported from East Asia.

"I'll be interested to see what's in these," Caslin said. "Something tells me it's not only nutrients."

"If I had to guess, I'd argue Moretti was a junkie, wouldn't you?"

"Yes, but somehow I doubt that was a decision of his own making. Let's get CSI in here."

"Caslin!" A shout came from below. Leaving the bedroom, Caslin made his way downstairs. He found Templer at the entrance to the dining room.

"What is it?"

"You need to see this." He beckoned him to follow.

Templer led them out of the set of French doors of the dining room and into the courtyard. Caslin was drawn to the pond. Clearly not well tended, the vegetation spread across the surface in a haphazard and aggressive manner. Kneeling, Caslin spotted what he would have thought were water lilies but now he knew better. They were lotus flowers. Standing up, he joined Templer at a timber door to an outbuilding, aged, rotten and with flaking green paint. The brick structure doubled as a coal shed and the outside toilet. Mounted on the exterior was a plastic box housing the electricity meter. It was heavily damaged, as if it had been violently forced open. The door hung on its hinges and Caslin eased it open.

An enforcement notice was taped to the interior indicating it had been replaced with a prepayment meter. Such action was only ever done for non-payment of outstanding bills. The date on the notice was only a fortnight ago. Templer gestured for Caslin to enter. Inside, he was acutely aware of the smell of damp along with another, intense and recognisable smell that he would never forget. A chest freezer dominated the space and, glancing to his colleague with an inquisitive look, Caslin approached warily.

Using the edge of his hand to lift the lid, Caslin jumped back, startled.

"Strewth!" He threw a hand across his mouth and nose. Meeting Templer's eye, he misread the younger detective's expression. "Fowler?"

"No, it's not him. I've no idea who this is."

Caslin peered into the freezer. The capacity was barely enough to contain the body of a grown man. By the way he lay inside, it was reasonable to presume several of his limbs were broken in order to cram him into the available space. For what purpose, he couldn't begin to imagine. The urge to return to fresh air was overwhelming and, using his elbow to close the lid, the slapping sound of the seal engaging carried through the silence.

CHAPTER TWENTY-ONE

"DI Caslin, North Yorkshire Police." He held up his warrant card.

"What can I do for you, Inspector?" Caslin took in his measure. He was an ascetic-looking man in his late fifties, stiff, immaculately presented and unfazed by their presence.

"We need to speak to you regarding Alessandro Moretti." At mention of the name, colour drained momentarily from his features and he ushered both Caslin and Hunter away from waiting patients and through a security door towards the consultation rooms.

"I thought the investigation was concluded." The man was irritated by their presence without having heard why. Opening the door to an office with a sign matching his name, William Logan, the practice manager, held the door for them. Upon their arrival, he'd been summoned as soon as they mentioned to the receptionist why they were there. His frustration at the recurrence of an inquiry he thought long buried appeared to frustrate him.

"Does it bother you to discuss it?" Caslin sensed the reluctance.

Logan pulled out his chair and sat down, offering them a seat opposite at the same time. "It is not that it bothers me, Inspector.

There has just been so much upheaval since the inquiry. Patients were unsettled, as were the staff... the practice also changed hands as a result. Despite assurances to the contrary, there existed a perceived failure in the leadership."

"Failure?" Hunter asked.

"Unjustly, in my opinion." Logan's reply was somewhat haughty.

"The criminal investigation found insufficient evidence for the CPS to bring a prosecution," Caslin said.

Logan scoffed. "Nor did the *General Medical Council* but that is nowhere near the same as a proclamation of innocence. The inquiries took months and we all had to work under a very dark cloud indeed."

"And the families were left to wonder as to how their loved ones died," Caslin replied, irritated by the man's attitude.

"Yes... of course." Logan dropped much of the attitude, meeting Caslin's eye with a flicker of regret in his own. "I was speaking from a purely professional... operational, point of view."

"Moretti?"

"What is it you want to know that hasn't already been investigated? You're not opening up more cases are you? I thought—"

"No, this is another associated inquiry. Alessandro Moretti died late last night."

Logan was visibly shocked. "That's awful. May I ask what happened?"

"He was hit by a car," Hunter said.

"Awful," Logan repeated. "Here, in York?"

"Yes," Caslin confirmed. "You seem shocked by that."

"I am. I thought he had returned to Italy months ago."

"Is that what he told you his plans were?"

Logan shook his head. "No, not at all. We were never friends, not really. I... we... all thought that's what he would do. What with taking the suspension so badly."

"Did he? Take it badly?" Caslin asked.

Logan nodded. "To be expected. No one likes to be accused of professional misconduct."

"He was investigated for far more than that. Three counts of murder were on the cards at the beginning."

"And none were proven," Logan reminded them. Caslin felt he was still endeavouring to protect the reputation of the practice. "I know Alex... Alessandro... felt aggrieved but there was little option under the circumstances. We were advised not to communicate with him until the GMC, as well as yourselves, were finished with the inquiries."

"When was the last time you spoke with him?" Caslin asked.

Logan thought hard. "Early last year, I should imagine. I'm not sure exactly."

"Around the time of his suspension?"

"Yes. Like I said, we were asked to keep away. Once the case was settled, there was the opportunity that he would return but none of us really thought he would come back."

"Why not? You thought him guilty?"

"Certainly not." He was indignant. "But mud sticks, Inspector. Patients were already requesting to not be seen by him if he returned. The contract of trust had broken down. His position would have been untenable."

"You expected him to move on then?" Hunter asked.

"Why, yes. It's not like he was a partner in the practice. He was a junior GP, recently settled in the UK and we thought he would go home... well, back to Italy anyway."

"And no one followed up with him... even after he was cleared in the investigation? Not particularly caring, was it?" Caslin pressed.

"You must understand the internal workings of the practice, Inspector," Logan said, taking on a conciliatory tone. "The suspicions were first raised by fellow practitioners. Alex's own colleagues brought it to the attention of management and the GMC. Many bridges were burned in the exchanges. There was little love lost between Alex and the staff."

"Who accused him of murdering his patients?" Caslin said the fact aloud that Logan was dancing around.

"Assisting their suicides would be more accurate," Logan said, lowering his voice despite no one else being present to overhear their conversation.

"Nonetheless, Dr Moretti was investigated for potentially murdering three elderly patients in his care. Your colleagues, those who raised the alarm, felt that some of these deaths were somewhat surprising as well as untimely. Other cases were also investigated, we understand."

"That is true," Logan agreed but raised a finger, wagging it like a parent does to an unruly child. "No further cases were brought before the GMC or prosecuted as well you know."

"The doctors who put up the flag," Caslin asked, "are they available to speak with us?"

Logan shook his head. "I'm afraid neither of them is still with us. It was a trying time, as I'm sure you can understand, but I can give you their contact details."

"Thank you," Caslin said. "Before this whole mess developed, what was your impression of Dr Moretti?"

"A diligent practitioner. Very capable with a bright future."

"Were there any threats made against Dr Moretti either before the investigation or during it?"

"Not that I am aware of. Many of his patients expressed quite the opposite. He was a popular young man, particularly among the elderly. Alex would often go the extra that many others wouldn't."

"In what way?"

"After hours home visits. If a patient couldn't make it in or if there was no availability within the appointment schedule."

"Sounds like the type of GP everyone needs," Hunter said. Logan did not disagree.

"Thank you for your time," Caslin said as he rose. "If we need anything further, we'll be in touch."

Logan accepted Caslin's offer of a handshake, appearing

confused. "I don't understand why you are asking these questions. I thought you said Alex was struck by a car."

"He was, Mr Logan. He was."

"Cause of death was certainly the result of being struck by the car," Dr Taylor explained to Caslin whilst Hunter was scanning the initial autopsy report. "Aside from a fractured skull that led to a bleed on the brain, he suffered massive internal injuries to the abdomen, several ribs punctured his left lung and his spleen ruptured. Even had he been in decent physical shape, which he wasn't by the way, I'm not sure he would have made it."

"Nasty." Caslin looked the body up and down. In the artificial light of the pathology lab, Moretti appeared far older than his thirty-two years, an emaciated, skeletal figure with the skin drawn tightly around his frame.

"If it's any consolation, I doubt he would have known much about it," Dr Taylor said, turning and crossing to her workstation. Returning with a print out, she passed it to him. Caslin cast an eye over the detail – a list of drugs as far as he could tell.

"I recognise the heroin," he said, glancing up at her.

"To name but one of the opioids in his system," she explained. "This man was under the influence."

"And when you say *under the influence*?"

"High as a kite, is probably more apt. Not only from heroin but his blood toxicology results revealed high levels of both *Fentanyl* as well as *Carfentanyl*. They are synthetic opioids that I presume you remember from—"

"The house at Stamford Street, yes, I remember," Caslin confirmed. "The dealers often cut them with the heroin to increase the street value of their product."

"Right," Dr Taylor said. "You don't need a pathology qualification to realise this man had a history of drug use, you can see it with your own eyes."

"Not according to his medical records," Caslin said. "His performance evaluations were exceptional and nothing in his background leads us to believe he was a recreational drug user let alone an addict."

"I can see that. If you look at his wrists and ankles." She indicated the specific areas with a pen. "You will note abrasions and bruising consistent with the application of repeated pressure. Presumably some kind of restraints."

"We found those at his house."

"He was a heavy drug user," Dr Taylor continued, "but whether he was voluntarily doing so is for you to investigate."

"You don't believe so?" Caslin asked.

"I deal in facts, Nate. I leave the speculation to you... most of the time." She glanced in his direction through the corner of her eye. "The drugs in his bloodstream would prove fatal to many, so there is the likelihood he built up quite a resistance to them. Helped by the fourth drug on that list you have."

Caslin read further down. "*Naloxone*. What's that?"

"It's an opioid antagonist medication, specifically designed to block or reverse their effects. It has a high affinity for opioid receptors, where it has an inverse reaction, causing the rapid removal of any other drugs bound to these particular receptors. As you know, if heroin reaches the level of an overdose it can lead to respiratory depression, absent pulse rate and a reduced heart rate to name but a few symptoms."

"Ultimately leading to death," Caslin said quietly.

"Exactly. *Naloxone* causes a rapid reversal of the depression of the central nervous system. It saves lives."

"Somehow, I don't see Dr Moretti administering this to himself," Caslin theorised. "Rather, he was being forcibly addicted to the heroin but at the same time monitored so as he didn't overdose."

"I think you're right," Dr Taylor agreed. "Whoever was... I don't want to say *caring for him*... administering to him is probably a better description, took great care to ensure he didn't die during the process."

Caslin thought on the information. Something didn't make sense to him but it was Hunter, apparently thinking along the same lines, who responded first. "We saw dash camera footage of his last moments before he was run over and his movements were erratic. Hardly in keeping with cognisant thought."

"That's not surprising," Dr Taylor said. "He could well have been entering a state of severe psychosis."

"He may have overdosed, even if he hadn't run out into traffic?" Hunter asked.

"That would be quite possible, judging from the state of his heart as well as his circulation. Quite frankly, I'm amazed he was still alive last night."

"In your opinion, Alison, how likely is it that a man with these levels of intoxication could escape from restraints and run from a would-be killer?" Caslin asked, seeking clarity.

Dr Taylor considered the question. "I doubt he was thinking clearly at all. We cannot underestimate the basic human survival instinct but I would be reaching if I suggested that as a reason for his escape."

Caslin exhaled deeply, passing back the paper in his hand. "Thanks, Alison."

"I'll get my final analysis on Moretti over to you as soon as I can," she replied. "In the meantime, I'll move onto the victim you found in the deep freeze."

Hunter's phone rang and she answered it, stepping away. "Where are you with that?" Caslin asked, looking around.

"It took Iain Robertson and his team hours to get him out of the chest freezer. Other than the fact he didn't have a digit missing, I'm afraid you'll have a few hours to wait before I can tell you more than you know already. He was severely bloated, indicative of having thawed out days before."

"Yeah. It looks like the power company had cut him off. Probably would have been worse in the height of summer. Thanks, Alison. We'll speak soon."

Hunter fell into step alongside him with both of them leaving pathology together, Caslin holding the door open for her. She hung up on the call as they walked, their footfalls echoing on the polished floor.

"That was Terry," she said. "The killer has uploaded his latest video."

"Footage of Moretti being run over in the street," Caslin replied without looking at her.

"Yeah," she said, surprised. "How did you know?"

"He let him go and then followed." Caslin sounded bitter. He was. "I'll bet the car was a bonus. You heard what Alison said, if not the car then the drugs would have taken him. He'd already removed the finger and staged the house for us to find. We're the mouse to his cat. The bastard's toying with us."

"We've managed to ID the body in the freezer too. His prints were on file from a decade ago when he was pulled over for driving under the influence."

"Who is he?" Caslin asked, stopping and turning to face her.

"Christopher Maitland. Aside from the twelve-month driving ban and a nominal fine, he has no other prior arrests or convictions."

"What else do we know about him?"

Hunter consulted the brief notes she'd taken during Holt's telephone call. "He was fifty-two. Divorced. He is listed on the electoral register in Sheffield and until recently held a position at *The Post*."

"What position?"

"News Editor," Hunter confirmed.

"Jimmy said the previous editor was sacked because of the paper's poor performance."

"Where could he fit in to this?"

"Let's get a bit of background." Caslin took out his mobile. He scrolled through his contacts and selected Sullivan's number.

Moments later, he hung up, frustrated. "Straight to voicemail." Caslin checked the time on his watch. Choosing another entry, he dialled again, only this time calling the journalist's desk extension. The phone rang without reply and he was about to give up when the call was answered. "Jimmy—"

"No, sorry, it's Katie. Jimmy's not at his desk. Can I help... or take a message?"

Caslin remembered her from an earlier meeting, although they'd never spoken directly. "Katie, it's Nathaniel Caslin from Fulford Road. Is Jimmy around? I need to speak to him about something."

"No. I've not seen him at all today and he hasn't called in. If you do get a hold of him." She lowered her voice to not be over-heard. "Can you let him know he's in the shit with the boss?"

Caslin laughed. "Not for the first time, I'm sure. Likewise, if he surfaces can you let him know I need a word?"

"Will do, bye."

Caslin put his mobile away, looking back down the corridor as if something occurred to him.

"What is it?" Hunter asked.

He shook his head. "Did Holt say what number came up at the end of Moretti's video?"

"The number one. Why?"

"That's *do no harm to living things*."

"If he judged the doctor guilty, then Moretti certainly failed that one."

"Which leaves us what?" Caslin asked out loud.

"The fourth?" Hunter said, trying to remember. "But what happens after that?"

Caslin let the question hang. One thing he could be reasonably sure about was this killer was too controlling and manipulative to have not considered his next move. Whatever was planned, they needed to stop him before he reached that point.

CHAPTER TWENTY-TWO

PRESSING THE BUZZER ONCE MORE, only this time holding it for three or four seconds before releasing it, Caslin stepped back and looked to the first floor. Still there was no sign of movement from within the apartment. The curtains remained drawn and no one responded on the intercom. Glancing at his watch, he pursed his lips as the gnawing sensation he was missing something reasserted itself with a vengeance. Taking out his mobile, he called Sullivan's number again, only this time, straining to hear if it rang inside. The call rang out, passing to voicemail as it had done with each attempt.

A woman appeared in the communal hall beyond the security door. Approaching the entrance, she eyed him warily as he put his phone away and waited expectantly for her to open the door. She was elderly and her movement was frustratingly slow. Assessing him with a watchful eye, standing outside in his suit, she must have judged him non-threatening, disregarding his obvious impatience, and addressed him directly.

"Can I help you?"

Caslin took out his warrant card. "Police, madam. Do you live here?"

"I do, yes. In apartment two."

"Have you by any chance seen Mr Sullivan today?"

"James?" She thought about it for a moment. "Can't say I have seen him for a while. You're more than welcome to go in and try yourself."

Caslin thanked her, holding the door open to allow her to pass before entering the building. Taking the stairs two at a time, he reached the door to Sullivan's apartment. Hammering on it with a closed fist, he waited. When there was still no reply, he looked around. It was mid-afternoon. Most residents were still at work and a glance through the window of the communal landing to the outside revealed few cars parked below. Sullivan's SUV was visible, parked in his allocated space. Reaching into his pocket, Caslin took out a small leather pouch. With one last furtive look around, he opened it, withdrawing two slender metal instruments. They were slim, to the untrained eye they would look like dental tools. The first had a thin paddle at one end while the other, a small hook.

Kneeling, Caslin slipped them into the lock, one atop the other. It took a few minutes of patient exploration for he was out of practice, but soon the reassuring sense of the mechanism moving as each point fell into place, came to him and he smiled. Seconds later, the lock disengaged and he stood. Slipping the picks back into his pocket, he grasped the handle. With one last furtive glance over his shoulder, he opened the door and entered Sullivan's apartment, closing the door behind him.

The interior was dark. Every curtain in the small apartment was drawn. The air was stuffy and in desperate need of an open window. Making his way along the corridor, every room within the apartment sprang off it and his senses were heightened. Listening out for anything untoward, Caslin heard nothing but the ticking of a clock hanging on the wall a few feet away. Despite not having anything to justify the sensation, something felt wrong. Reaching the first doorway, the entrance to the kitchen, he poked his head in and scanned the interior. Alongside the sink, stacked on the countertop, were some dirty crockery appearing to contain the remnants of what was an evening meal. Upon closer inspection, it was probably the previous night's.

Moving on, he pushed open the door to the bathroom. It too was empty. A dirty towel was cast over the side of the bath and the air still smelt damp. The next room was the solitary bedroom of the apartment. Sullivan was divorced, never one who seemed bothered about relationships, and Caslin knew he saw nothing of his children despite the occasional text or phone call. One bedroom was more than adequate for his lifestyle. The bed was unmade with the duvet thrown back. A few items of clothing were scattered around. Retreating, Caslin turned right as he re-entered the hall, heading for the living room.

Entering, he found the room to be much as it was on the occasion of his last visit. Jimmy Sullivan was the middle-aged bachelor of stereotype. If anything, the place was tidier than Caslin had come to expect. Crossing to the nearest window, the first of two, he pulled back the curtains. The grey light of an overcast sky filled the room and he surveyed the scene. There was nothing out of place. The furniture was undisturbed. The remote controls for the television and satellite television sat on the coffee table alongside a tea-stained mug. Nothing present should concern him and yet… the unsettled feeling would not subside.

The silence broke with the sound of a ringing mobile. Reaching into his pocket, Caslin eyed the screen and breathed a sigh of relief, answering the call.

"Jimmy, where have you been?" His sense of relief dissipated as quickly as it had arrived. No voice came down the line but a muffled sound, similar to someone struggling in the background was all that he could make out. Listening acutely, Caslin felt his stomach tighten as a knot of fear took hold. There was movement but unsure of whether it was someone walking or background noise, Caslin frowned. The sounds became starker, the muffled noises louder but were now accompanied by ragged breathing and what he thought was a gurgling noise. He couldn't discern what it was. Silence followed and Caslin listened, wondering for a moment if the call may have disconnected but checking the screen, it hadn't.

A high-pitched scraping sound shot through the earpiece and Caslin winced, pulling the mobile away from his ear momentarily. Someone picked up the handset. Now, he heard measured breathing, controlled, and yet clearly the result of the expenditure of significant energy. Moving to the window, Caslin scanned the outside. Unsure of what he was looking for, he waited, his heart pounding in his chest.

"Jimmy?" he asked quietly. The response was sneering. A dismissive gesture that struck fear into Caslin's heart.

"He's not available. Come to the chapel." The voice was condescending, cold and firm. The line went dead.

Caslin stood staring out into the empty car park, a sense of dread seizing him. An all-encompassing paralysis, even the inability to draw breath lasted until the mobile, still cupped in his palm, rang once more. The sound brought him out of his mental state, the paralysis replaced by a flash of searing anger.

"*Now, you listen to me–*" he snarled.

"Sir? It's Terry Holt."

Caslin was thrown, his confusion offsetting his rage. "*Terry…*"

"He's online again, sir."

"Uploading?" Caslin turned, picking up his pace, he set off for the front door.

"Not this time, sir. He's streaming – *live,*" Holt explained with obvious excitement. "We've got him. We know where he is."

"York Cemetery Chapel," Caslin stated, leaving the apartment and running down the stairs as fast he dared. His voice echoed in the stairwell.

"Yeah…" Holt replied, stunned. "How did—"

"Never mind, Terry. Get as many bodies as you can and flood that area immediately. Approach with caution and be advised there is a possible hostage situation in progress." Caslin thundered through the communal entrance, sending the door bouncing against the jamb as he charged it.

The cemetery was barely a four-minute drive from Fulford Road Police Station but Caslin was closer. Sullivan's apartment block was south of the city, along the Barbican Road. Clambering into his car, he fired the engine into life and put his foot down. The wheels spun and the tyres shrieked in protest as the car accelerated away. An oncoming vehicle swerved to avoid a collision as Caslin turned across the oncoming traffic. The driver of the vehicle responded with a blast of the horn by which time, Caslin was long gone. Swerving in and out of traffic, he sought to cover the distance in the shortest available time.

Through gritted teeth, he took the turn into the cemetery following a risky overtaking manoeuvre that saw him mount the kerb, collecting part of a hedge and almost clipping the stone archway of the entrance as he passed through. Flooring the accelerator, Caslin flew down the access road, coming from beneath the canopy of trees and into the parking expanse in front of the old chapel. The car skidded to a halt on the gravel and Caslin was out of his seat without applying the handbrake. The sound of approaching sirens met him as a police car tore along the road behind him, also sliding to a halt.

The two uniformed officers within leapt out, running to the rear and lifting the boot. Caslin set off for the entrance, an imposing double door, dwarfed by the massive stone columns to the frontage supporting the pediment above.

"Sir, wait!" one of the officers shouted as he strapped on his body armour. The second was already preparing his semi-automatic rifle. The armed response unit was the first deployed vehicle in attendance and they intended to take the lead but Caslin ignored them, running for the entrance.

Slowing as he came before the doors, he approached with caution. The right-hand door was cracked open and he tentatively peered through into the interior. He had been here before for a colleague's funeral and now, he wracked his brains to remember the layout. The thought came to him that the building was recently renovated, although he recalled there was only one way in or out and he was standing before it. Despite the neo-classical construction, imposing in both height and grandeur, the chapel only consisted of one room with large sash windows set high in the walls to every aspect, bar the frontage. If the killer remained then Caslin stood between him and escape. *If* escaping was his plan.

Reaching for the door, Caslin felt a firm hand on his shoulder. Glancing back, the armed officers joined him and the first indicated for him to step aside with a silent two-finger gesture, pointing towards his right. Allowing them to lead, Caslin watched as the door was pushed open and the two men entered. Their movements were precise and controlled. Caslin slotted in behind them. Their stealth was wasted. Inside, the black and white polished marble floor and stone walls reverberated even the slightest sound, magnifying the sound of their presence as it echoed throughout the interior.

The room was one large expanse, open to the apex of the roof. The huge windows, three per aspect, allowed any light penetrating through the trees outside to pass into the interior, casting shadows and eerie reflections across the surfaces. The building appeared empty, aside from a solitary figure seated with its back to them away to their left, at the far end. The uniformed officers altered their angle of approach, putting a little space between them, as the three men ventured farther. They kept watchful eyes in every direction, as well as above, as they made their way. Caslin felt the adrenalin building. His heart was thudding within his chest and his mind saw danger in the flicker of every shadow cast from the surrounding trees.

Moving closer, they could see the figure was male, sitting upright, arms dangling by his side. His head hung to the left, unsupported. The pool of crimson spreading out around him in an ever-increasing circle across the smooth marble was indicative of near death if not already passed. The sheer volume of blood lost, Caslin judged, was enough to almost guarantee death. The uniformed officers indicated to each other for one to provide cover whilst Caslin and he inspected the body.

Coming around to the face the man, Caslin slipped as he inadvertently stepped in the growing pool of blood despite his best efforts, his attention consumed by the horror before him. Jimmy Sullivan's lifeless eyes stared at him. Although the flow had apparently ceased, the journalist's beard was matted with blood. The flow passed down across his chin and his upper body. Caslin fought to tear his eyes away but he couldn't. He was transfixed. Sullivan's lips were parted and a rag of cloth had been stuffed into his partially open mouth. This too, was soaked in crimson. His throat had been slashed almost from ear to ear and the subsequent blood loss had soaked into his clothing, almost from head to foot, now pooling on the floor below.

Caslin reached forward and tried to find a pulse despite knowing it to be a futile gesture. Glancing to the floor, next to Sullivan's right foot and floating in his life blood, lay a blooming lotus flower. The petals were streaked with blood. The index finger of his right hand was missing and the blood dripped onto the flower below. Scattered randomly around it, or possibly strategically placed for it was impossible to tell for sure, Caslin noted a number of coins. Dropping to his haunches to inspect them, they were silver and of varying denominations. Caslin's catholic school upbringing flashed the connection in his mind. *Thirty pieces of silver.* The symbolism was strong; a reference to the selling of principles. Standing, tears welled in his eyes and he clenched his teeth as he shuddered involuntarily.

"Bastard!" Caslin shouted. The sound carried all around them, echoing, bouncing off ceiling and walls. The two officers accompanying him exchanged concerned glances before continuing their sweep of the room. Caslin remained where he was, staring into the eyes of his dead friend. "I'm so sorry, Jimmy," he whispered. His mobile rang. At first, he chose to ignore it but eventually rewarded the caller's persistence and answered.

"Sir."

"For fuck's sake, Terry, what is it?" Caslin snapped.

"He's still streaming, sir." His tone was apologetic, almost embarrassed.

"What do you mean?"

"The feed… it's still up. You're… *you're live on the internet*, sir," Holt said awkwardly.

Caslin hung up. Putting his phone away he sought to quell the rising fury within. Looking around for the source of the feed, he wanted to kill it immediately. There were few places to hide a camera with so little furniture present. It didn't take long. Caslin caught sight of something against the wall in the corner, barely eight feet away. Crossing to it, he found a mobile phone strapped to the wall with gaffer tape. The screen was covered but following the camera's line of sight, it was positioned to have a perfect view of both the entrance as well as their approach to Sullivan.

Caslin took a tissue from his pocket. Leaning in closer to the phone, he stared into the camera.

"I will find you. I promise you that." His words were cold, measured, belying the unchecked rage building inside him. He spoke with assured certainty. Using a finger, covered by the tissue, to press and hold the standby button, he powered down the device. More sirens could be heard approaching. Given the all-clear to approach by the armed response team, they were now bringing their presence closer and securing the scene. Looking back to his friend, Caslin took a deep breath and whispered, "I will find him."

CHAPTER TWENTY-THREE

THE BARMAN SET the glasses down in front of him. Caslin passed a ten-pound note across the bar and picked up the chaser. Seeing it off in one swallow, he placed the glass down just as his change arrived.

"Same again." The barman nodded, albeit with an awkward accompanying smile as his gaze lingered on him. Caslin watched as he poured out another double measure of *Edradour*. He returned and Caslin scooped up the scotch along with his pint, left coins on the counter and set off back to his booth in the lower bar. Descending the steps on unsteady feet, his wayward movement saw him spill the top of his beer. The foam ran down the glass and across the back of his hand. He was relieved to slip back onto the safety of his seat. Shaking off the excess, he wiped his hand on his jacket before picking up the beer and taking a mouthful.

Opening the book on the table before him, he caught sight of the bar staff looking in his direction. They were hardly subtle regarding their discussion. There was no doubt in his mind that they were talking about him. Whether it was the lack of his usual affability or they had seen the viral clip of Jimmy Sullivan's murder, where he'd played a starring role, he wasn't sure and if the truth be known, he didn't care. Seeking out the bookmark, a fragment of a torn receipt, Caslin located his place.

The tome Chen Tao lent him was proving fascinating but somewhat gruelling to get through. More of an encyclopaedic collection than a narrative, Caslin was finding it difficult to find what he was looking for. Therein lay the problem, *he didn't really know what he was looking for.* The basics were fairly clear. The study of the teachings of the Buddha alongside their application in a person's life would guide them along a developmental path, improving them spiritually and leading towards a state of enlightenment. Provided that is, if they could devote themselves to the path and be prepared for the process to take a lifetime, if not several. Caslin felt somewhat impressed by those who walked the path. The modern world, particularly western society, gravitated towards immediate gratification.

Chen Tao's insight on the violent beliefs held by practitioners of certain traditions was eye opening, if not disturbing. Until that point, Caslin was unaware such extremes existed within Buddhism. Turning his thoughts to their target, he considered that at some point he had chosen a path steeped in the harmonisation of the body, speech and mind, only for it to warp into a twisted reality that sought to justify acts of barbarity that made sane people retch. The truly frightening prospect was that he was not insane at all, but cool and calculating, in full control of his actions and beliefs. Caslin was banking all along on him making a mistake for they usually did. *How many more would die before the window of opportunity presented itself? Could he have acted differently?*

Picking up the scotch, Caslin tilted his head back and drained the glass. Closing his eyes, he savoured the taste alongside the fleeting burning sensation spreading across his chest. Returning the empty glass to the table, he realised someone was standing next to him. He hadn't seen her arrive. Blowing out his cheeks, he forced a smile in greeting.

"Hi Nate," Alison Taylor said. "I figured I would find you here."

"Hey, Alison."

"I'd say I'll get you another but by the looks of it, you're doing okay already." She took off her coat, threw it across the back of the seating and slipped into the booth opposite him.

"I'm doing all right," he whispered, picking up his pint, avoiding her gaze.

"Are you?"

He inclined his head to one side and eventually was compelled to meet her eye. "I've had better days."

A member of staff appeared alongside them, smiling at Alison but glancing nervously at Caslin. "A dry white wine for me, please."

"And a—"

"Just a dry white wine." Alison cut Caslin off before he could order another scotch. The waitress left and neither spoke until she was out of earshot.

"I think the management will be concerned that the staff are spending a lot of time on social media," Caslin said, looking out of the corner of his eye towards the bar.

"Or they are simply observant." Alison casually pointed to his left hand.

Caslin glanced down and saw nothing. Lifting his forearm, he looked on the underside. Blood had soaked into the cuff of his shirt. "Scotch would fix that."

"Don't you dare, Nathaniel."

The hostility in her tone caught him off guard. "Dare what?"

"Sit here drowning in scotch and your own self-pity, that's what." She snapped at him, reminiscent of how she once did when they were together. Alison was never one to pull her punches with him. He needed that. He respected it. "What happened to Jimmy *is not your fault*. Do you hear me?"

"That's funny," Caslin replied, picking up his pint and sipping at it, frowning. "Because I sort of see that it is, really."

"He's to blame. The sick bastard who did it. Not you."

Caslin sat forward in his seat. She appeared startled by the aggression in his eyes. Putting his pint aside, he leaned forward and focussed his attention on the book, leafing through the pages to another bookmarked spot. Spinning the book to face her on the table, he gently pushed it towards her. Alison looked down and scanned the page. "See?" he said. "*My fault.*"

"No, I don't see," she countered.

"The Fourth Precept," Caslin stated emphatically. "Or, as they refer to it in there." He indicated the book. "The principle of truthfulness. With every single one of the Five Precepts there are both positive and negative forms."

"Go on." Her drink arrived and she thanked the waitress, drawing the glass towards her and cradling the stem, looking for Caslin to continue.

"In the negative form practitioners must undertake the training to refrain from false speech."

"I see where you're going," Alison said, sipping at her wine.

"It's not a case of where I'm going," he argued. "I put Jimmy up to that interview. I put him front and centre, spinning a yarn about how this guy is some pathetic weirdo. I stoked the fire and therefore, it's on me."

"Jimmy knew what he was doing."

"That doesn't matter," Caslin snapped. "I put him in that predicament."

"So, by your logic, you had Jimmy put out a pack of lies or suppositions to instigate a response," Alison said, raising her eyebrows, "in order to rattle this guy's cage."

"Exactly."

"And it brought Jimmy into the firing line."

"The body in the deep freeze was Jimmy's former boss."

"I know," Alison said.

"I reckon he was the intended victim for the fourth precept, the archetypal news editor who spreads rumour and gossip, but then…" Caslin said, his voice tailing off as he broke eye contact. "Then I brought him Jimmy."

"No. *You brought him you,*" she countered.

That got his attention. "What the hell are you talking about?"

"You wanted to provoke a response and you got one. You were hoping it would push him into making an error and it has. You just haven't managed to exploit it yet."

"You've lost me," Caslin said, returning to his pint.

"This wasn't about Jimmy. This was about you. You presented yourself as the authority figure. The man with the moral superiority and that goes against everything in his make up."

Caslin sat forward, intrigued. "How so?"

Alison sat back, nursing her drink. "Serial killers represent a dual failure, both of their own development as fully fledged, well-rounded and productive individuals, as well as a failure of the culture and society they develop in. In a materially focussed society, such as we have, social anomies proliferate."

"Meaning?"

"The usual ethical and moral standards within a group can go missing. Studies have shown that in this scenario, psychologists see a pattern of what they call malignant objectifiers growing in numbers – people devoid of empathy."

"Narcissists?"

"Exactly. The killer's megalomania manifests against your challenge to his moral framework, which he sees as far superior to yours. It's no surprise that he is using the teachings of wisdom set out over thousands of years as a cloak to justify his actions. He believes he is more knowledgeable, ethically pure and morally on a different level to you. To all of us. The fact no one else can see this will only enrage him further."

"Why focus on me?"

"You challenged him. You judged him and that's antagonised him. Perhaps it has driven him on in order to prove you wrong."

Caslin nursed his drink. "This doesn't alleviate my guilt."

"The point is, it doesn't matter whether it was Jimmy," she said, holding up her hand to dampen his protest. "It could have been any of us, anyone important *to you*. You're the counterpoint to his quest, his mission. You are the authority figure. That's why he keeps coming back at you. That's why he's taunting you."

"He's emboldened. The stunt today with the live streaming shows his confidence is growing."

"As is his recklessness," Alison replied. "He's building up to something. Up until now, he's been methodical and calculating. Every step has been planned in great detail, weeks if not months, in advance. Now, he's starting to make it up on the fly." She sipped at her wine while Caslin worked through her logic. "The change of plan regarding the victim. How long did he have the editor locked up?"

"He hadn't been seen by his neighbours for over a month. Everyone thought he was taking an extended holiday after the events last year when he was sacked." Sullivan had been right. The paper had been in a spiral of decline for some time. Dwindling circulation saw failing advertising revenues and a demand from the ownership to stem the flow. The editorial staff shifted focus, looking for headline grabbing material. They believed they'd stumbled across a real scoop involving private enterprise and local government corruption, running the story without fully verifying the facts. The subsequent lawsuit almost put the paper into bankruptcy.

"So, no one who knew him missed him?" Alison asked.

"That's right. He was never reported missing because no one knew he was. Unmarried, single and not particularly sociable – a perfect candidate."

"And yet the killer changed his plan at the last moment, substituting him for Jimmy. Once he was no longer needed, he killed him and stuffed him in the deep freeze without a second thought."

"Where is he taking it now?" Caslin wasn't expecting her to know, he was thinking aloud.

"My theory is that the plan he's been working to has changed. Most likely due to more than merely your interference. The repeated acts of escalating violence, alongside the culmination of his well-made plans are failing to alleviate an almost over-whelming anxiety and depression. This is a very damaged individual."

"He's approaching his end game."

Alison drank her wine, sitting forward and placing her elbows on the table. She took a deep breath, meeting his gaze with a stern expression. "Whatever he is working towards... and it will be something... you will be at the centre of it. You have to be careful, Nate."

Caslin held the eye contact. He sensed there was more she wanted to say, to communicate to him but the moment passed and she placed her drink down on the table before standing up. Picking up her coat, she put it on. Leaning down, she kissed him on the cheek and left without another word. Watching her mounting the steps, Caslin mulled her theory over in his head. Thoughts passed to his family, considering their safety if he was indeed a target but he dismissed the notion. If Alison was right, the killer wanted his attention, not to punish him. There were no indications that Caslin himself was facing a moral judgement. She could be right in that as the principle lead in the investigation, the killer wanted Caslin to understand the motivation, to agree with him, or at least respect the man's actions.

Pushing his drink aside, Caslin returned his focus to the book. Revisiting the chapters relating to Buddhist ethics, he flicked ahead of where he'd last read, passing the precepts themselves in search of references to justice. His working theory was one of a maligned individual, meting out punishment on the morally corrupt. In which case he wanted to see what punishments were considered by followers. Skim reading, he found a section describing the purpose of punishment was *only a requirement when it came to reforming character* which Caslin found wholly unful-filling as an answer. Glancing at his watch, he considered picking Chen Tao's brains but it was far too late in the day.

Continuing on, he came across a character by the name of *Angulimala,* a revered figure spanning multiple Buddhist traditions in relation to childbirth and fertility. However, it wasn't those associations that drew Caslin's interest. Nor was it the fact he was widely regarded as an example of a complete transformation, the power and influence of the Buddha's teachings. The literal translation of his name pulled Caslin from the drunken malaise he was sinking towards. It was the name, *Angulimala – he who wears a finger necklace*.

His phone rang. Reluctantly, he tore his attention away from the pages to answer it.

"Nathaniel, are you okay?" a female voice asked. It was Michelle. His heart leapt at the recognition before a wave of guilt washed over him, the fleeting joy in stark contrast to the cloak of shame he insisted on carrying since Sullivan's murder. "I saw you… on the television news, just now. I mean, I recognised you in the background."

"This guy's making me famous," Caslin replied, ignoring her initial question.

"You looked so upset. I'm not surprised," she added swiftly. "Anyone would be but… did you know him? The man who died."

Caslin bit his lower lip and he found himself fighting back tears, not for the first time that day. "Yes. He was a friend of mine. A good friend."

"Oh, Nate. I'm so sorry. Is there anything I can do?"

"No!" Caslin responded, realising immediately that he was unintentionally curt. "I'm sorry, I didn't mean to sound dismissive."

"That's okay. Would you like to come over? Carly is sound asleep. We could talk." Caslin said nothing. The silence carried. "Or, we could say nothing and just sit," Michelle added, lightening her tone.

"No. I would like to but I have work to do."

"You sound like you're in a bar."

"And… you sound like my ex-wife," Caslin replied without hostile intent.

Michelle laughed. "Duly noted. I'll be up for another couple of hours if you change your mind. Otherwise, I'll speak with you soon?" Her tone was born of optimism rather than a statement of fact.

"Yes, of course," Caslin replied. "Goodnight."

"Take care, Nate."

He hung up, placing the mobile down on the table. Pulling the book into his lap, he sat back and retraced his finger to the beginning of the story.

The parallels were stark. The story dated back over two thousand years. *Angulimala*, born in the ancient Indian city of *Sāvatthī*, into the priestly caste to a father who served as a king's chaplain. Sent to study as a young man at the hands of a famous teacher in the Brahman priestly traditions, he excelled, rapidly earning both favour and extended privileges from the teacher, much to the jealousy of his fellow students.

Such was his favoured status, his peers schemed to curtail his progress, alleging an affair between the latter and their teacher's wife. Caslin found himself wondering at the accuracy of events, whether they could be after such passage of time. Returning to the story, he read how the teacher was unwilling to confront the younger man, either for fear of *Angulimala's* status or personal strength, the book didn't say. The teacher fabricated a conclusion to his student's *Brahman* training, telling him his studies were nearly at an end. In order to complete them, *Angulimala* must provide the traditional offering... the gift of a thousand fingers. Only then would his training be complete.

Caslin reached for his pint, momentarily distracted by a couple taking their place in the booth adjacent to his own. Returning to the story, he sipped at his drink while he read. *Angulimala* protested the request, claiming to be from a peaceful family but his teacher insisted, finally persuading him. The young student then set out on his mission leaving his teacher comfortable in the belief the younger man would eventually be killed in the process. He preyed on travellers, becoming ever more successful, and brutal, as he honed his skills. The story told how people avoided the roads only for the killer to enter villages and drag victims from their homes, murdering them in the street.

Carefully bookmarking his place, Caslin stood, putting on his coat. Every direction in which he looked there were people enjoying the end of their evening. His thoughts passed to the many occasions he and Jimmy had propped up this very bar, staggered between the levels and helped one another home. Lifting his glass, Caslin tilted it in a silent toast to his friend and drained the remainder in one motion. Tucking the book under his arm, he climbed the steps to the lower bar and headed for the exit and his apartment in Kleiser's Court. The story about the ideological young man reinforcing his beliefs through murder, turning over and over in his mind as he walked.

CHAPTER TWENTY-FOUR

PLEASED to find the team already at their desks when he arrived, Caslin clapped his hands together and grabbed their attention. Despite the fog clouding his thoughts, an aftereffect of the previous night, he was drawn to revisit their suspect with renewed vigour.

"So far our suspect is still a ghost to us. Pull your case notes together because we are going back to the beginning. We know he's meticulous in his planning, leaving nothing to chance. Locations are scouted, he knows where to expect the security cameras to be, how we can trace people through his vehicles or contacts but—" Caslin raised a finger for emphasis. "He spends a great deal of time either with his victims or researching them prior to killing them. That suggests they are not random targets or at least, they aren't by the time he kills them."

"So, he's either a friend or colleague?" Hunter asked.

"Correct," Caslin replied. "Perhaps not long term though. Maybe he was a temporary employee or a delivery driver. Someone who could potentially have had minimal contact with the victim but their paths have almost certainly crossed. Our suspect is somewhere in these files." Caslin slapped a hand down on a folder on the table in front of him.

"What makes you so sure of that?" A voice came from the other side of the room. All heads turned to see the arrival of Kyle Broadfoot. They were all so focussed on Caslin, no one heard him enter.

"It stands to reason, sir," Caslin argued. "To get as close as he needed to, to find out their darkest, most intimate secrets requires time and personal contact. Either with the victim or with someone within their inner circle. We may not have the suspect's true name on file but he's in there. I'm absolutely certain."

Broadfoot inclined his head. Leaning his back against the wall, he folded his arms in front of him and gestured for Caslin to continue. "Carry on. Don't let me interrupt."

"I want us to revisit the statements you've all taken from family, friends and work colleagues. Similarly, workplaces, hobbies, any opportunity for them to have either met new people or been introduced to friends of friends," Caslin stated, watching them for a reaction. Not one of them appeared angry at being asked to return to square one. Each and every member of the team was focussed on getting a result. "Hunter, revisit Kelly Ryan's life, both professional and personal. Find the link."

"Do we look again at Thomas Ryan, sir?" she asked.

"We look at everyone again."

"I'm on it," Hunter said, reaching for the corresponding paperwork.

"Terry, I want you on Andrew Connolly. You've got his computer and we all know what he was up to. Perhaps he's the one victim where there is a digital fingerprint linking him to the killer."

"I didn't find anyth—"

"Look again." Caslin cut him off. He was adamant they'd missed something, not necessarily through incompetence but perhaps it appeared insignificant at the time. They needed to revisit the case with a fresh approach, disregarding any conclusions they'd already reached. "Likewise, see how *Child Protection* are getting on with identifying Connolly's victims. Are there aggrieved family members or even grown up victims who might fancy some retribution?" Holt raised his eyebrows but didn't protest. "Maybe it's a long shot, Terry, but do it anyway."

"What about me?" Templer asked, sitting forward in his chair. Caslin lowered his gaze to his fellow DI. Of all of them, perhaps besides Caslin himself, it was Craig Templer who appeared to have found the case the most draining. Unsurprisingly. He was still missing a colleague and they were no closer to finding out his fate, let alone knowing if he was dead or alive.

"Revisit the Moretti inquiry. If I'm correct, then he's close to it."

"That was a very public investigation," Templer argued. "High profile. He could just have easily read about it in the papers."

"True." Caslin tilted his head to one side. "But everything else we know about him suggests an intimate knowledge, a close connection. He killed Jimmy Sullivan to draw me further into his world. He's making it personal. To me, that says this entire mission of his is personal."

"That means family members," Templer said, thinking aloud. "Those who feel the police or General Medical Council didn't do what they were supposed to."

"Not only," Caslin added. "Put Moretti's colleagues on the list. It was them who blew the whistle in the first place. Subsequently, the case was not proven and the whistle blowers were hauled over the coals, professionally destroyed, even when they made the correct moral call. On this occasion, Moretti was ruled innocent. The practice manager of Moretti's surgery said the colleagues who pointed the finger moved on due to the stress of it all. What's the betting they weren't given a great deal of choice in the matter. They could have an axe to grind."

"Got you," Templer said, his body language demonstrating he was up for the challenge.

"Regarding Kelly Ryan, sir," Hunter said. "I got the impression from one of her colleagues that she knew more than she was letting on. I'll give her another squeeze."

"Good. Push her hard. We only need to crack the link with one victim and then the others will follow. I'm certain. Then, once we've done all of this, we're going to do what we didn't do and should have done so already – and that's catch this man before anybody else gets killed. Understood?"

The team replied positively, in unison, and Caslin stepped away. Broadfoot lifted himself off the wall and crossed the room. Signalling for them to move into Caslin's office for a private word. Caslin caught Hunter eyeing them with a sly sideways glance as they entered his office. Closing the door behind them, Caslin offered his superior a seat but Broadfoot chose to stand.

"I am sorry for what happened to your friend." Broadfoot's tone was heartfelt and genuine.

"Thank you, sir." Caslin appreciated the sentiment but didn't want his focus clouded by grief. Mourning the dead would have to wait. He glanced out of the window. Rain was steadily falling.

"I have been speaking with the chief constable." Turning his back to Caslin, Broadfoot observed the team through the internal glass divide. Glancing at him sideways, he continued, "He has raised concerns over the handling of this case."

"*My handling*?" Caslin clarified, biting his lower lip and flicking his superior a contemptuous look.

"Yours specifically, yes. But don't imagine that his focus on you deflects any disproval away from me," Broadfoot countered, turning his gaze inwardly to the room. "When things start to go bad, there is always a tendency for some to look at shifting the chairs around."

"Shifting the blame more like."

"To be candid, yes. That's true."

"Are you here to replace me, sir?"

"Don't be such a child, Nathaniel," Broadfoot said, "you have my backing as much as at any time previously."

"But…"

"Your set up here is rather unorthodox in that you don't have the respective layers of command that you should."

"I'm well aware of the latitude, sir."

"Then you will appreciate how easy this is to maintain when things are going well. Should that not continue... well, you know how political things become around here."

"In your world."

"You need to bring closure to this case soon," Broadfoot said, turning to face him and bordering on losing patience. "Otherwise, it will be taken out of my hands and neither of us want that. The knock-on effect will be damaging to both of us."

"Understood, sir." Eyeing Iain Robertson entering from the corridor, Caslin checked whether their impromptu meeting was at an end and Broadfoot indicated it was. Caslin left his office, acknowledging Robertson's greeting.

"I've got the preliminaries from the chapel. Would you like to go through it now or I could leave it with you?"

"No, let's run through it now while everyone is here," Caslin replied.

Broadfoot came alongside him. "Keep me in the loop, Nathaniel."

They waited until he left the room before Robertson passed out copies of a two-page document to all those present. It was a summary of his initial findings. The last person to receive a copy was Caslin himself. As he took a hold of it, Robertson held his grip. "Are you sure you want to do this now? The rest of the team and I can..."

Caslin cut a half-smile, one of resignation. "I need to do this, Iain, but thanks."

Robertson nodded and released his grip on the paper. Turning, he pulled out a chair and sat down. Caslin scanned the summary. The details were graphic, hard for him to read but he meant what he said. This was something he needed to hear.

"The victim," Robertson began, choosing not to mention Sullivan by name deliberately, thereby maintaining objectivity, "suffered a sustained and brutal attack. Dr Taylor will confirm, I'm sure, but we've documented defensive wounds to both hands and forearms.

There is evidence of one heck of a struggle, but it didn't take place at the chapel. Rubber streaks were found on the marble flooring." Robertson reached into a folder and withdrew a set of crime scene photographs, placing them on the table for others to see. "Near to the entrance. I should imagine he was dragged into place in the chapel."

"If he was unconscious, could he have been killed elsewhere?" Hunter asked.

Caslin cut in. "No. Too much blood. He died in the chapel."

"Correct," Robertson agreed. "The victim sustained a beating but we do believe he was unconscious or unable to resist. That sets the killer as quite a large man or at least, very strong. The victim weighs over seventy-eight kilos and that's a lot of dead weight..." Caslin drew a sharp intake of breath. "Sorry, Nathaniel. The victim was a large man. Moving someone of that size is damn difficult unless you have a lot of upper body strength. Not to mention technique."

"Cause of death was blood loss, I'm presuming?" Caslin flipped to the end of the report.

"You'll have to wait for Alison, I'm afraid," Robertson said, glancing awkwardly across at him. "I've spoken with her this morning and it is possible he was asphyxiated. The killer..." Robertson hesitated.

"What is it?" Caslin pressed.

"The killer removed his tongue... and forced him to swallow it."

Caslin missed the wave of revulsion expressed by his team, such was the depth of his own reaction. Moments later, he recovered his composure. "Then his throat was cut."

"Aye, it was," Robertson said. "Judging from the passage of the blade and the... smooth nature of the wound, Alison and I believe the victim most likely lost consciousness prior to it happening."

"He did it for the presentation value," Caslin said aloud.

"That was all for the cameras," Robertson said.

"As well as for me," Caslin replied. "Any DNA, trace evidence?"

"No. I'm convinced your suspect knows what we look for."

Caslin resisted the temptation to focus on that last point. Grasping for leads could have led them towards someone with forensic know-how or law enforcement experience but Caslin knew better. Their processes were detailed on multiple websites, and modern dramas did a half decent job of recreating police procedures these days. He saw fit not to read too much into the comment.

"What about Sullivan's apartment? We don't know how or where he was abducted. His car was still outside his apartment. Have you been through his place?" Caslin asked.

"We have, yes. Pulled a number of prints, some of which are unidentifiable. However, we got a partial I'm convinced belongs to the killer."

"How can you be so sure?" Caslin asked.

"There was a match with another smudged partial taken from Alessandro Moretti's residence. It's the only plausible explanation. It looks like a thumb print." Robertson fished out the copies, handing them to Hunter. "We ran them through the system but there were no hits."

"One partial thumb print?" Caslin asked. Robertson nodded. "That guy must have been either living at Moretti's house or at least visiting it frequently for months and you've only found one print."

"Partial," Robertson said, wishing to be clear.

"I went through Moretti's financials," Templer interjected. "How long did Dr Taylor reckon he was incapacitated for, while he was being pumped full of heroin and Fentanyl?"

"Months," Caslin said.

"His bank account and credit cards have been active in that time. Repeated withdrawals of cash at various times every week. Not to mention regular payments to supermarkets and other online retailers. If Moretti hasn't been capable, then who's been using his money?"

"That's how he's living under the radar," Caslin said. "No one's been shielding him, no one has a friend who has been acting weird. He is effectively off the grid, living somebody else's life and money. Get onto the bank—"

"Find out which ATMs he's been withdrawing the cash from." Templer finished for him. "Maybe the security camera on the cashpoint got a decent snapshot. The supermarket purchases are also on a regular fortnightly pattern. That suggests to me they're home deliveries. He wouldn't be stupid enough to walk into a building with a sophisticated CCTV system and use Moretti's credit card for his groceries. Utilising home delivery means he gets one delivery driver, probably different each time, who is making multiple drops and unlikely to remember him if asked months later."

"Possibly at night too," Hunter added.

"We should ask the drivers, anyway. It's worth a shot," Templer stated.

"Good thinking." Caslin turned back to Iain Robertson, raising his eyebrows. "One print?" he repeated, incredulous. "He couldn't live with gloves on all the time, surely?"

"I'm at a loss," Robertson replied. "I can only tell you what I found. Why just the one and from a thumb... I don't understand how he managed it. He can't have been sweeping the prints away because we have multiple other sets."

Caslin thought on it but in the end, he was merely going around in circles, so he chose to move on. "Craig, while you're looking at financials. Pull everything for the man in the deep freeze as well. Perhaps he's been making a habit of living like this."

Templer made a note. "If the money was running out, that would explain why the power was cut off and why he was bleeding money from Andrew Connolly. He needed funds to live off but, in that case, why would he leave the final pay off behind?

And why not take the money from the dealers at Stamford Street? I don't understand."

Caslin was equally confused. Templer had a point. "Before, he was playing the long game. Maybe something has changed. Find out if Moretti had a car. I don't see Jimmy going anywhere quietly, so he must have had transport. If there's a print in his apartment, there was no altercation inside because I've been there and seen it for myself. It stands to reason he's using some kind of vehicle. Maybe it's Moretti's. If so, he might still be driving it."

"Give me half an hour," Templer said.

"There's something else, Craig," Caslin said. The edge to his tone made Templer stop as he was about to crack on. He sat down again, looking inquisitively towards Caslin. "It's tough but I have to ask. Your man, Ben Fowler. How well do you know him?"

Templer looked confused. "Well enough. Why do you ask?"

Caslin glanced away and then back again. "We are yet to find him... or any evidence of what has happened to him... if anything."

"Don't go there, Caslin."

"We have to consider the possibility."

"I've worked with him for over a year as his handler," Templer argued. "I have no doubt that he's not gone rogue."

"He's been under a long time," Caslin countered. "Living that way. A high-pressure double life will exert a lot of stress."

"You said it yourself, Caslin. This is personal," Templer stated. "There is nothing personal to Ben about these other victims. Let it go."

Caslin had to admit it, he had a point. Despite allowing the matter to drop, the question regarding where Fowler was couldn't be so easily put aside.

CHAPTER TWENTY-FIVE

"I don't understand what I'm doing here? I answered all of your questions and gave you everything you asked for."

Caslin sat forward in his seat. The interview room had no natural light. The room was purposefully cold. Caslin turned the heating off with the deliberate intention in mind to make the conversation as unpleasant as he possibly could.

"I don't understand what I am doing here, I really don't."

Simon Alexander, Kelly Ryan's line manager, shifted nervously in his seat.

"And yet you failed to mention how you and Kelly were involved," Caslin said, folding his arms across his chest.

"Involved? We were—"

"You were lovers, Mr Alexander."

He stammered. "I... I... don't know where you heard that."

"It's common knowledge among your staff," Caslin said.

"Gossip..."

"Don't lie to me," Caslin barked, slamming a flat palm against the table. Alexander jumped in his seat, startled. "People are dead! Stop lying to me."

Alexander took a deep breath, holding his hands up in supplication. His nervous mannerisms appeared to magnify. "All right... all right." He looked across at Caslin, hunching his shoulders conspiratorially and gently shifting his head from left to right, as if frightened someone might overhear.

"You were in a relationship," Caslin told him. It wasn't a question. "Why did you keep it from us?"

"I didn't think it was relevant. It isn't relevant."

"I'll be the judge of what is and isn't relevant. How long were you seeing each other?"

Alexander shrugged, demonstrating a degree of petulance. "The past year on and off. No big deal."

"Your staff seem to think it is."

"People love to talk," Alexander said. "They'd do so whether it was true or not."

"Who knew?"

"About the relationship?"

"Yes, obviously."

"I don't know... maybe Kelly told someone else as well."

"As well as who?"

Alexander looked momentarily confused, his eyes moving to the ceiling. "I... erm..."

"You said she may have told *someone else*. The time for secrecy has passed. You need to talk to me."

"He came to visit me, at the office," Alexander said quietly, resigned to revealing the nature of the tryst. "A few months back. Her husband. Kelly's husband."

"Thomas Ryan?" Caslin asked, genuinely surprised. Alexander nodded. "Specifically, about the affair?" Alexander nodded but said nothing. "How did he know?"

He shook his head, turning the corners of his mouth down in an exaggerated manner. "Kelly must have told him. I never called her at home or after hours, and it's not like we met all that often for someone to... catch us. There's no other way. She must have done."

"What did he want when he came to see you?"

"To tell me to stay away from his bloody wife! Like it was all my fault."

"Are you devoid of blame?" Caslin asked, raising his eyebrows.

Alexander responded with further childish petulance. "She *pursued* me. I was a married man."

"You could have said no," Caslin countered, masking his incredulity.

"Kelly wasn't a woman who took no for an answer." His response a mixture of denial tinged with a dose of excitement at the memory.

"Did he threaten you?" Caslin asked.

"Not as such… He was angry… sure, but…" Alexander paused, as if a realisation was dawning on him. "Do you think he did it?"

"The visit he paid you, did that put a stop to the relationship?"

Alexander shook his head. "No, of course not. If anything, Kelly upped things a little. I think… she enjoyed it… the thrill was everything for her. It needn't have been me. If not me, then it would have been someone else."

"Where did you used to meet?" Caslin asked.

Alexander appeared irritated at having to discuss the subject. Caslin sensed animosity. "Various places. Sometimes we would get a hotel, others… well, wherever. You know how it is."

Caslin didn't reply but he remembered his own days of infidelity well. Creeping around, experiencing the thrilling sensation of the forbidden fruit, feeling that curious mixture of achievement and shame in almost equal measure. *Almost.*

"Did you ever meet in the countryside?" Caslin asked, watching closely for a reaction.

Alexander averted his eyes from Caslin's gaze. "Occasionally."

"Where?"

"We found a little place where we could be alone." His reply came with obvious reticence and an associated nervous cough. "Near to the Derwent, on the outskirts of a village."

"Westow?"

Alexander snapped to attention, tilting his head to the side. "Yes. How… how did you know?"

"That's where we found Kelly. In a small clearing alongside the river."

"Oh…" Alexander said, his head sinking into his hands.

"Sound familiar?"

"Yes." Alexander nodded solemnly. His expression switched from guarded embarrassment to animated shock. "Listen. You don't think he's going to come for me, do you? I mean, the things this man has done are terrible. What if he comes after me? You need to protect me."

"I should think if he was looking to punish you, then you and I wouldn't be having this conversation right now, Mr Alexander. Kelly is dead. She suffered, perhaps, so you didn't have to."

"Oh, right. Yes, of course. Dreadful business," Alexander said, shaking his head. "I… I don't suppose we could keep all of this out of your investigation, could we? Like I said, it's largely irrelevant."

"And you wouldn't want your wife to find out, would you?"

"No, certainly not."

"I'll see what I can do, Mr Alexander," Caslin said, standing. "You hang on here for a bit and we'll get you home later."

Caslin glanced sideways at the man and then up towards the camera, mounted in the corner where two walls met the ceiling, as he left the room. Although far from a shrinking violet and guilty of his own extramarital affair in the past, Caslin still found this particular individual worthy of his contempt. Even now, he was still seeking to protect his own marriage and reputation at the expense of a murder investigation. The murder of his lover no less, and offering no thought to anything but his own desires. Caslin was met in the corridor by DS Hunter who was watching via a monitor in a separate room. She fell into step alongside him.

"What do you want us to do?" she asked.

"Get Thomas Ryan in here. He's another one who's been lying

to us and I wouldn't mind knowing why. You never know, there may be a few other details his mind has let slip recently."

"What about him? I don't think he's involved, do you?" Hunter indicated towards the interview room where Simon Alexander waited.

"No. He's certainly not involved. An utter waste of oxygen. Have Terry Holt take his statement again. I want all of what he just told me on the record. His wife will no doubt find it an interesting read when it's read out in court."

"Right you are," Hunter said, smiling.

"We'll leave him to stew on things for a bit. Have uniform put someone in there with him but make sure they don't talk. That'll make him feel uncomfortable."

"You're cruel."

"How did you get on with revisiting Kelly's caseload?" Caslin asked as they made their way to the stairs.

"Repossessions are far from the peak levels experienced a few years ago but her team were busy. No one they came into contact with was happy about the process but aside from the verbal abuse the staff have come to expect, there didn't appear to be anyone who ticks the boxes."

"No threats?"

"None specifically aimed in her direction, no, and none that were given anything but passing credence."

Holt met them when they were halfway up the stairs.

"Sir, I've just heard back from *Child Protection*. I asked for an update on their identification of the victims in the Connolly investigation."

"How are they getting on?" Caslin asked.

"Slow progress, sir. They've positively identified six of the children thus far. Four of whom are currently attending the centre where Connolly worked. They've started with the most recent and are working backwards but as I said, it's slow progress."

"Background checks on the victims' family members?" Caslin

asked as they re-entered their investigation room. Templer acknowledged their arrival.

"I've run the names through the *PNC* and none have returned any hits regarding violent history or criminal records," Holt explained. "We'll have to go out to them and take fingerprints in order to compare them with those Robertson lifted from Moretti's house."

"What about the addicts at Stamford Street?" Caslin asked.

Holt returned to his desk, retrieving a sheet of paper. "You'll not be surprised to find each and every one of them has a place in our rogues' gallery. However, none can be judged as anything other than petty criminals. I went back over every name but turned up nothing new. We have arrests and convictions for robbery, theft and assault. All of which arguably stem from the need to service their addiction."

Caslin took the offered paper, glancing over at the whiteboards mounted on the ops room wall. "Any crossover with other victims or known associates?"

Holt shook his head. "No, sir. None that we can see. Maybe they're not related in any way and he's selecting them at random. He's methodical, willing to take his time. These religious funda-mentalists can harbour things for years before they crack."

"Let's hope you're wrong, Terry," Caslin said, shooting him a sideways glance. "Besides, I don't think we have a fundamentalist on our hands. At least, not a devout one anyway."

"What makes you think that?" Templer asked. "He's throwing the imagery at us each time he orchestrates something."

"He's throwing us part of it," Caslin countered. "None of what he does has a place in the devotion to Buddhist traditions. This man isn't a zealot. At best, I believe he's acting out his twisted world vision using the religion as a shroud to either justify it, or to try and demonstrate a moral superiority."

"A lot like a religious zealot, then," Templer stated.

Caslin couldn't disagree. "I still think despite the obvious planning and the creative vision he employs we are dealing with a lay believer, and that is why he will have an association with one of the victims that will take us to him. Craig, what can you tell me about the Moretti investigation?"

Momentarily distracted by some shouting from the street outside, Caslin turned back to Templer as he crossed to a board where he'd already detailed the associations of the key names in the investigation.

"Moretti's colleagues, two of them, raised concerns regarding a number of cases in which patients of the good doctor appeared to have died relatively unexpectedly."

"Relatively?" Caslin queried.

"They were all elderly patients suffering from various ailments associated with old age," Templer explained. "Most had multiple conditions, either being treated on an outpatient basis in conjunction with the local hospital, or directly by staff at the medical centre Moretti worked at. The problems were that none of those who died were thought to be at risk."

"The CPS focussed on three cases, I believe?" Caslin asked.

Templer nodded. "That's correct. However, they considered up to six more. Four of those were cremations, so there was little or no forensic evidence to work with. The investigation team, working out of your sister station at Acomb Road, applied to investigate further back to his time in Italy where he originated from."

"What happened with that?"

"Judged unnecessary. I imagine the cost implications were considered too high. There may have been a different outcome if the case had gone to trial and delivered a guilty verdict," Templer said. "As it stands, the details were passed to the Italian authorities and they were left to do their own investigation. No idea whether they acted on it though."

Caslin glanced to the window again as more shouting carried to them. The disturbance seemed to be growing but he pushed his curiosity aside. "What of the three cases?"

"They were burials, so the team applied for exhumations with the approval of the families, although the decision was not uniformly welcomed by all according to the case notes. Further autopsies were carried out. Higher levels of painkiller medication were found than expected in all three, whereas in one case, a medication used in the treatment of acute schizophrenia was found in a patient who had never been prescribed the drug."

Templer picked up a marker. Underlining the first name, he turned to face them. "Iris Baker," he said, tapping the name for effect. "Suffering from arthritis, a thyroid complaint and dementia, died within three hours of a home visit from Moretti. He administered a dose of steroids, according to her medical notes. At the time, her age, frail nature and long medical history didn't cause an alarm to ring."

"Who signed the death certificate? Moretti?"

Templer nodded. "Correct. The family called the surgery when Iris took a turn for the worse and Moretti paid them a second visit, by which time she had already passed. There were no suspicious circumstances noted."

"What about the next?" Caslin asked.

"Peter Scarrow. An eighty-four-year-old man diagnosed with COPD, a chronic lung condition that left him in almost permanent need of extra oxygen. He was pronounced dead following his arrival at Accident and Emergency." Templer shrugged, picking up a summary document and passing it to Caslin. "Been in and out of hospital on several occasions in the prior months due to his condition."

Caslin speed read the sheet. The cause of death was noted as a cardiac arrest, brought on by continual stresses placed on the heart by his condition. He couldn't help but wonder if the conclusion may have been reached too hastily.

"Don't tell me, Moretti paid him a visit as well?" Caslin asked, flipping to the photographs of the deceased. All three images depicted smiling faces. Despite their age and varying levels of infirmity, all appeared content in life and were surrounded by loving family members. That was part of what made the suggestion of murder even more unpalatable for the doctor would need to have the trust of not only the patient, but their relatives as well in order to get close enough to kill them.

"Right, yeah. You're seeing the pattern. Moretti saw him that afternoon. Going downhill shortly after, he needed to be admitted to hospital and the family called for an ambulance."

"And the last one they investigated?" Caslin stood, feeling the onset of cramp. He had the urge to stretch his legs. The growing commotion outside drew him to the window overlooking the exit from the station out onto Fulford Road, and he observed a number of uniformed officers fanning out at the edge of his field of vision, but as to why, he had no idea.

"Eleanor C—" Templer was cut off by a ringing phone. It was the landline to Holt's desk and he apologised, rushing to answer it. Seconds later, Hunter's kicked in followed by Caslin's mobile. The team exchanged glances. Standing at the window, the setting sun dropped below the cloud line causing Caslin to raise a hand to shield his eyes from the glare.

"Caslin," he said in greeting, lifting his mobile to his ear, watching as more officers ran past from left to right below, disappearing from view.

"You're going to need to get down here." The familiar voice of a colleague came to him. The tone was strange, strained somehow with an intonation of stress. There was something of a ruckus going on in the background with several raised voices audible but Caslin couldn't make out what was being said.

"What is it?"

"It's one of yours… down here, out front." A scream carried through the mouthpiece. Caslin hung up, turning to his colleagues.

"Something's going on. We'd better get outside." Realising from the expressions on the faces of the team, their calls conveyed the same information as his.

CHAPTER TWENTY-SIX

By the time they descended the steps at the front of the building, at least a dozen uniformed officers were present. They were drawn to the commotion away to their right and ran in that direction. Rounding the corner, a startling scene lay before them. The officers were surrounding a lone man who was clearly in an agitated state. The image struck Caslin as similar to a wounded animal, cornered and afraid, unable or unwilling to recognise the help on offer. The man, stripped to the waist, spun in eternal circles in an attempt to find an escape route. Every avenue was closed off. Officers adopted nonconfrontational gestures, offering soothing voices, attempting to talk the man down from his apparent mania.

"He's off his face," Holt said aloud, drawing a glance from Caslin.

"That a technical term is it?" he replied wryly. Holt wasn't far off with his assessment as Caslin quickly reached the same conclusion. The man was pale, his face drawn, sweating profusely despite the cool breeze of the afternoon and his minimal clothing. Heavily tattooed, Caslin didn't recognise him and the man was distinctive enough that if they'd met, Caslin would be sure to remember. The reason his team were summoned downstairs was obvious with only a cursory assessment.

The man crouched or was about to topple over, Caslin couldn't say which but he threw his arms about wildly in an attempt to ward off the surrounding ring of blue. Two officers jumped away, attempting to avoid the arc of blood flowing from a flailing arm. Even from this distance, the missing index finger of the right hand was clear. Streaks of blood ran from wounds to his upper body but such was his animated state, it was very difficult to see the true nature of the injuries. The nearest officers had donned blue latex gloves, standard procedure to avoid contact with bodily fluids.

"Dear God," Templer muttered under his breath. Caslin looked at him, seeing the mask of abject horror in his colleagues face as the wild-eyed man lunged at the nearest officer. A guttural scream of anger emanated from his mouth, lips curled, reminiscent of a rabid dog. Templer was transfixed, rooted to the spot. *"Ben..."*

Caslin returned his attention to Ben Fowler, the undercover detective missing from the house at Stamford Street. He was struggling. The exertion of his efforts to avoid capture were such that his strength was failing. He staggered and then lurched sideways to avoid two sets of hands seeking to grasp hold of him. Stumbling backwards, he fell against the exterior wall of the police station. His legs gave out from under him and he slumped downwards, eyes rolling as he sank down.

There was a moment that followed where time appeared to stand still. The sheer electricity present in the air mere seconds earlier now replaced by an eerie silence. The passing traffic on the Fulford Road all that could be heard as normality continued around them. The officers exchanged glances and one made to step forward but it was Templer who intervened, forcing his way past and standing between them and their stricken colleague.

Kneeling alongside him, he gently reached out. Fowler's eye followed the path of the approaching hand but didn't react in any other way. "It's me, Ben. It's Craig." He placed the palm of his hand affectionately on the man's shoulder. Attempting to make eye contact and seeking a sign of recognition, Templer forced a smile. "You remember?"

Fowler's gaze fell upon him but if he recognised his handler, he didn't let on. His eyes glazed over, as if staring off at some random point in the distance. Caslin came near, dropping to one knee.

"Ambulance is on the way," he said. Casting an eye over Fowler, Caslin noted the ragged breathing and rapid heart rate. The heart was beating visibly under the skin at a rate of knots far in excess of what could be considered regular. Now better able to assess Fowler's injuries. They looked fresh, crude, as if someone had taken a sharp blade to the man but intentionally refrained from going too deep with each wound. There was a noticeable level of bruising affecting both of Fowler's arms at the crook of each elbow. Scabbing was present alongside fresh needle marks. Fowler suffered a similar experience to Alessandro Moretti. Searching for a positive, Caslin concluded that at least he was still alive.

"What is it, Caslin?" Templer read his curious expression.

"Caslin!" Fowler barked, surging upright for a brief moment before falling back against the wall, accompanied by the press of a reassuring hand on the chest from Templer. "*Caslin...*" he repeated, mumbling.

"What is it, Ben?" Templer asked.

"I... I... a message," Fowler whispered, almost inaudibly. Straining to hear, Caslin looked to his colleague with an inquisitive expression.

Templer shrugged with a shake of the head. "You have a message?" he asked.

Fowler fought for breath, his eyes rolling until they eventually came to focus on Caslin. "*Message,*" he said, his head lolling to one side. Caslin reached up and placed a restraining hand gently against the side of his head, keeping him upright.

"What's the message, Ben?" Caslin repeated the question.

Fowler shook his head ever so slightly. "I'm… the message…"

Caslin exchanged glances with Templer. The shared fear that Fowler was slipping into unconsciousness struck them. Templer pressed for more detail. "What's the message, Ben? What do you have to tell him?"

Fowler's eyes closed and he passed out. Templer reached to his neck, searching for a pulse. Smiling, he announced he had one but it was erratic. The sound of an approaching ambulance could be heard, the sirens reverberating off of the buildings as it negotiated the rush hour traffic. Seconds later, the yellow vehicle appeared at the entrance to the car park. A uniformed officer directed them to the nearby group.

"That was incoherent," Templer said. "We need to know what the message was."

"He said *he was* the message," Caslin replied, frowning. The two men made room for the first of the two paramedics to reach them. A colleague joined her and Caslin stepped away, leaving Templer to fill them in on what they thought had befallen Fowler.

"Anyone see who dropped him off?" Caslin asked the assembled officers. There were blank expressions all round. Turning, he looked for Hunter. "Review the CCTV, maybe we can get a make of car and a direction of travel."

"Caslin! You need to see this."

He returned to where Templer stood. Fowler was laid out with the medics preparing to lift him onto a gurney for transport to hospital.

"Be quick," the first paramedic said to them.

Drawing back the blanket from beneath Fowler's chin to reveal his chest, Caslin was shocked. The blood across his upper body seeped from multiple injuries but the cuts were shallow. There was minimal blood flow. They were administered with a sharp blade, only stripping away the layer of skin and leaving much of the flesh beneath intact. Inclining his head sideways, Caslin could now see the cuts were, in reality, crudely shaped letters. The edges were ragged, more like barely controlled slashes than the result of focussed concentration. Perhaps Fowler didn't cooperate in the process.

"M.I.C…" he read aloud, struggling with the final letters.

"That's an *H*," Templer suggested, trying hard to read Caslin's expression. "And the last looks like an *E*… I would say. Wouldn't you? Is that the message?"

"He said the message was for me."

"Yeah. What does it mean?"

"Upstairs," Caslin began, the semblance of a thought forming in his mind along with a knot of fear in his stomach. "What were the names you had, particularly the one you were going to say before all this kicked off?"

Templer thought back to his notes on the three suspicious deaths in the Moretti investigation. "Err… Baker, Scarrow and… Eleanor something… Carter, perhaps. Sorry, not sure. Why?"

"Just a spark in the back of my mind," Caslin replied, trying to organise the jumble of thoughts flooding his mind.

"Come to think of it, it wasn't Carter. It was Cates, *Eleanor Cates*. She couldn't be related to…?"

Caslin met his eye, the links starting to come together.

"Do they… and that makes this *Miche*… what… who?" Templer asked.

"Michelle Cates. *Thomas Ryan's sister*," Caslin said quietly, "and he's telling me his next target."

Taking out his mobile, Caslin scrolled through his contact list and dialled Michelle's number. Pacing nervously as he waited for her to pick up, his anxiety growing as the call rang but without response, eventually passing to voicemail. He hung up and redialled.

"What is it?" Hunter asked, coming to join them and sensing something was wrong.

"Get the car," Caslin said, abandoning the call and putting his mobile away. "Get it now."

Something in his manner or tone hit home and Hunter turned

on her heel, setting off to the rear yard where her car was parked. Caslin turned to Templer.

"If I'm right, put out a *Bolo* for Thomas Ryan. Send some units to his home address. He should be approached with caution but I think I know where we'll find him."

"In that case we need to seal off the area—"

"He's on the edge of the centre." Caslin checked his watch. "At this time in the evening we'll have no chance of doing that quietly. There will be chaos if we try. We'll be tipping our hand."

"What are you suggesting?" Templer asked as the medics hoisted Fowler up onto the gurney and ushered them out of the way.

"I'm working on it," Caslin replied, spotting Hunter pulling up at the kerbside. He set off without another word, leaving the frustrated Templer behind.

"You've not even told me where you're going!"

Caslin ignored him, opening the passenger door and clambering in. Hunter pulled away. The last thing Caslin wanted was the entire station emptying and descending on the Cates' residence. Alison Taylor was right. He was at the centre of this and the killer *wanted* him there for the finale and Caslin intended not to disappoint. A flicker of panic rose within and he sought to quell it. *Would Thomas Ryan really kill his sister … his niece?* Without doubt, the man was certainly capable.

Hunter, sensing Caslin's requirement for urgency floored the accelerator, pulling out into oncoming traffic and forcing a path through. The evening rush hour was in full swing and the routes in and out of the city were approaching gridlock as usual. For once, Caslin didn't comment on her driving skills. The whites of his knuckles on show, he gripped the door handle and braced himself while Hunter carried out her particular brand of enthusiastic driving.

The blaring horns of terrified motorists sounded in front and behind them as they progressed. Despite Hunter's best efforts, the sheer weight of traffic on the approach to the centre eventually brought them to a standstill on *Fishergate*. Caslin shifted in his seat. They were a few hundred yards short of *Tower Street*. With a clear run, Michelle's house was a two-minute drive away or a five-minute walk.

Hunter swore. Viewing the road ahead, there was something blocking the nearside lane. A broken-down vehicle by the look of it. Caslin could wait no longer. He cracked open his door and was out before Hunter could object.

"Cas..." she shouted but let the call tail off. Reaching for her radio, she depressed the talk button. The radio crackled into life and she announced her location. Despite Caslin's fears regarding tipping their hand, she couldn't allow him to go alone. Knowing how rash he could be, a strength at times but incredibly risky at others, Caslin would be more than willing to go up against Thomas Ryan alone.

Breaking into a run, Caslin cut between two stationary vehicles and mounted the pavement. Passers-by stepped aside, some clearly startled by a grown man charging towards them. Heading left and over the bridge, Caslin sprinted across the road, narrowly avoiding those cars accelerating away from the traffic lights, seeking to gain an advantage on the other drivers around them. Descending the stone steps into the Tower Gardens, located alongside the river Ouse, Caslin was breathing hard. Stopping when he reached the ground level, the sound of traffic thundering over the bridge above him, Caslin caught his breath whilst eyeing Michelle's house on the far side of the gardens.

From his vantage point, he could see the glow from the light of the rear extension, visible above the perimeter wall. He knew time was limited. There was no way the panic button wouldn't be pushed, either by Hunter or Templer. They would be right to do so. That gave him a limited window in which to act. Resuming his route across the open space, Caslin ignored those on their way home from work, fleetingly jealous of their evening routine as the reality of his own situation fixed itself in the forefront of his mind. The notion he was walking... no, *running* into a trap was obvious.

Reaching the perimeter wall, far too high for him to climb over, he skirted along its length until he came to the rear access gate. Trying the handle, he found it bolted from the inside. He could hear the sound of sirens in the distance. Looking down to his left, he noted a chunk of brick missing from the wall alongside the gate. Using it as a foothold, he threw his arms over the top of the gate and levered himself up. Peering through the foliage he looked towards the house. His view was obscured. Night had descended and, confident he wouldn't be seen from anyone inside, he hoisted himself up and rotated his body over the gate, dropping to the path below.

Inching forward, he hugged the perimeter, using the bushes to mask his approach. The rear of the house came into view, all contemporary glass and aluminium. Caslin saw three figures sitting around the dining table where he'd shared a meal with Michelle only a few days earlier. She was sitting alongside her daughter, Carly, with another figure directly opposite her with his back to him. He wore a dark, heavy overcoat and sat hunched over. From his vantage point, he was unsure whether this was Thomas Ryan. His hair colour matched but the coat made his physical frame hard to determine and therefore confirm it was him.

Narrowing his eyes, Caslin assessed what was going on. He could see little or no conversation taking place. The three of them appeared to be waiting. Edging forward, Caslin took out his mobile phone, setting it to silent mode for fear of a random call giving away his presence. A few steps further and he was as close as he could get without risking revealing himself. The sounds of the city carried on the breeze. A light in an upstairs room flickered into life in the adjoining house. Caslin watched the curtains drawn as the inhabitants went about their routine, ignorant of the unfolding drama next door.

The sirens grew ever louder and Caslin knew he was at a crossroads. Either he backed away and awaited a trained negotiator, as would be the expectation, or he could enter the house. The latter filled him with a sense of dread. Observing those inside, the stronger he felt the likelihood was that they were waiting. Waiting for him. From where he knelt, Caslin couldn't see a weapon on the table. Nor could he see any immediate threat to Michelle or her daughter. Of course, that didn't mean they were in any less danger. Still unable to see or identify the man, Caslin looked at the remaining windows. All the rear facing rooms were in darkness. *Was he another hostage? Could Thomas Ryan be elsewhere, lying in wait perhaps?*

By entering the situation, as per the killer's intention, there was every possibility Caslin would set in motion the final stages of his scheme. Potentially disastrous for everyone present. Then again, were he to refuse to participate, an equal or even a worse outcome could materialise. His eyes fell on Michelle. Even from this distance, he could see she was crying.

Taking a deep breath, he rose from his position, stepping out and revealing himself. Advancing slowly towards the house, he was ten feet from the door when Michelle saw him. Her lower lip dropped slightly in an involuntary movement but it was enough. The man turned. Caslin stopped, standing still as their eyes met. Caslin had seen similar expressions before. He could never shake the memory of the piercing stare of a killer and it made his blood run cold. This was another of those times. He beckoned Caslin forward. All the while, his cold gaze never left him. Approaching, Caslin remained alert looking for a weapon and trying to work out what he was up against, different scenarios playing out in his head. There was no immediate threat. The man had his hands on the table in front of him, one atop the other. He seemed unfazed by Caslin's presence, returning his gaze to Michelle and Carly.

Reaching the patio, Caslin internally acknowledged his surprise. Somewhere along the line his logic had fallen down for whoever this man was, *he was not Thomas Ryan*.

CHAPTER TWENTY-SEVEN

THE FIRST OF the bi-fold doors was ajar. A distinctive smell drifted in his direction, carried by a through draft from within. Walking forward to the threshold, he paused. The overwhelming smell of petrol was intense. Caslin glanced at the floor. The tiles shimmered, reflecting the light from the fittings overhead. Inclining his head slightly, his eyes met Michelle's and she appeared to shake. Whether borne of a desire for him to keep away or an involuntary reaction to her predicament, he couldn't tell.

Michelle, aside from their first meeting, was a vivacious character, confident and a joy to be around. Here, now, her expression was unlike any he had seen before. A picture of focused control and yet fearful to the point that Caslin thought she may crack at any moment. Her complexion was pale, her make-up, usually classy and understated failed to mask how she must have been crying. Her mascara smudged around her eyes and tears welled, brimming to the point of flowing but Caslin recognised the iron will of her inner strength, a steadfast refusal to buckle.

Perhaps her motivation was her daughter. Carly sat alongside her mother. They clasped hands, her right held encapsulated by her mother's left. The grip so tight that Caslin wondered if the little girl might be in pain. For her part, she had also been crying.

Tears streaked the girl's cheeks and she tentatively glanced up at Caslin before looking away, back down towards the table as if frightened to make eye contact with him. She was still dressed in her school uniform.

Casting a look around, Caslin saw signs of a limited struggle. Broken glass lay near the entrance to the kitchen from the hall, alongside an overturned plant. He swallowed hard. The fumes were overpowering and he blinked, his eyes stung.

"Are you going to stand there all night, Caslin?" The man spoke in a calm, measured tone, sounding as if he was addressing a friend.

Stepping inside set off an expanding ripple outward in the pool of petrol. Only then did he notice multiple jerry cans, the metal type used by the military, two-foot-high and stacked against the far wall. One lay on its side but each can was missing the seal. They were empty, the contents poured all around them. The work-tops glistened. The build-up of pressure saw droplets run from the surface down the face of the cabinets, falling to the floor below.

Very deliberately, Caslin walked forward but careful to appear non-threatening. On the table lay a packet of cigarettes. The brand matched that of the discarded butts found in the garden all those nights ago. Atop the packet lay a wind-proof lighter. As if realising Caslin's thought process, the man smiled, reaching over and picking it up. The ends to his fingers were wrapped in fabric plasters, heavily stained and tattered.

"It's a funny thing... fire," he said, turning the lighter over and over in the palm of his hand. "So important to life. Warming. Welcoming. And yet, as much a method of intense destruction as it is renewal."

Carly burst into tears and her mother squeezed her hand tighter still, which Caslin didn't think possible. Michelle's lower lip quivered, clenching her eyes shut. The man looked at the girl. Reaching across with his free hand, he made to stroke her cheek.

"Don't you touch her," Michelle hissed at him through gritted teeth. Caslin admired her courage.

"We haven't met, have we?" Caslin asked, attempting to hijack their exchange and put himself into the centre of the dynamic.

"No, we haven't. Are you going to introduce your husband to your new lover, Miche?"

"You're... not my husband..." Michelle responded in a whisper. "He would never..."

"Don't lie!" He slammed his hand against the table in an instantaneous flash of rage. "I am your husband." Michelle jumped, startled.

Silence descended. Caslin felt the draught coming from the hallway. He could see the front door was ajar. Michelle and Carly must have been surprised as they entered the house.

"Despite my best efforts, you have me at a disadvantage." The couple shared an emotional connection and Caslin needed to assert some influence over the situation and deescalate the tension. He looked to Michelle, encouraging her with his eyes. She was silently pleading with him, her despair evident in her expression.

"This is Daniel, my ex... my husband," Michelle said, correcting herself. Flashing red and blue lights signified the arrival of the police units at both the front and the rear.

"Your friends have arrived in time," Daniel said.

"In time for what?" Caslin asked, fearful of the answer. Daniel smiled but it was one without genuine humour. No answer was forthcoming. "You've gone to great lengths to... educate... to demonstrate... your belief in the Five Precepts. You've been on quite a journey."

"The path is lit for those willing to see."

"You're not quite the scholar of Buddhist practice that people believe, though, are you?" Caslin sought to focus the conversation on what was driving his behaviour. An attempt to engage with Daniel Cates's warped world. He glanced towards Caslin but said nothing. "I came across your inspiration. Is that the right word?"

Cates fixed him with a lingering stare, a narrowing of the eyes but still offered no response. Daniel returned his gaze to Michelle. She looked to her daughter.

"Your reading of *Angulimala* is far from accurate."

"How so?" Cates asked, finally interacting. If he was surprised by Caslin's knowledge then he didn't show it externally, but there was a spark of interest in the eyes, Caslin was certain. Michelle flitted between the two of them, trying in vain to keep track but clearly lost by the reference.

"His brutal mission was brought to an end upon his meeting with the Buddha. *Angulimala's* path to enlightenment followed his conversion away from *Brahmanism* and his rejection of violence, *not* as a result of his passion for it."

Cates locked eyes with Caslin. He placed the lighter on the table before him. Caslin calculated his potential for success if he made a move for the lighter. Without weapons, neither held a distinct advantage over the other but Cates was a physically imposing man, easily taller and of greater stature than himself. Going toe-to-toe with this man would be a major risk. Reaching up, Cates grasped the zipper of his coat and slowly drew it in a downwards motion. A crudely fashioned leather cord looped around his neck, hanging almost to his waist. Threaded through were severed fingers in a macabre, ghoulish presentation. Several were blackened, a result of decomposition, while to the ends of others strings of withered flesh protruded. Michelle gasped.

"Don't look, Carly." Her tone was sharp. The words harsh. Carly turned away screwing her eyes shut, on the verge of tears once more.

"He reached his goal, as I shall mine," Cates said, defiant.

"Why stop now? *Angulimala* was tasked to collect a thousand. He had a lifetime of indoctrination in dogmatic religious belief and the pressure of royal duty to spur him on. *What do you have?* A failed marriage? Forgive me but that doesn't make you special—"

"I *show* people the way!" Cates retorted. A flash of the deadly personality contained within showed through his controlled exterior. "You dare to judge me? Those people lack the purity of their *body, speech and mind*. The *doctor* who took lives having sworn an oath to heal and care for them. Harming those who relied upon him... the frail and the weak."

"He took your mother." Caslin's tone was nonconfrontational, seeking to connect on an emotional level. Cates met his gaze and for the first time, Caslin saw what he thought was a spark of humanity. A depth of genuine pain as opposed to twisted rage. "Doctor Moretti took her from you before her time. The others... were they all worthy of such wrath? Those dealing with addictions—"

"Intoxicants cloud their minds, harming their spiritual development. Their slavish commitment to their craving is their weakness."

"Addicts fight battles every day," Caslin countered thinking of his own struggles.

Cates shot him a dark look. Rising, he unhooked the last section of zipper and slid the coat off, tossing it aside. Defiantly, he turned his left hand, palm showing, dragging his sleeve up with his right, revealing the crook of his elbow. The action revealed scarring, long since healed but indicative of a former habit.

"Their failure shows a lack of spirit... of conviction." Cates was cold, unsympathetic.

"No one is perfect. Everyone in this world is in a state of suffering. If not, we would all be enlightened."

"And there are those who require a forced renewal." Caslin saw a marked shift in his demeanour. The spark of defiance passing to anger and then finally to reflection. "A man devoting his life to caring for the most vulnerable children in our society, only to use it as a cover to satisfy his own perverted desires. A man willing to starve his family of every penny in order to hide his darkest secrets."

"Not everyone is as deserving of your anger," Caslin argued. It was certainly true that very few people, if any, would spare much sympathy for the plight of Andrew Connolly. A man who committed such vile actions against innocent children.

"You are cowed into submission by your conditions. They manifest in your hypocrisy."

Caslin shook his head in disagreement. "Not so. I've spent my adult life hunting down people like him—"

"I am honest and open about my desires!" Cates barked at him. "At the very least, Connolly knew who he was… *what he was*. If he'd had the courage of his beliefs, then he wouldn't have felt the need to hide."

Caslin saw the expression of belief in his moral superiority. The perception of a higher knowledge and understanding. Not only did Cates see himself as possessing a transparency to be admired but he found Caslin's apparent disdain to be somehow irritating. Almost interpreting it as a display of ingratitude of his efforts.

"Your protests are so predictable." Cates was dismissive, shaking his head.

"What about Kelly? Did she deserve her fate?" Caslin asked, taking a risk. Of all the victims, she was family. A close relationship ended in the most brutal of fashions. Aware of Carly's presence, he glanced sideways at Michelle who understood, reaching across and drawing her daughter into her arms. Cates looked but didn't raise an objection. Caslin took it as a sign he was making inroads into the man's psyche, deflecting his focus away from his family.

"A woman with such low morality? Profiting from those who fall below the unachievable standards set by supposedly faceless corporations. People talk about corporate greed but there is no such thing." Cates fixed Caslin with a stare. "Corporations are abstract concepts. They are run by people. Policies are set by people. *Corporate greed* is interchangeable with *personal greed*. That's what Kelly was."

"She was doing her job!" Michelle whispered, her daughter

buried her head into her mother's chest. "Daniel, how could you?"

Cates appeared hurt. Stung by his former partner's criticism. "The likes of her took our home! That woman made your brother's life a misery. She couldn't keep her clothes on for—"

"That's not for you to judge," Michelle countered.

A flicker of movement caught Caslin's attention. With Cates distracted by Michelle's challenge, he chanced a sideways glance. Craig Templer stood in the hall, hugging the wall as he inched forward out of sight from those seated at the table. Upon seeing Caslin, he stopped, inclining his head and indicating pointedly in Caslin's direction with two fingers. There were officers taking position along the perimeter wall. No doubt, sharp shooters. That filled Caslin with a sense of dread. The amount of petrol in the room, coupled with the intensity of the fumes, meant the slightest spark would see the house explode with extreme ferocity.

All Caslin could do was hope Templer would realise and get the word back to the officer commanding.

"The journalist. What about him?" Caslin asked.

Cates maintained his gaze on Michelle for a few seconds longer before he turned. "The principle of true speech is far more powerful than many believe. Above all else, the spoken word must be beneficial to those who hear, if not to those who speak. The motivation for journalism is to speak the truth to power. *Your friend did not uphold that tradition.*"

"I placed him in that position."

"And by doing so, *you*, and you alone, charted his course," Cates told him.

"He was a decent man."

"And not my intended target," Cates replied, grinning maniacally. "I chose his former boss. The man who destroyed my career with unfounded lies. *Can you imagine that?* Spending your life in a profession, working hard, only to have it ruined by one man and his pursuit of a readership. They took my pride, my self-respect…" He looked to Michelle. "As well as my wife and family.

And then you brought Jimmy Sullivan to me, an equally suitable candidate who came with added motivation."

Caslin felt a flash of anger surge within. Once again, he considered launching himself at the man and pounding him into the ground. As if he was able to read his thoughts, Cates lost his grin. He stared at Caslin, almost willing him to make the move. Reaching for the lighter, he scooped it up. Gripping it between thumb and forefinger, top and bottom, he squeezed. The cap of the lighter pinged open. Caslin had seen it before, a deft little party trick. Cates placed a thumb on the wheel, a moment away from sparking the flint.

"I understand the craving," Caslin said, thinking on his feet. Cates held their eye contact but his thumb remained poised to strike the flint. "Didn't the Buddha say that we live in an imperfect world? In the second of his *Four Noble Truths*, he recognised the world will always be unsatisfactory. There will always be pain and suffering. We cannot escape this reality."

"You speak of *tanhā*," Daniel said and Caslin nodded. "The thirst for sensual pleasure, to both exist and to not. The principal cause of *dukkha*."

"Yes. There will always be suffering," Caslin agreed. "We live in an imperfect world. No matter what we do or how many of us try to walk the path to enlightenment, we will always see chaos and suffering all around us. I understand the craving, the longing for it to end. Believe me."

"The craving grows harder to manage," Cates said, staring off at some imaginary point in the distance. "The world is ever changing… and is innately unsatisfactory."

"Bringing more pain by way of arguments and conflict between individuals." Caslin tried to remember all that he'd read. This was his way in to the conflicted mind of this killer.

"Which is why we must renew, liberate ourselves from this material existence and continue on the spiritual path," Cates said quietly.

Caslin could tell Cates had slipped into an understanding of the *Dharma* warped by the successful spread of the teachings. By the time Buddhism reached Tibet, it had been heavily influenced by Hinduism. The concept of rebirth, the passing of a soul from one life to the next had taken root. The understanding of reincarnation interpreted in another light. Caslin understood his endgame. The Five Precepts were marked and his mission complete. Now, he sought to journey to the next life, to continue on towards enlightenment only this time, he would take his estranged family with him. They had all wondered what the Sixth Precept would be. Daniel Cates intended to mark his passing in spectacular fashion.

"But they won't see a rebirth, will they, Daniel?" Caslin said, adopting a conciliatory tone. "The Buddha spoke not of a rebirth but more of a *re-becoming*. As one candle burns to the base, the flame is used to ignite the next but what remains of the first? The passage into the next life is assured but the only way to develop spiritually is to walk the path of life, earning karma that will ripen either in this life or the next. There is no shortcut. Our spiritual path is for us and us alone. You cannot make this decision for anyone but yourself."

"Did not the *Bodhisattva* sacrifice himself as a supreme offering to the Buddha? His body flamed for a thousand years before he was reincarnated and burned again for thousands more, allowing many to reach enlightenment before he was restored."

"Your desire for self-immolation, the craving of total annihilation is admirable…" Caslin began, drawing a fearful look from Michelle. She was staring at the lighter. "But this is not for your daughter to see. She must learn from her teachers. You, her father is one of those. You must allow her the chance to walk the path."

Cates's head sank. Caslin could see his grip on the lighter tighten, the whites of his knuckles showing. His hand shook. It was a few seconds before Caslin realised the man was crying. Not openly sobbing, but tears streamed unrestrained down his face. His one weakness revealed in an otherwise impenetrable armour.

"Let her walk her own path," Caslin repeated.

Cates mumbled, the words almost inaudible and Caslin wondered if it was even coherent, let alone meant for him to hear. The words grew louder with each repetition. The same phrases over and over again.

"The world is impermanent, insubstantial, incapable of fulfilment."

Caslin had heard them before, he must have read about them but the reference was lost to him. Glancing to his left, Templer stood at the entrance to the kitchen, as close as he dared to be without revealing himself. The man's bravery was to be admired. He signalled to Caslin that everything was under control with a thumbs up gesture. Drawing Michelle's attention, Caslin silently gestured for her to stand. The legs of her chair scraped on the tiles as she did as he requested. She froze. Carly, her arms and legs wrapped around her mother, instinctively clamped herself even tighter Cates didn't react.

Caslin sensed this was their one window of opportunity.

CHAPTER TWENTY-EIGHT

MICHELLE INCHED TOWARDS CASLIN. He stepped between them and Daniel Cates. The latter dropped the lighter and it clattered against the surface of the table. Placing his head in his hands, he began to weep uncontrollably. Encouraging her in the direction of the hall, Caslin pointed to the waiting Templer. The desire to run screamed to make itself known in his mind, but he was concerned that a sudden change in atmosphere might trigger an irrational move from their captor. Templer stepped forward, taking Carly from her mother's arms and smiling in order to reassure the girl everything would be okay.

Michelle looked over her shoulder, realising Caslin was not following. He still stood between them and her husband. She mouthed to her daughter, allowing her grip of her hand to slip as Templer set off for the front door. She reached out and touched Caslin's arm.

"Don't!" she whispered, imploring him with her eyes. "Please… he was a good man once but let him go if that's what he wants. It is his choice…"

"*Go now*," he replied. Moving away from her grasp, he pulled the chair out that she had vacated. Michelle hesitated for a second and with a slight shake of the head, she moved away. Caslin didn't see the pained expression on her face.

Despite Daniel Cates being what he was, Caslin could see the broken man on the inside. A man who couldn't cope with what life threw at him. If not for a freak set of circumstances bringing Caslin himself back from the brink, only a few short years ago, maybe it would have been his mind that seemed irrecoverably broken. Sympathy was non-existent, empathy... possible but what was strong in Caslin was the need for this man to face justice for his crimes. He should spend the rest of his natural life in a cell and Caslin intended to ensure it would happen.

Sitting down opposite Cates, the man lifted his head. His face contorted in pain, eyes bloodshot and swollen. Something was lost in his expression, his mind seemingly on the verge of collapse.

"You should leave too," he said quietly, reaching for the lighter. He clasped it in his palm and closed his hand into a fist.

"*Angulimala* is revered by Buddhists the world over... an example of how even the most damaged minds can be transformed."

"Not this time... not by you," he replied.

"What is it that you are looking to achieve? Everyone has a purpose in life, a career, a family, or a goal they are seeking. Tell me yours? You haven't done any of this on a whim."

Daniel Cates looked into his eyes. The stare was hard and unforgiving. "There is great evil in this world. All that we are arises with our thoughts and with our thoughts we shape the world."

"And you feel your journey towards enlightenment is somehow benefitted by highlighting the precepts and the lack of adherence to them by society?" Caslin asked, genuinely trying to understand, to build some kind of a bridgehead into this man's troubled mind. "The Precepts are but guidelines, are they not? You choose to ignore the positive aspects and focus on the negatives, ignoring the presence of the *Worldly Winds*."

"I see you have been studying the *Dharma*, Inspector." Cates smiled at the reference. Caslin found it unnerving. "Pleasure versus pain. Praise and blame. Fame and dishonour."

"*Gain and loss.*" Caslin completed the list.

Cates inclined his head. "But have you only memorised the words or can you apply an interpretation?"

Caslin saw the challenge. Cates wanted to know if he was debating an equal or someone attempting to deceive. "For me, the truth, and make no mistake for it is a truth, is that you are correct. There is a tremendous amount of evil in this world. But evil in of itself is an abstract construct. There is no entity, being or force in which this label applies. All we have is the sum of the acts carried out throughout history and around the globe. The choice we have as an individual is whether we will choose to add to that or to walk a different path. *Angulimala* realised this truth. He chose to revere life over death."

"*And accepted responsibility* for his past actions and how he would be treated. The people beat him with sticks, punished him for his past transgressions *despite* his transformation to follow the *dharma*."

"The Buddha always said practitioners must live within the constructs of society. The same rules apply to them as everyone else."

Cates appeared to be thinking hard. Caslin was making inroads, he could sense it.

"Which is why you need to leave," he said, locking eyes with Caslin. Something changed in his expression, a veil of darkness appearing to sweep over him as he spoke. "*While you still can!*" He hissed the last comment, almost through gritted teeth.

Caslin stood slowly. "There is still time for you… what lies ahead will only cause you more pain. Either in this life or the next, unless you walk out with me now." Cates was unmoved. Caslin backed away, watching for any sign from him, any indication of what he planned to do but there was none. He remained, staring at the table in front of him.

Turning as he reached the hall, he trotted to the open front door. Reaching the threshold, he sucked in a deep breath of fresh air. It tasted sweet. The petrol fumes were still present and he felt nauseous. Caslin looked towards the assembled emergency services within the nearby cordon. An ambulance, two fire brigade appliances and multiple police cars lined the quayside. Hunter was visible, beckoning him to descend the steps to safety. The quay was taped off at both ends, no doubt the neighbouring properties had already been evacuated. People were gathering nearby. The pub on the corner had emptied to watch the spectacle unfold.

Perhaps it was because of a perceived affinity or a sign of the sheer stubborn, bloody-mindedness he was famous for, but Caslin thought that bringing Cates back from the brink would somehow lay the ghosts of his own past to rest, a sense of closure maybe. Regretting his inability to do so, he stepped forward.

There was a rush of air from behind him, similar to a fan starting up on a hot day. The warm breeze reeked of fuel. Caslin heard no sound, nor did he see the fireball surge in his direction. The pressure wave struck and he felt momentarily weightless as air escaped his lungs. His vision swam, becoming a blur of coloured lights only to be replaced shortly after by darkness. The warm breeze on his skin was now as cold as stone. The embrace of the silence was a comfort, an all-encompassing sense of belonging. Then he felt nothing. Nothing at all.

A PERSISTENT RINGING echoed in his ears. Opening his eyes, Caslin could see movement above him. Seconds passed and details emerged as shadows coalesced into shapes. Attempting to move released an intense burst of pain. It rippled along his arm before cascading down his spine. Caslin cursed although he didn't hear the words. Hunter was knelt by his side, placing a restraining hand gently on his chest. Her lips moved but it was another minute before his senses righted themselves and he could understand what was being spoken to him.

"Don't try to move," she told him, repeating herself for the second or maybe third time, he wasn't sure.

Disregarding her advice, he rolled on to one side. The pain was less intense on this occasion and he levered himself up onto his elbow. Strewn around him were assorted pieces of debris. Some were still flaming, and almost all were unrecognisable in relation to their origin. Glancing back at the house, flames licked at the exterior from the open doorway and shattered sash windows. The crews from the fire brigade were advancing on the house, attempting to suppress the fire before it could take hold and spread to the adjoining terrace.

Closing his eyes, Caslin fought a wave of nausea that washed over him. His head throbbed and something cool was running down the inside of his shirt at the base of his neck. Moving to touch it released another wave of pain and he gave up, cursing under his breath.

"You should listen to me once in a while, you know?" Hunter chastised him.

"Michelle and Carly?" Caslin asked, looking past Hunter in the direction of the nearby melee, a hive of uniformed activity.

"They're fine."

Caslin spotted the two of them, seated in the back of a parked ambulance. They were draped in a blanket, Michelle with a comforting arm around her daughter, stroking her hair and kissing the top of her head.

"Daniel Cates?" In all honesty, he already knew the answer to that particular question. Hunter shook her head. "Released from his suffering after all."

The reference was lost on Hunter, who smiled, relieved to see he was not as badly injured as first feared. Caslin looked around. He was twenty feet away from the base of the steps to the Cates house, and barely five from the river.

"That must have been some explosion." Caslin felt thankful

not to have ended up in the water. A police boat approached the nearby jetty, picking its way through the debris being carried away by the current of the Ouse.

A paramedic arrived but Caslin shrugged him off, choosing to stand against the advice of those around him. He braced against Hunter, who helped him to his feet. His legs felt wobbly and every movement was painful. There was no arguing. He would need to attend the hospital. Catching sight of Michelle, he thought she was staring in his direction. Whether she recognised him or it was merely coincidence, he couldn't tell. Raising a hand, he waved, forcing an accompanying smile. She remained impassive, still staring straight ahead as the doors to the ambulance were closed and she disappeared from view.

His smile faded. Hunter noticed.

"Give her some time, Nate," she said reassuringly. He glanced at her, nodding. She knew. How she knew, Caslin could only guess. Maybe it was how they left the house together. Maybe Hunter knew him better than he realised.

"I can do that."

"She was distraught when the house went up."

"Not surprising, it was her home." Caslin looked back at the house. A ruin of its former grandeur.

"No, Nathaniel. She thought you were dead," Hunter replied, placing a warm hand on his shoulder. "And she's not the only one." She patted him gently. "Just give her some time."

Caslin watched as the ambulance moved off, carving a path through the voyeurs. For the first time in a long time, his thoughts were for anything but the job.

FREE BOOK GIVEAWAY

Visit the author's website at **www.jmdalgliesh.com** and sign up to the VIP Club and be first to receive news and previews of forthcoming works.

Here you can download a FREE eBook novella exclusive to club members;

Life & Death - A Hidden Norfolk novella

Never miss a new release.

No spam, ever, guaranteed. You can unsubscribe at any time.

ONE LOST SOUL - PREVIEW
HIDDEN NORFOLK - BOOK 1

HOLLY WAS GRATEFUL FOR the shelter of the dunes. The wind had a habit of rattling along the coastline, sweeping across the flatlands and cutting through even the hardiest of winter clothing. Where they were sitting, beyond the thick pine forests of the Holkham estate, there was shelter of sorts. She watched the others building a fire on the beach below, gathering driftwood and any fallen branches scavenged from the nearby woods. In the summertime, the estate routinely sent groundskeepers out to ensure open fires were not set but not at this time of year. Early spring could be lovely on the Norfolk coast, bright sunshine, warming on the skin. As long as the prevailing wind wasn't whipping in off the North Sea, at least. The sun had long since set and the chill of the evening was beginning to bite.

In a month or so, the tourist season would begin. All the local businesses running skeleton opening hours over the winter would be up and running once more. The seasonal workers would soon return, maybe. There was a lot of talk amongst the locals that this year would be different. Applications for job vacancies were down on last year and her father commented that even agencies were struggling to fulfil the roles.

It must be amazing to be one of those people with the freedom to travel beyond the confines of where they grew up, able to go to another country and experience different lifestyles and culture. The prospect of learning a new language, trying strange food or simply watching the sun set over an alien landscape was exciting, exotic. One day that would be her. Not that she could tell anyone, nor would she when the time came. She would vanish on the breeze, carried away by an unstoppable force. Maddie came to mind, watching her as she danced with her friends a short distance away. What will become of her when I leave? That last thought dampened her enthusiasm, tempering the future vision.

The fire was lit now. They were singing, the others. It wasn't a song she cared for, not one she even knew the words to but it was popular. Their shadows danced on the sand around the fire as they moved, linking arms and singing louder as more voices joined in the chorus. Holly felt a hand on her shoulder. The touch was gentle. She didn't look round. Mark slipped his arm across her shoulder, coming to sit alongside her on the blanket he'd laid out for them. Part of her wanted him to suggest they move closer to the flames. He didn't and she knew why. He would no doubt try to slip his tongue into her mouth soon. To be fair, it was to be expected. The location, the fire, and their being alone, away from the others and sitting in the darkness made for quite a romantic setting. She would probably oblige.

Mark was a nice guy. Most of their year group steered clear of him but that was less to do with his outbursts and more to do with the family reputation. If she knew of anyone less deserving of such scorn, then it would be news to her. Releasing his grip on her shoulder, Mark retrieved a bottle from a plastic bag at his side and unscrewed the cap. He offered it to her first. She could smell the alcohol and it made her stomach churn. The waves of nausea were getting more frequent but she kept quiet. The last thing she needed was another lecture on visiting the doctor. How could she? The thought of drinking made her feel worse and she declined the offer. He said nothing, sipping from the bottle and pulling an odd face as the liquid burned his mouth. That was the issue with Mark. Immature.

The bonfire was well underway. The colours, the crackling of the wood and the spiralling wisps of smoke and flame dancing into the night sky with the waves crashing on the beach was somewhat hypnotic. Holly imagined her fears being consumed by the heat, with the glow at its heart a depiction of her dreams and fantasies. One day soon she would leave this place and everyone in it behind, travel somewhere where no one knew her and become an artist, make things... jewellery perhaps. All of this would be but a memory.

She felt Mark's hand stroke the small of her back. Looking to him, he smiled. She said nothing, returning her gaze towards the bonfire and spying the whites of the breakers beyond as they approached the shoreline. Mark was a nice guy. Even so, he still couldn't come with her. There was no place for him. There was no place for any of them.

One Lost Soul
Hidden Norfolk Book 1

ALSO BY J M DALGLIESH

The Hidden Norfolk Series

One Lost Soul

Bury Your Past

Kill Our Sins

Tell No Tales

Hear No Evil

The Dead Call

Life and Death*

*FREE eBook - A Hidden Norfolk novella

Visit jmdalgliesh.com

The Dark Yorkshire Series

Divided House

Blacklight

The Dogs in the Street

Blood Money

Fear the Past

The Sixth Precept

Box Sets

Dark Yorkshire Books 1-3

Dark Yorkshire Books 4-6

The entire Dark Yorkshire series is available in audio format, read by the award-winning Greg Patmore.

Divided House

Blacklight

The Dogs in the street

Blood Money

Fear the Past

The Sixth Precept

Dark Yorkshire Books 1-3

Dark Yorkshire Books 4-6

Hidden Norfolk

One Lost Soul